# Vashua's Messenger
## Book 2 of the Vadelah Chronicles

# VASHUA'S MESSENGER

## Book 2 of the Vadelah Chronicles

## Julie Rollins

PUBLISHING

Belleville, Ontario, Canada

# Vashua's Messenger
## Book 2 of the Vadelah Chronicles
### Copyright © 2005, Julie Rollins

Scripture quotations marked NASB are taken from the *New American Standard Bible*, copyright © The Lockman Foundation 1960, 1962, 1963, 1968, 1971, 1972, 1973. All rights reserved.

**Library and Archives Canada Cataloguing in Publication**

Rollins, Julie, 1961-

Vashua's messenger / Julie Rollins.

(The Vadelah chronicles : bk. 2)

ISBN 1-55306-941-2

I. Title.  II. Series: Rollins, Julie, 1961- . Vadelah chronicles ; bk. 2.

PS3618.O549V38 2005     813'.6     C2005-905913-3

*Essence Publishing* is a Christian Book Publisher dedicated to furthering the work of Christ through the written word. For more information, contact: 20 Hanna Court, Belleville, Ontario, Canada K8P 5J2.
Phone: 1-800-238-6376 • Fax: (613) 962-3055
E-mail: publishing@essencegroup.com
Internet: www.essencegroup.com

Printed in Canada
by

# Dedication

To those who live in the difficult places—laboring beneath the threats of beating, imprisonment, and death—to bring the light of Jesus where few know Him. Your steadfastness, courage, and love for the lost inspire me. I dedicate this book to you.

# Introduction

When college students David Decker and Todd Fox first found Gyra, a marooned space alien, they were terrified. But driven by his Christian compassion, David took Gyra in and hid him from dark government forces. Gyra wasn't easy to hide; the phantera looked like a giant white pigeon with arms.

As the phantera learned English, he blundered into trouble at every turn, becoming entangled in a brawl at a bar, a scuffle at an abortion clinic, a riot at a UFO convention, and a fiasco with the dolphins at Marine World.

But, in the midst of all this, David learned something amazing. After lending Gyra his Bible, David woke up the next day to find the phantera had become a Christian. Gyra explained that his people believed something significant had happened on *Trenara* (Earth) about two thousand years previously, rendering the phantera sacrificial system obsolete. The old phantera prophets were told to wait for a messenger from Earth who would explain the great mystery to them. Gyra believed Christianity was the revelation many aliens had longed for. The phantera explained that God's moral laws applied to all sentient beings.

Gyra revealed some of his kind's unique abilities. The scaly skin on his hands was remarkably heat-resistant. By activating a special organ called a *crealin* while he touched someone's head, Gyra could perform *rhutaram* and instantly absorb the person's language. Or he could engage in *falarn*, sharing a person's mental thoughts.

But David had little time to ponder those abilities. The government was closing in, and David had become a wanted man. In an act of great sacrifice, David's roommate, Todd, allowed himself to be captured so David and Gyra could fly away.

During their disastrous escape, a sniper shot Gyra. David had to carry the unconscious phantera into his repaired ship. Uncertain about Gyra's condition, and unwilling to face his pursuers on Earth, David fled to the alien's home planet, *Arana*.

Because Gyra was in a coma of undetermined origin, the local phantera were unwilling to do rhutaram on David, forcing him to learn *Ramatera,* the common trade language. Philoah, Gyra's brother, was assigned to watch David and teach him. In the course of learning the language, David was informed he would stand trial for Gyra's injuries.

Philoah led David on a long journey through the desert to the Pendaram's City for his trial. Shortly after entering the city, an old phantera prophet named Rammar met David. The black phantera announced that David was the *vadelah*—Vashua's messenger.

Gyra, having finally emerged from his healing coma, arrived at David's trial in time to clear him. Pendaram Ariphema, ruler of all Arana's phantera, then asked David to reveal the mysterious events that took place on Earth.

While David explained his Christian faith, a *naharam* Pentecost occurred, similar to the Pentecost of the early church. David felt the Ramatera language fused into him as strongly as a native tongue.

Rammar the Prophet then declared that David must share the "Great Revelation" with the three dark planets most hostile to *Yavana* (God).

As the leaders prepared to spread the Great Revelation, hostile alien ships attacked their city. After the enemy ships were defeated, Rammar the Prophet raised his hands and looked up at the sky.

"We have drawn up the battle plan for delivering the Great Revelation. Now the war is upon us."

# 1. A Moonlight Trip

"News of the scrimmage spread rapidly," Gyra told David at dinner. "Four squadrons of *delahs* were sent up to patrol the planet in case the *crullahs* return. The phantera in the chambers have finished viewing your books and they all know English now. Some have left to take it to the other provinces."

Carrying his dirty bowl over to a large basin, David began to wash it. "So, what are the rest doing?"

"Meditating on what they've learned."

"Well, I'm ready to hit the sack. I'm exhausted!" David placed his cleaned bowl on the drying rack and staggered off to his bed. The spongy plant fibers cradled his weary frame. Closing his eyes, he sighed, drinking in the gentle aroma of dried *alawa*.

Distant murmurs and cries rode the night air. The phantera were "reading" Trenara's Scriptures—weeping over the depth of human sin and rejoicing in Yavana's love for His people.

The volume steadily increased. Tossing and turning, David pulled the cloak he used for a cover over his head. Brusaka hummed from the dining room. David smothered beneath the cloak. Sighing in exasperation, he flung it off, rose, and paced the floor.

Agaria, Arana's larger moon, bathed the pool in a cool light. Soon her little red sister, Dilari, would join her. Sitting down on the edge of the pool, David dangled his feet in the warm water, troubling it. The moon's reflection danced as he listened to the cacophony of noise. Singing, weeping, shouts of surprise, whoops of joy, they all mixed with the cool night air—along with the constant drone of Brusaka's humming.

"Phantera can sure be emotional at times," he muttered.

A cloaked figure appeared at the far side of the pool. "David?"

"Yeah, who is it?"

"Gyra. You're having a hard time sleeping."

"Is it often this noisy at night?"

"No, David, I've never heard the city so stirred. Many of the *haranda* have fled for the sea because they can't sleep."

"I'm glad I'm not alone!"

"The phantera will be finished by morning."

"Gyra?"

"Yes?"

"How did you keep silent after you read the Scriptures?"

Treading lightly around the rim of the pool, Gyra crouched beside David. "It was hard, but I didn't wish to disturb you. I was in your world, in your culture. Here, phantera can be themselves. We have our own culture."

Brusaka's humming stopped. "Oh, Israel! When will you learn? Why do you continue to turn away?" The black phantera fell silent.

Gyra placed his hand on David's shoulder. "Since you can't sleep, would you like to go for a moonlit ride on my *duca*?"

"You have a duca?" David almost shouted.

"Of course. Almost every phantera does. Didn't Philoah tell you?"

Scratching his full beard, David said, "I guess we didn't get around to that. I'd love to fly on your duca."

"Grab your cloak and follow me."

Leaving the guesthouse, they stepped into the street. Phantera stood scattered among buildings, beside fountains, on street corners, and under the large *dowels* lighting the city.

Gyra paused and gazed at his meditating brethren. "It is a sight, isn't it?"

They continued to the moonlit lawn where two ducas waited side by side.

"Gyra, if phantera can tolerate hot and cold climates, why do you wear cloaks?"

"To protect our feathers from wear and keep the dust off. After several *shartaras*, our feathers can become quite ragged. Also, the fibers in our cloaks make it harder for enemy ships to pick us up on their sensors."

David watched as the two ducas nibbled each other's necks, rumbling contentedly. "Is it a *he* or a *she*?"

Smiling in the moonlight, Gyra said, "Mine is a *he*; Philoah's is a *she*."

"Philoah's? I thought this was Gilyen's."

"They do look similar," Gyra noted.

Raising their heads, the ducas became attentive. Gyra's duca bore a knife-shaped crest, like a *pteranadon*.

"Do phantera name their ducas?" David asked.

Gyra scratched his feathered chest. "Yes, but not in Ramatera. We name them in our native tongue, *Dalena*."

David realized that Dalena was the melodic bird-like notes he had first heard when he landed on Arana. The phantera had switched to Ramatera, the universal trade language, to accommodate him. Unlike humans, most naharam had a single unifying language named after their home world.

Looking up at the ducas, David asked, "Can you give me a rough translation of their names?"

Gyra gave a cooing laugh. "I can with some of them, but others won't work. How do you translate the name

*Rhoda* or *Jeff*? Even your name doesn't translate into Ramatera, unless it has a meaning I'm unaware of."

"Many of our names do have meanings, but in my country we don't give them much thought. Mine means *beloved of God* in Hebrew."

Gyra raised an eyebrow. "So, there is more than you've told me. Well, I will attempt to tell you my duca's name." Turning to his duca, Gyra sang a few notes. The large bird waddled closer.

"That is my duca's name in Dalena. A rough translation would be *knife air cutter*."

"And Philoah's?"

Gyra sang another melodic line and the tube-crested duca drew near. "Philoah's does not translate at all!"

"What do you mean?"

Wearing a subtle phantera smile, Gyra said, "He gave her the name because he liked the way the notes sounded. It has no meaning."

David looked up at Philoah's duca. "I wish she had a name in Ramatera. I'd like to know what to call her. Maybe I can give her a name."

Gyra wagged his head. "*Myute*, only Philoah can give her a name. He is her owner. If you like, you can ask him tomorrow to give her a second name. I don't think he'll refuse you."

"What about your duca?" David eyed the bony blade on the bird's head.

"I can give him a name. How about *Treasar*? It combines *trean* for knife and *wesar* for wind."

"*Knife wind*?"

"Actually, I was thinking more like *wind knife*."

"Treasar," David mumbled. "It sort of sounds like *dinosaur*. Well, ducas do remind me of dinosaurs. I like it."

Gyra had the duca lower his massive head. Placing his hand on the great yellow bill, the phantera spoke in Dalena.

He ended, saying, "Treasar," and released the duca's head. Raising his powerful neck, the duca trumpeted.

"There, now he will respond to both names," Gyra said with a satisfied smile.

"I feel honored to be the first human to witness the naming of a duca," David teased.

"You should; it's a very private ceremony. Usually it occurs with only the owner and the duca present."

David blushed. "Gyra, I didn't know!"

"I realize that, David. I wanted to honor our friendship this way. Now, would you like to go flying?"

"Oh, no! I don't have any goggles! I won't be able to keep my eyes open, I'll—"

The phantera dangled a pair of goggles before David's face. "I got these from Gilyen."

Laughing, David slipped them on. "Gyra, you think of everything!" He looked up at Treasar, but saw nothing to grasp. "I don't know how I'm going to get up. Gilyen's had a leather vest I could climb."

"I guess you'll have to mount him *haranda* style." Gyra sang a few bird-like notes.

Lowering his head, Treasar opened wide his mighty bill.

David stepped back. "Wait a minute! There's got to be a better way to—*ahhh*!"

The great bill seized him in a firm yet gentle grasp as the rubbery tongue cushioned David's rigid body. He was too shocked to speak. The smell of soured alawa turf permeated Treasar's steamy breath.

The bill opened, dropping David onto the springy feathers of the duca's back.

Gyra fluttered up and landed beside David. "Treasar is wearing a leather girth under his feathers. You can hang on to it." Probing around, David found it, along with several loose thongs that he wrapped around his hands.

"Are you ready to go?" the phantera asked.

"*Dala!*"

The duca ran across the lawn, gaining momentum, as the rushing wind obscured the racket from the city. They climbed in a slow spiral above the bright lights. Beyond the city, the two moons illuminated the land and the crashing surf, bathing them in a ghostly glow.

Treasar turned toward the mountains. A silver river shone as it wiggled from the foothills to the sea.

"Gyra, where does all the water come from? I've never seen it rain on Arana."

"We get rain, plenty of it too, but you came at the beginning of our dry season. Soon, the *shardrea* season will come."

David didn't ask what shardrea meant. *Drea* was water and *shar* meant to mix as in a storm. Hence, a shardrea must be a rainstorm. How big did they get? The river below was a mere trickle compared to the width of its banks.

Treasar climbed higher. Forests and shrubs carpeted the foothills. In a clearing, a flock of ducas grazed in the eerie moonlight. The cool white brilliance of Agaria and the rosy glow of Dilari created twin shadows, adding to the dream-like appearance of the night.

The air grew cold and thin, stinging David's nose as they rose above the mountains. He could see a great distance down their long jagged spine. What was it Philoah had called them? The *Majeram Amada-ba*? A strange name. *Amada* was mountain and *ba* was the suffix for plurality. So *Amada-ba* meant a mountain range.

David shouted against the wind. "I know these are the Majeram Amada-ba, but what does *Majeram* mean?"

Leaning closer, Gyra answered, "In English you would call them the Lookout Mountains. They're one of the places where we watch for attacks. The *ma* stands for four of the question words: *manar,* what, *maha,* who, *marana,* where, and *matrel,* when. These are the things we need to know when the *mel-naharam* launch an attack."

"What about *balute*, the word for why?"

"We know why the mel-naharam attack us, David. The *je* is an abbreviation for *jea*—to see."

"And *ram* means high or height," David finished.

Bringing in his wings, Treasar aimed for a narrow valley high in the mountains. The wind buffeted David so strongly that he grasped the riding straps in terror.

The duca slipped between two sheer cliffs—silent granite sentinels guarding the entrance. A small valley spread out before them. Tree-sized exotic plants crowded the valley floor, and a small lake nestled against one of the steep walls.

The wind fell as Treasar glided over the shimmering waters and landed on the sandy shore.

Gyra's voice pierced the stillness. "Philoah said you complained about Arana's deserts. I thought you might like to see some of our *tearel*, our plant life."

Sliding off the duca, David answered, "I know what tearel means." It was farther to the ground than he thought! He landed on his rump with a thud. At least the sand was soft.

"Are you all right?" asked Gyra, peering down from Treasar.

David groaned. "There's got to be a better way to do this." Rising stiffly, he brushed the moist sand from his clothes. "Are there any dangerous *dalam* or tearel around here?"

Laughing, Gyra fluttered down. "I brought you here to enjoy yourself, not to let a *melcat* chase you! There are no dangerous dalam in these mountains. Its one reason the *lampar* like it. As for tearel, you needn't worry unless you eat a poisonous one."

Sighing with relief, David headed toward the forest. The light of the two moons exaggerated the bizarre appearance of the plants. One "tree" billowed up like an enormous cauliflower. Another resembled stacked table-sized mushrooms. Rising several stories high, a huge tree reached upward with barren twisted branches. Was it dead?

Little feet pattered all around. They were not alone. A flightless bird burst from a bush and darted past him. David yelled even though the bird was only the size of a chicken.

"Perhaps this is not as relaxing as I'd hoped," Gyra commented.

David caught his breath. "No, it's okay. I really am enjoying myself. It just takes a while to get used to it all."

Bobbing his head, Gyra smiled. "I was terrified when I first landed on Trenara."

"You should have been!" David crept deeper into the forest. A large shrub glowed in front of him. Its folded wrinkled surface reminded him of brain coral as he stared, mesmerized by its aqua light.

"We use extracts from this tearel to make underwater lamps," Gyra said. "Some naharam visit the submerged part of the city, but can't see well in the depths without a lamp."

Pointing out various plants, the phantera gave their names and uses. The giant cauliflower plant was a *corune* tree. Gyra described how the phantera carved its hard blue wood into tables, bowls, and other objects.

As they wandered back to the lake, the reflections of Agaria and Dilari danced on its smooth surface. A winged creature darted across the water, chirping as it went. David was glad there were no mosquitoes on Arana.

"We should go back now," Gyra spoke, breaking the stillness.

"Before we leave, I've got to find a better way to get on and off a duca!" David insisted.

"Perhaps I can help." Gyra instructed Treasar to sit and lower his head to the ground. David grabbed the bony crest and the duca swung him onto his feathery back.

Treasar stood and wagged his tail. "That was better," David said. "Now, how do I get off?"

Gyra peered up from below. "It's too difficult for you to jump down?"

"Both times I've tried have been painful."

The phantera uttered a few notes. Treasar squatted until his stiff tail touched the ground. David slid down the duca's long back. It wasn't very dignified, but it didn't add any bruises to his body.

He remounted the duca, ready to go home.

"Perhaps I could teach you how to ride a duca without a belt," Gyra suggested.

"Is it as hard as mounting one?" asked David warily.

"Not at all! Reach down and grab a bunch of feathers with your hands. Make sure you have several feathers and not just one or two—ducas do molt on occasion. Pull to see if they're firmly rooted."

David did. He decided to bury his legs too. Lifting the feathers before him, he eased himself down. Treasar's coat was amazingly thick. The skin vibrated as the duca gave a low rumble. Treasar's great head swung around, eyeing him.

"Did I do something wrong?" David asked.

Chuckling, Gyra said, "You're tickling him. He's not used to riders burying themselves in his feathers. His skin is sensitive, but don't worry, he'll get used to it."

Gyra gave a command and Treasar leaped into the air.

## 2. A Time to Rest

A nagging soreness roused David from his slumber. He remembered his wonderful flight on Treasar—and his fall beside the lake.

With a grunt, he forced himself up and stripped off his outer clothes. His stiff legs staggered to the atrium.

Hissing, he slipped into the sunlit pool. The warm water and gentle swimming motions slowly massaged the stiffness out of his limbs.

Brusaka's head popped out from behind an archway. "Are you finally up? I was beginning to wonder if you were hibernating."

David smiled at the black phantera's English. "You can still use Ramatera around me. I don't want to grow lazy and forget what I've learned."

"Do humans forget so quickly?" Brusaka raised an eyebrow.

"We don't have the memory of a phantera. Ask Gyra about it some time." Pulling himself out of the pool, David dried off. He dressed, donned his cloak, and headed for the table.

Philoah and Gyra were discussing the events of the previous day. Philoah stopped and turned toward David. "Did you sleep well?"

David glared at him.

"Well, you did get some sleep," Gyra commented.

David helped himself to the cooked vegetables and dried *fala* fruit. "So, what happens today?"

Gyra rubbed the end of his pink bill. "Today Pendaram Ariphema wishes to ask you questions about Trenara."

David swallowed a mouthful of vegetable far too large for his throat. He grimaced from the pain. "Are they waiting for me, like last time?"

"Of course," Philoah said, preening a flight feather.

David dashed for the doorway, but Brusaka beat him to it. Blocking the way, the black phantera stared down at him. "Go back and finish your breakfast! They will wait a little longer. We don't want the vadelah fainting from hunger."

Meekly, David returned to the table and wolfed down his food.

"I didn't know humans could eat like that," Philoah commented as David crammed his mouth with one cooked vegetable after another.

Opening his eyes, David stared at the ceiling of his room. If only he could just lay here all day! In his mind he still saw a sea of phantera and haranda faces, watching him, listening to his rambling explanations of human affairs. If today was just like the last three—how long could this go on? *Lord, I wasn't made for these grueling lectures. By the end of the day my feet ache and I feel like a road kill.*

He rolled over and sighed. If Pendaram Ariphema asked him any more questions about American government, David's ignorance would be exposed for all to see. Yesterday was bad enough; trying to describe bureaucracy and the legal system was a joke. David wasn't a political science major and he couldn't explain what he didn't understand! Perhaps today they'd ask him about something simpler—like brain surgery. Getting up, he wandered into the dining room.

Mojar stood at the table. "Pendaram Ariphema said you looked tired yesterday." She opened her medical bag. "I came to see if you are well."

David smiled. "I haven't had a chance to speak to you since I arrived in the city. I want to say *Ramara* for helping me when I first came to Arana."

Mojar assembled an instrument and approached him. "I wish I could have given you a local anesthetic when I took those first blood and tissue samples. I didn't because I was afraid you might have a reaction. Some naharam die when given the wrong anesthetic."

Placing the end of an instrument into David's ear, she glanced at the reading. Mojar picked up another instrument and wrapped a cord around his arm. "We have learned a lot about your physiology since you left."

"How is that?" David asked before he opened his mouth for her.

Rubbing the inside of his cheek with a padded stick, she placed it in a sterile container. "We have the skin culture we grew. Your DNA is quite curious. I wish we had samples from more humans so I could run a comparison.

"Our analysis indicates it would be difficult for a human to live beyond 125 of your years. We were amazed at your short life spans. According to Trenara's Scriptures you used to live much longer, but after the Flood, your life spans decreased dramatically. Why?"

"I wish I knew," David replied.

"Your sun's radiation could do a lot of damage," Mojar whispered, picking up another gadget. David flinched. He recognized the instrument. Mojar dabbed a cool numbing liquid onto his neck.

He swallowed. "Some people think Trenara's atmosphere was much different before the Flood, that it blocked out much of the sun's harmful rays." David tried to focus on the issue rather than Mojar's work on his neck. "Trenara's climate and surface were vastly changed."

Mojar finished drawing blood from his neck and inserted her sample into a portable machine. "That would fit with our Scriptures," Mojar affirmed with a nod. "Long ago, a phantera prophet told of a terrible calamity on Trenara. Yavana showed it to him in a vision."

After scanning David, she glanced at her machine. "How do you feel?"

"Like I need a vacation!"

"Do you think you can last one more session?" She watched him with her red eyes.

David rubbed his forehead. "Yeah, I guess so."

"Then tomorrow you will begin your *enar*," Mojar said with an air of authority.

He blinked. Did she say enar? Music to his ears! *Enar*

meant rest or vacation. It was the Phantera equivalent to a Sabbath, but without rigorous rules. "Ramara, Mojar. You just made my day."

Packing her instruments with deft hands, she remarked, "It wouldn't be wise for us to question the vadelah to death!"

David awoke early the next morning, as was his habit, but this time he lay in bed and smiled. After a good fifteen minutes, he ambled into the eating room.

Gyra, Philoah, and Brusaka stared at him with silly grins on their faces, their hands hidden in their cloaks.

"Okay, guys, what's up?"

Brusaka spoke first. "David, human naharam of Trenara, chosen vadelah, I beseech you to accept this humble gift as a token of my endless gratitude for the Great Revelation." Withdrawing a hand from under his cloak, he held up a folded piece of thick material.

David shook it open to reveal a heavy cloak.

The black phantera bobbed his head. "You can use this when you travel. It will keep you warm."

Running his fingers over the soft material, he nodded. "Ramara, Brusaka, I'm honored. My old one has quite a few rips in it."

The black phantera beamed.

Gyra spoke next. "David, friend to the friendless, protector of Yavana's wayward phantera, please accept this gift as a token of our friendship." He held out a shirt and a pair of pants, faithful duplicates of David's clothes, only sturdier.

"Oh, Gyra!" David cried and gave his friend a hug. He examined the pants. "They're wonderful. I was beginning to wonder what I would do when mine wore out. Ramara, Gyra."

Philoah wore a wide grin—for a phantera. "David, human student, slayer of the melcat and master of the Ramatera language, please accept these gifts as a token of our friendship." He held up socks and two pairs of under-wear. "I noticed your underwear was wearing rather thin because you rarely take it off, so I made two pairs for you."

David's face ached as he struggled to keep from laughing. Philoah's sincerity and innocence were priceless.

"See how he likes my gifts!" Philoah cried in triumph. "He's smiling so wide his face will break!"

At that David did break, laughing until tears came to his eyes. "Ramara, Philoah," he finally stammered.

After breakfast, Philoah turned to David. "What do you plan to do for your vacation?"

David glanced up at the ceiling. "I don't know. How long do I have?"

"That is for the vadelah to decide," Brusaka stated.

David eyed Gyra. "Don't they need me to answer more questions?"

Wagging his head Gyra replied, "Myute, Pendaram Ariphema will be leaving today for Dalena. When the Council of Pendarams meets, he will give them the Great Revelation. May Naphema bless it with His presence as He did here! The council will last a few days. There will be no more questions until Pendaram Ariphema returns."

"What about the other leaders?" asked David.

"The *delaram* have all left. They called their ducas and flew out this morning to spread the knowledge throughout Arana. The *talaram* of the city is translating the rest of Trenara's Scriptures into Ramatera. He will be busy for quite a while."

Philoah leaned toward David. "When do you leave for the mel-naharam?"

David walked from the table to the pool's edge. "I don't know. The time doesn't seem right. I know I've got to go, but not yet."

"Good!" Gyra cried. "Then we can go on the trip."

Whirling around, David asked, "What trip?"

Philoah grinned. "We thought we'd take you to see more of Arana."

Gyra bobbed his head. "Todd said you love to camp."

"And we can travel by duca," Philoah added.

"You could see the tearel in the daylight," Gyra cut in again. "Their colors are brilliant."

"Wait a minute!" David silenced the phantera with a raised hand. "This sounds like a conspiracy. First the new clothes."

Brusaka blinked and scratched his neck.

David narrowed his eyes. "Then you secretly find out if I have to speak for the next few days. After that you probe to discover when I will be leaving for the mel-naharam. Finally you try to persuade me with 'Todd said you love to camp,' and 'We can travel by duca,' and 'You could see the tearel in the daylight.' I tell you, this smells like a conspiracy."

He took his new clothes and stuffed them into his leather bag. The three phantera exchanged glances.

"Did we offend you?" asked Philoah.

Locking eyes with Philoah, David smiled. "Not at all. Let's go!"

"Have a good enar, David. You need the rest!" Brusaka called after them. "Yavana *hamoth*."

As they stepped onto the street, David asked, "How come Brusaka isn't coming?"

Gyra led the way. "Brusaka stays at the guesthouse until his allotted time is up."

"I heard how Gyra gave his duca a Ramatera name," Philoah told David as they approached the landing lawn. "I decided to give mine a second name too, but hers is in English." Beaming, he looked toward his duca. "I named her Echo."

David looked up at Echo. "That's a nice name."

"And an interesting translation of her Dalena name," Gyra added with a bird-like chuckle.

Treasar lowered his head to help David mount. In one swift movement, David was on the duca's back.

"I've never seen anyone mount a duca like *that*!" Philoah cried.

"Wait until you see how he gets off," Gyra replied, with a twinkle in his eye.

"David! I have something for you," Mojar called from the edge of the landing lawn. She hurried over to them.

"Here." She tossed up an instrument the size of a fat marking pen. "It's a food tester, programmed to detect toxins. Just press the button, ram the point into whatever you're sampling, and the display window will tell you if it's safe to eat. It will also rate poisons as to how toxic they are. Gyra can explain the details to you."

"Ramara, Mojar," David said, bobbing his head. Clipping the instrument onto his belt, he lowered his goggles, muttering, "I still say this is a conspiracy."

After Gyra settled in behind David, the ducas raced over the lawn and rose into the air.

David grasped Treasar's leather belt. The wind hissed by his ears, cooling his curly head. How things had changed from his first days on Arana! Not only had he survived, he was beginning to thrive here. He held fast to the riding straps as the wind tugged at his curls.

Treasar's great white wings flashed in the morning sun. The duca rose with labored strokes, circling the Pendaram's City.

"Where are we going?" David asked his guide in Ramatera.

"First to the valley I showed you a few nights ago," came Gyra's voice. He was hard to hear because of the wind.

David looked down at the vast *Adrana Agera*, the Great Sea. It shimmered clear aqua near the shore and the geometric shapes of submerged buildings glowed in the shallows.

In the inky-blue depths, the underwater structures were harder to distinguish.

Echo flew ahead of Treasar, and Philoah waved from her back.

After they gained several thousand feet in altitude, Echo and Treasar peeled off for the mountains. The woolly foothills rolled beneath them. Ducas grazed among the trees. One of the crested birds raised its head and called out a greeting. Treasar and Echo trumpeted back.

The dusty-green hills rose, changing to mottled peach and pastel blue, until they merged with the lavender mountain slopes. Different plants dominated each elevation. The highest peaks glinted with ice and gray granite, barren of *tearel*—plant life.

A slit opened between two towering crags, revealing a growing sliver of the narrow valley. The more David saw, the more amazed he was by the valley's transformation. It was a riot of brilliant colors shimmering in the sun, a living impressionist painting. Splashes of blue, accents of red, dashes of yellow, green, and orange—the festive hues of the plants would put a parrot to shame.

Diving through the granite gateway, Treasar glided over the lake.


That evening, David lay down beneath a canopy of stars. The strange whistles, chirps, and clicks of the night animals were a constant reminder of the alien nature of his campsite. Since there was no campfire or light, the creatures were not as shy as their Earth counterparts. Hidden animals rustled through the undergrowth while flightless nocturnal birds fished in the lake's shallows.

David gazed at the flickering stars. Where was Earth, his home? "Gyra, do you know where *Trenara* is?"

"Dala, but you can't see her sun. It's too far away."

"Do we live in the same galaxy?"

"Dala. Arana is on the far side of what you call the Milky Way Galaxy."

"What do you call it?"

"The *Cirilla Pala*."

"The Silver Plate? That's an interesting name. Can you show me where Trenara is?"

Turning to face the east, Gyra pointed to a section of the Milky Way near the horizon. "Do you see that dark area? It looks like a hole. That's the Myudo Nebula. Above it and to the right is Trenara, just below that red star. Sanor, your sun, is too faint to see."

"Ramara, Gyra, now I know where to look when I get homesick."


Bird song awakened David.

Perched on top of a towering red tree, Gyra and Philoah sang in Dalena as they greeted the dawn. When the sun touched the upper peaks, the phantera brothers fluttered down. David and his friends ate a leisurely breakfast and mounted the ducas.

"Today we have a treat for you," Gyra told David. "We're going to the Valley of the Ducas."

David buried his waist and legs beneath Treasar's wonderful soft feathers. The lakeshore was too curved to serve as a runway. The last time they left the valley, his back nearly snapped when the duca jumped into the air. Grabbing a bunch of feathers in his hands, David leaned forward. This time he would be ready.

With a great leap, Treasar launched into the air. They rose above the valley floor and traveled east along the jagged mountains. Other valleys crept into view; vibrant flowerpots of color nestled among the gray granite teeth. Slivers of ice and snow still clung to the highest crags and lurked in deep crevasses.

The ducas winged their way over ridges, weaving

around perilous peaks.

The icy wind stung David. Thankful that Brusaka had given him an extra thick cloak for this journey, he wrapped it around his upper body, which was not shielded by the duca's feathers.

The mountain range broadened, revealing a great high valley. Blue forests, silver rivers, and a large lake adorned the lush bowl. Nestled between two peaks, a melting glacier gave birth to a stream. The cascading water plunged over a cliff, feathering into the valley lake below.

Treasar brought in his wings, and the wind roared. They plummeted toward the high plain. A blue corune forest grew on the edge of the valley. The cauliflower-shaped trees formed a lumpy canopy.

Gesturing toward the blue woods, Gyra said, "The ducas like to nest in the corune forest. It's dark and easy for them to hide in there."

A flock of over a hundred ducas grazed on the plains. More bathed in the lake, dabbled on the mud flats, and wandered through the brush.

Treasar and Echo trumpeted. A few of the ducas answered back from below.

"The *balith*, the master-breeder is here!" Gyra shouted as they landed. Nearby, a duca with a butterfly shaped crest balanced on one leg while a cloaked phantera examined the raised foot.

"Balith Orajar, have you been left alone?" Philoah called as he hopped down.

"Everyone else went off to spread the Great Revelation," the balith answered without looking up. "Someone had to stay and tend the flock."

The trio dismounted.

Philoah walked over to observe Orajar's work. "Sore callus?"

"Dala. This one is getting old—and fat. Too much pressure on the joints." Orajar had his back turned to the new-comers, but this was not considered rude among phantera. He was preoccupied with delicate surgery.

"What's he doing?" David whispered to Gyra.

"He's removing part of the overgrown callus."

David watched, fascinated, as the phantera cut away the troublesome callus with a laser, pulled the skin together with an odd stapler, and swabbed the area with disinfectant. The duca appeared to be more interested in David than in the operation on her foot.

Unrolling a large piece of material, Orajar sang an order and the duca spread her toes. He covered the bottom of the foot with a special glue and pressed the material in place. The balith spoke to the duca in Dalena.

"He's telling her to stay out of the water and return in the evening for pills," Gyra translated.

Rumbling a response, the duca limped off toward the plains.

Orajar pulled back his hood and faced the travelers. The silver phantera bobbed his head when he saw David.

"This is Vadelah David," Gyra began.

"The human naharam from Trenara," Orajar finished. "What brings the vadelah here?"

"We do," answered Philoah. "He is enjoying an enar. We're showing him a little of Arana."

"David, come here. I want to show you something," Gyra called.

Puzzled by his friend's eagerness to lure him away, David followed, leaving Philoah and Orajar. "What do you want to show me?"

The phantera led him into the flock of grazing ducas. "Look at their crests."

David squinted. "Are they different breeds?"

"Myute, it is the way they are. You never know what the offspring will look like. Brothers and sisters may be similar, but the children are almost always different from their parents."

Like great cows, the giant waterfowl eyed David as they grazed on the lavender turf. They bore curved crests, tubular crests, double crests, and wavy crests. "Hey Gyra, look! There's one that doesn't have any crest."

The phantera smiled. "That is a very rare duca. Back when we sacrificed *chelra* and *dalam*, the duca with no crest was the most costly sacrifice. We called them *Vashua's ducas.*"

As if responding to some unheard call, Gyra did an about-face. "Wait here." He marched back to Philoah and Orajar.

David meandered in and out among the giant birds. He was a little apprehensive now that he was alone. At least they seemed to be benign. He'd hate to be the first human hors d'oeuvre.

He spied the duca with the patch on her foot. What were Gyra and Philoah up to? Another conspiracy like his "spontaneous" vacation? Creeping back to the three phantera, his suspicions rose. Philoah and Gyra were talking in low voices with Orajar.

"I think she'd be perfect," Orajar stated. "She's healthy, intelligent, and has a good temperament. Someone would have claimed her long ago, but she won't respond to Dalena. I suspect she's part deaf. I had to use—"

"David, back so soon?" Gyra said in a loud voice. The others fell silent.

"All right guys, what's up?" David asked in English. Philoah and Gyra looked at each other. They turned to Orajar.

"This was your idea, you explain it!" Orajar retorted.

Snapping his jaw, Gyra said, "We wanted to get you a duca."

"You *what*?" David broke into a laugh. "That's wonderful, but I don't think I can take one with me. It wouldn't fit in a *delah.*"

"Delahs come in many sizes," Gyra offered, "And you can use her while you're here."

"Dala," Orajar agreed. "You can even take her home with you after you finish your tasks on the three dark planets...if you survive."

Gyra and Philoah scowled at Orajar.

"*Shalar* Orajar," the silver phantera apologized, his eye-rings blushing a deep red. "I did not mean to discourage you."

"She would be a perfect match," insisted Gyra.

David raised his eyebrows. "She?"

"And she's young, only twenty circuits old," Philoah added enthusiastically.

Folding his arms, David asked, "How old do they get?"

Gyra's red eyes regarded him. "Most last two hundred of your years. A few reach two hundred and seventy."

David whistled. "So she'll probably be around long after I die."

"Dala," Gyra replied.

After a long pause, David said, "Well, let's see this duca."

Orajar summoned a duca with a wavy crest. It waddled out from the flock to the silver phantera.

"Is this the one?" David asked.

Philoah shook his head. "Myute, he's just a messenger duca. The one we were discussing is part deaf. She doesn't respond to Dalena so Balith Orajar trained her using Ramatera. Since you can't speak Dalena, and she can't hear it, you're a perfect match!"

Orajar warbled a command and the wavy-crested duca flew off across the valley.

"You make it sound like I'm getting married," David said with a laugh.

Gyra raised a scaly finger. "The bond between a duca and its master is deep, but not *that* deep! This duca will serve you as long as she lives."

"Or as long as I live," David added dryly.

"She is very intelligent—for a duca," Orajar stated. "She's a quick learner, healthy, and has good blood lines. Her mother is a Vashua's duca."

"The duca I saw with no crest?" David asked in surprise.

Obviously pleased, Orajar smiled and bobbed his head rapidly. "You have seen her! They are very rare."

David eyed the grazing flock. "Gyra said most of the phantera have ducas. How many of these have masters?"

"The majority. Those that don't are too young, deformed, or old. A few of the aged ones have outlived their masters. Yavana has blessed you with a young well-trained one. She was not taken because phantera like to speak to their ducas in Dalena."

David spied the rare duca in the flock. "Who owns the crestless duca?"

Chuckling, Orajar placed a scaly hand on David's shoulder. "What do we call the duca with no crest?"

"Vashua's duca."

"And that is who owns her," Orajar answered.

"The messenger duca is flying back with the candidate," Philoah announced.

Like a lumbering bomber, the messenger duca turned aside and swooped back into the flock, but the new duca landed before the master-breeder. Her great blue eyes noted the phantera visitors. Spying David, she stretched out her neck as if to get a better look. Her bony crest fanned out behind her head like the shield of a triceratops, but this "dinosaur" had no horns.

David approached the curious duca. As he circled her, she tried to circle him. Seeing this was fruitless, David stopped to let the duca look him over. When she finished, he walked around her.

"She's beautiful," he whispered in Ramatera. The duca rumbled and bobbed her head.

Frowning, David asked, "Did she understand me?"

Orajar laughed heartily this time. "Dala, she knows crude Ramatera."

David looked at the master breeder. "How will she tell me her needs?"

Orajar beamed. "She'll tell you in Ramatera."

"You taught her to *speak* Ramatera?" Gyra exclaimed.

"Myute," Orajar said, eyes glowing with pride. "She taught herself! That's how I discovered how smart she is."

"Amazing," Philoah cried.

Orajar approached the duca. "They learn Dalena, why not Ramatera?" Staring into the giant bird's eye, he pointed to David. "Duca, do you like naharam David?"

"Dala," the duca answered in a warm low voice.

"You called her *duca*, but doesn't she have a name?" David asked.

Orajar laughed. "Myute. She has no name because she has no master."

Feeling pity for the beautiful unclaimed chelra, David announced, "I will give her a name."

"Then you will take her?" Philoah asked, head bobbing like a piston.

"Dala."

Philoah clasped his hands. "We will leave while you name her."

"Myute, please stay and watch," David begged. "I don't know how to do this."

"Are you sure you want us here?" Orajar asked.

"Dala, I know this is supposed to be a personal time, but I'd like to share it with my friends."

"We are honored," Gyra responded. "To name your duca, place your right hand on her bill and say 'Duca, I name you...' and then say her name."

Orajar made the duca lower her head. David drew in a deep breath and released it slowly. The duca's head hovered before him, watching. Was that a sense of longing in her eyes?

Stepping forward he placed his right hand on the smooth warm bill and felt it quiver. "Duca, I name you...*Arachel*."

Arachel raised her head and trumpeted with such force David covered his ears.

"What a beautiful name," Philoah exclaimed. "Where did you come up with it?"

David wore an embarrassed smile. "I don't know. It's a combination of *ara* and *chelra*. The word just came to my mind as I put my hand on her bill." Why did he name her "sky chelra"?

Orajar slipped away and returned with a large leather strap. "To complete the ceremony, I give you her working belt."

The silver phantera handed it to David. The thick leather strap felt heavy in David's hands, as was the new weight of responsibility.

Arachel wiggled her stiff tail. David told Arachel to lower her head, and he solemnly slipped the belt over her head. When she raised her neck, the belt slid in place. Looking down at David, Arachel growled happily.

"All that's left is for you to ride her," Gyra whispered.

"Oh, no!" David cried in English. "How am I going to mount her?"

Rumbling, Treasar looked at Arachel. David's duca rumbled a response and lowered her head.

"Did Treasar tell her what to do?" David asked.

Gyra wore a satisfied smile. "Dala, in duca language."

David grasped the large feathered crest. Lifting him gently from the ground, Arachel deposited him on her back.

"Hoowah!" Philoah cheered.

David settled into the duca's feathers, hoping she wasn't ticklish. *Here goes my first solo flight on a duca.* Lowering his goggles, he grasped the leather strap. "Let's fly around the valley, Arachel."

The duca ran across the turf and eased into the air.

# 3. The Valley of the Ducas

David whooped as Arachel climbed above the valley. *The thrill of getting my driver's license was nothing compared to this!* Would the FAA require a pilot's license to fly a duca on Earth? What would his friends and family think if they could see him now?

The cool, fresh wind was exhilarating. David directed Arachel to turn left, right, dive, and climb. Obeying instantly with smooth precision, Arachel glanced at her passenger from time to time with her soft, blue eyes.

"*Ramara, Yavana*!" David crowed.

Arachel gave three long bugles as she descended. Most of the flock below stopped grazing and called back in a noisy chorus.

"Land near Balith Orajar," David instructed.

Arachel brought in her wings and the wind became a thundering wall of resistance. They shot over the flock, low and fast. Like a jumbo jet, the duca flared, her proud head rising higher and higher as the wind diminished. Treasar and Echo trumpeted as Arachel touched down. David exhaled in amazement. Arachel's landing had been the most gentle he had ever experienced.

"How was she?" Gyra called from below.

"Wonderful!" David cried.

Philoah fluttered onto Echo. "We'll go over all her abilities later. Arachel has had special training; she really is perfect for you."

Mounting Treasar, Gyra guided his duca to Arachel's side. "Do you want to learn to steer her without vocal commands?"

David rubbed his throat. "Dala, I was going hoarse up there. It's hard to shout into the wind."

Gyra smiled. "Let's begin with ground maneuvers."

"Enjoy your duca," Orajar said. "I have to make some medicines for a few ailing ducas."

"Ramara, Balith Orajar!" David called after him.

Philoah and Gyra instructed David in duca riding. He learned hand signals for when he was not on the duca and foot signals for when he rode her.

Tossing David a coin-sized object, Gyra instructed, "Clip that onto your robe, near the neck. When you want to call her, press it firmly until you hear it click. She will come."

"What is it? Some sort of beeper?" David examined the flat egg-shaped device. It shone metallic blue.

Gyra cooed. "It's similar to a beeper. Its signal is picked up by the receiver in her crest."

"Do all the ducas have a receiver?"

"When they are old enough to work, it's implanted in their crests. Only ducas without crests aren't implanted."

"*Balute?*" asked David.

Gyra wore a wry smile. "Because they are Vashua's ducas. He has no trouble calling them."

"Oh," David said in English. *Dumb question.*

Philoah spoke up. "Look who's following us."

David signaled Arachel to stop as the crestless duca ran toward them. Ducas did look funny when they run. "What does she want?"

Philoah moved Echo out of the way. "She's come to see her daughter off. Ducas have strong bonds with their mothers."

The rare duca's unusually dark blue eyes scrutinized David. She nibbled Arachel's bill and Arachel nibbled back. The two ducas bobbed heads and the crestless duca trotted off.

"That's it?" David blurted.

Philoah smiled. "They are only chelra, not naharam."

Moving Treasar ahead, Gyra said, "Let's show David where the ducas nest."

David practiced guiding Arachel as they headed toward the corune forest. The blue trees towered higher than the ancient walnut grove at Whitefield Park. Blocking most of the sunlight, the succulent leaves and thick branches formed a nearly impenetrable ceiling.

Philoah steered Echo into the cavern-like interior. "The canopy keeps out most of the rain during the wet season. Ducas prefer to nest in dark dry areas. Back on Dalena, they must hide their eggs from predators, so they nest in caves and dense foliage."

The stale air and eerie blue light created a somber atmosphere in the dark silent woods. David guided Arachel around a corune trunk, guessing its girth to be about thirty feet.

"Are there other forests like this?" he whispered to Gyra.

"Dala, but the trees here are larger than most."

Heading back, David smiled when the sun bathed him in its warm light.

"Ready to learn aerobatics and special maneuvers?" Gyra asked.

David was ready for *terra firma*. Two grueling hours of unusual attitudes, rolls, stalls, and vertical takeoffs had left him exhausted. Gyra and Philoah were great encouragers, but he could only endure so much. It was late afternoon when they landed beside the lake in the Valley of the Ducas.

"You have learned all the basics," Gyra said as Treasar made his way toward the shore. "Now, you need to take

Arachel into the water." He glanced at Philoah and gave David an odd smile.

Nudging Arachel with his toes, David directed the great, waddling bird into the lake where she floated like an enormous swan.

"Tell her to bathe," Philoah shouted from shore.

Without thinking, David gave the command, and the duca plunged her head under the surface. David realized his predicament when she yanked her crested head back up.

Arachel flung the water onto her back and shuffled her wings, dipping her body with each plunge. She was ducking...like a duck! David was drenched.

"Stop! Stop!" he cried uselessly in English. After three more soakings, his wits returned. "*Bot, Arachel!*" The duca ceased and eyed him, growling affectionately.

Philoah and Gyra whooped and shouted from shore.

Steering Arachel back to land, David dismounted and let her finish her bath. Then he faced the two phantera.

"Hoowah! Congratulations," Gyra began. "You've successfully completed the ceremony."

Wringing out the bottom of his shirt, David remarked. "I thought it was finished when she got her riding belt."

"Officially it did end there, but unofficially it's not considered complete until you share the same water."

He rubbed his dripping beard. "Kind of like a marriage isn't complete until you share the same bed."

"Dala."

"I just wish I didn't have to get so wet. That water is cold!" David stripped off his soggy shirt.

Philoah pulled out another set of dry clothes, identical to David's soaking ones.

David eyed him. "A second set? You just happen to have a second set made just to fit me? This is a conspiracy!"

Philoah and Gyra turned their backs to David while he changed.

"Who thought of all this anyway?" David asked as he pulled on a dry shirt.

"Brusaka," the two phantera said in unison.

In the evening light, David gazed across the watery mirror.

A distant cascade rumbled as it fell into the lake, breaking the inverted sky and blazing clouds into dancing ripples. Small flying reptiles darted across the water like bats, but there were few insects in this part of Arana. Chirping and squeaking, the long-faced creatures plucked tiny fish from the shimmering surface. A few more "singers" joined them as the sun died.

A low cooing echoed from across the lake. Above, a creature whined as it flew through the darkened skies, too high to see.

And then there was the gross belching noise bursting from the shrubs. Lying down on the alawa turf, David tried to tune out that dissonant sound.

As the last light of day faded, the Milky Way spanned the sky above and his thoughts drifted toward home. How long had he been away? What was everyone doing now? Did they ever figure out what had happened to him? Did they think he was dead?

His mind returned to Arana with a jolt as something cold and wet slid over his arm.

"Ahhh!" He leaped up.

The ducas raised their heads and Arachel stood.

"*Sarena*, David. It's just a *boolee*," Philoah said with chuckle.

A loud obscene belch roared from the unseen creature. Groping around, David found his tool belt. He removed his dowel and turned it on.

A black worm-like creature recoiled from the light. David had never seen such a mollusk before. The two-foot long clam shriveled back into its shell. Its massive foot, which had touched him, was as big around as his arm.

"What is it looking for?" David asked in a shaky voice.
Gyra blinked in the light. "Food. It likes alawa turf."

"Great," grumbled David, "It's eating my bed."

Arachel's bill nudged David.

"What does *she* want?"

Philoah smiled. "She wants to eat the boolee. Ducas love them."

"*Boosah*, gross," David muttered. "Go ahead, Arachel, you can have it."

Arachel pounced on the black mollusk. David cringed at the staccato crunching of shells as she devoured her snack. The duca raised her head as a large lump crept down her neck.

Waving his hand, David said, "You can have any others you find around here. Just keep them away from me."

He lay down and tried to sleep. Just as sweet oblivion began to steal him away, shattering shells jarred him awake. Arachel had found another boolee.

After two more obnoxious interruptions, David ordered Arachel to stop. He mounted the duca, curled up on her back, and slipped into a peaceful sleep at last.

Awakened by a faint rocking, David sat up on Arachel's feathered back. "I don't believe it!" His mount was swimming in the lake.

Alarmed, he ordered Arachel back to shore. She had walked all the way to the water without waking him! Her gait was much smoother than Treasar's.

Gyra and Philoah prepared breakfast as David dismounted.

"Sleep well?" Gyra asked.

David stretched. "Fine, once I climbed onto Arachel." He sipped the cool morning air.

A large flock of ducas noisily dabbled their bills in the mud flats.

David frowned. "What are they doing?"

Giving him a piece of *horlah*, Gyra explained, "They're looking for food."

"What type of food?" David bit into the vegetable.

"Boolee," answered Philoah.

David's stomach tightened. Painfully, he swallowed his bite and stuffed the remains of his vegetable into a pocket.

"The boolee hide in the mud during the day and come out to feed at night," Philoah explained.

"I understand," David mumbled. He covered his mouth and held up a hand to silence Philoah.

"Arachel is hungry. Are you going to let her eat?" asked Gyra.

David wiped his mouth. "Of course!"

"Then you had better tell her."

"She won't eat *unless I tell her*?"

Gyra fingered his bill. "You told her to stop eating last night. Did you forget?"

"No, I thought she understood I meant while I slept!" He turned to Arachel. "*Shalar* David, go and eat."

Arachel cocked her head and ambled off for the mud flats.

David rubbed his hairy chin. "Why did she look at me like that?"

Philoah put a hand on his shoulder. "She does not understand the word *shalar*. *Sorry* she understands, but forgiveness is too complicated for a chelra. Only naharam can really comprehend it."

"And some naharam understand it better than others," Gyra added. "The phantera have a harder time forgiving the mels than humans do."

David stiffened. "I don't know about that! Humans find it pretty hard."

Gyra's round eyes blinked. "Dala, but, among the phantera, forgiveness toward the mels was unthinkable until you came. It is still hard for us to grasp. The Great Revelation has astonished us."

After David finished breakfast, they mounted their ducas and flew out of the valley.

Traveling east along the jagged range of granite teeth, David mulled over Gyra's words. *Forgiveness. Now there's a two-edged sword. It's humbling to ask for it, but even harder to give it. Sure it's easy to cover over minor offenses, but in the really heinous acts, the ones that really count, it's more difficult to give than to receive!*

# 4. Like Falatirah Upon the Ground

Sitting on a rock, David wrote in his journal as the sun heated the thin morning air.

> *Yesterday we visited several small villages. The phantera always greet us speaking Dalena until Philoah shouts "Ramatera." Then the villagers switch to the trade language.*
>
> *Although every phantera on Arana knows English by now, Philoah is encouraging me to use Ramatera as much as possible. "The vadelah must be completely fluent by the time he goes to the melnaharam," he says.*

A duca trumpeted in the distance.

Looking up, David spied the great bird approaching from the west with a rider. He closed his book and stuffed it in his bag. The visiting duca landed beside Treasar.

Philoah bobbed his head. "It's Gilyen."

Now David noticed the difference between Gilyen's and

Philoah's ducas. The tubular crest on Gilyen's duca curved down, while Echo's crest curved up."

"What news do you bring?" Gyra called.

Gilyen hopped down. "Pendaram Ariphema is still gone. We received word that the council went well, but I have no details. Pendaram Ariphema will fill us in when he returns."

"Where are you off to now?" asked Philoah.

"I'm on enar, so I'm going back to my village. Do you have time to come?" Gilyen eyed David. "We would be honored if the vadelah visited."

"We are on enar too," Gyra answered. "We'd be happy to come—if the vadelah approves."

Standing, David said, "Dala, let's do it." He mounted Arachel.

"Nice duca!" Gilyen commented. "I heard they were going to get you one."

David shot a mocking glare at Gyra, but the phantera only smiled.

"Her name is Arachel," Gyra told Gilyen. "She is the daughter of a Vashua's duca."

Gilyen raised both his feathered brows. "Yavana has blessed you, Vadelah David! What an honorable gift." He flew onto his mount.

The four ducas ran over the clattering stones and rose into the air. Gilyen led them north to a narrow valley. They set down in a barren rocky gorge.

"Why are we landing here?" asked David. "I don't see a living thing."

"My village raises lampar in a canyon," Gilyen explained. He pointed to a narrow gap between the sheer opposing walls. "We will walk in that way."

David scowled. "But why did we land here? Is the canyon too small?"

"Myute, David," Philoah said in a low voice. "Lampar are skittish and startle at the sight of a duca. Four ducas

would send them into a stampede. The lampar would trample
their young. This is the only way into the valley on foot."

"We also have a cirilla mine," Gilyen said.

David looked at Gyra. "The phantera seem to mine a lot
of silver."

Gyra fingered his pink bill. "Dala, we make alloys
with it."

Leaving the ducas, they followed a steep trail that was
actually a dry creek bed littered with boulders. The canyon
walls closed in until they were twenty feet apart.

David felt the chill granite wall. It sapped the heat
from his fingers. Tucking his hand into his pockets, he
walked through the cold shadows. A faint wind brushed
the hair on the back of his neck when he emerged from the
gap into the valley.

"It's so quiet," Philoah observed. "Where is everyone?"

Cocking his head, Gilyen answered, "I don't know. A
lot has happened recently."

A small steep hill blocked their view of the valley floor.
Gilyen's nails clattered as he raced ahead, crested the hill,
and looked down. His body went rigid. The feathers on his
head shot up. Throwing back his head, Gilyen released a
shrill wail. The eerie sound seared itself into David's mind.
Gyra and Philoah flew up and joined Gilyen, feathers rising
on their heads as well. Snapping his jaw, Gyra glanced at
David, pink eye-rings drained of all color.

David scrambled up the slope. Looking down, he covered his mouth. Bodies littered the valley, dozens of them.
David hardly recognized the skinned phantera remains.
Just below him, a grotesque corpse stared up at the sky.
Young and old, male and female—their killers had been
indiscriminate. Blue-purple phantera blood spattered the
rocks and stained the ground. It ran in little rivulets and
pooled into puddles, a silent testimony against the mel-
naharam. Gilyen wailed out of control, blue tears turning

purple. David knew if they went red, the phantera was as good as dead.

"Gilyen!" Philoah yelled. Grasping his friend, Philoah placed a hand on the shrieking head. With his fingers positioned for falarn, Philoah cried, "Share it! Share it!"

"Will he die?" David asked.

Philoah's voice rose to a wail, matching Gilyen's in pathos. They both shed purple tears.

"Philoah has penetrated Gilyen's mind," answered Gyra. "Now they share the grief. They will both live."

Pulling a small disk-shaped communicator from his bag, Gyra alerted Arana's communication net of the massacre. He hooked the device onto his cloak.

David locked eyes with Gyra. "Why did the mels do this? Why? Did they have to kill the little ones too? Did they have to butcher them like dalam?"

Gyra looked away. "Come help me gather the bodies." He started down the hill into the valley of carnage.

David's stomach twisted. He didn't want to follow Gyra. He wanted to run, find Arachel, and fly away from this place of horrors, but he knew he could not escape the sorrow that pierced his heart, even if he fled across the galaxy. Taking a deep breath, he followed Gyra as a numbness set in.

The ducas circled the valley, keening. Gilyen's wail must have summoned them. Gyra directed the ducas to land on the hill beside Philoah and Gilyen, but the ducas continued to keen. The walls reverberated with the cries and wails of the mourners, adding to the morbid scene.

David helped Gyra pile the bodies in stacks of five or six. The corpses were not heavy, but it was wearisome work for a burdened heart.

The sound of the mourners finally diminished as Philoah and Gilyen wept and the ducas moaned.

Gyra was the first to speak. "These were killed recently, perhaps early this morning."

David reached for a stiff leg. "How can you tell?"

Gyra held the head of the corpse as they lifted it. "They have not begun to decay and the blood is still fresh."

Staring at the purple puddle marking the body's place, David said, "It looks like *falatirah*."

"Dala, Vadelah David. 'Like falatirah upon the ground.'"

David remembered the phantera Scripture. "Why were they skinned?"

"The *mel-dijetara* wanted the hides, but these were not killed by them. This is the work of the *mel-hanor*."

David grimaced. "They look like they were…tortured."

"That is the way of the mel-hanor," Gyra reached for a slender body.

Looking away, David tried to disengage his mind from the horrific images. "Why don't I see any lampar?"

"The mel-hanor took them. They will use them for sport back on their dark world."

They moved to another area and Gyra paused as he examined one of the bodies. He snapped his jaw.

"What is it?"

Gyra straightened up. "The *mel-balahrane* were here as well. This phantera is missing organs, and she was killed with a knife."

"Why?"

"They offer the organs to the *mel-aradelah*—their demon-gods. The mel-balahrane use knives on their sacrifices."

"*Boosah*," David muttered.

"I believe a better word is *castulshep*," Gyra stated.

"The English word *abomination* is appropriate too," David spat. He helped lift the carcass. It was much lighter than the previous ones.

They found others opened up by the mel-balahrane. A few phantera had tried in vain to hide behind rocks and in crevasses from their relentless enemies. Traces of the deadly net that once covered the valley still clung to the sharper ridges. Gyra directed David to search the west side of the valley for more bodies while he combed the east side.

Weary, David stumbled onto a ledge and found the rigid form of a slender phantera. Judging by the faint blue tone left in her eye-rings, the corpse was a female. He lifted her stiff form. A second small body lay underneath. David wept as he removed the battered corpse of the phantera child. The poor mother couldn't save her son.

A faint warble came from the granite wall on his left. He restrained his weeping to hear what it might be. There it was again! Standing up, David held his shaky breath, listening. Another soft warble.

"Who is it?" he asked in Ramatera.

The warble changed to muffled words. Following the voice to a crack in the rock wall, David pressed his face against the rough rock.

"Dahmoo...dahmoo...," a soft voice called. *Dahmoo* was Ramatera for mother. A child had seen him and was asking for her mother!

"Gyra, come here quick!" Gazing down at the female corpse on the ledge, he spoke in a tight voice, "Perhaps Yavana has spared one of your children."

Gyra alighted on the ledge, saw the two bodies, and sighed.

"There's a survivor!" David cried, pointing to the crack in the wall.

Gyra sang a few notes. A melodic line answered back.

Searching along the crack, Gyra wagged his head, scanning the rock. "It's the door cover to the silver mine." He pressed his hand against the stone door and slid it aside.

A fuzzy phantera chick stood before them, blinking in the light.

Gyra picked her up and cradled her. "Ramara, Yavana, for saving this little one," he whispered.

The child reached toward the skinned contorted bodies. "Dahmoo."

David clenched his jaw to stifle a scream. He wanted to hide the child from her mother's brutal death.

Pointing to the corpse, Gyra said, "This is dahmoo's body, but dahmoo is not here. Just like a broken eggshell, your dahmoo has left her body behind and is with Vashua."

"Dahmoo has hatched?" the child asked with blinking blue eyes. "Nest brother too?"

"Dala, they have hatched into *cerepanya*. You will not see her or your nest brother until you are hatched too. We will miss them." Setting the chick down, Gyra placed a hand on her head. "I will share your grief."

David turned, gathered the body of the child's brother, and carried it down to the valley floor. As he laid it beside a pile of corpses, the cry of the child rent the air.

He stared at the destruction around him. David didn't want to speak to the mel-naharam; he wanted to kill them! "God, why didn't you annihilate them?" he cried in English. "Why didn't you stop them from killing so many of your people? Will You gain glory from *this*?"

He climbed up to Gilyen and Philoah. Arachel approached David and nudged him with her bill. Feeling very lonely, David rubbed the duca's warm beak and hugged her head.

About a half-hour later, Gyra returned with the child. Gilyen was comforted by her presence. Calling the child, he placed a hand on her head. "Wenlan, because you have neither father nor mother nor any other closer kin, I will cover you with my wings. I will be your father, and you shall be my daughter."

The child's pale-blue eyes blinked. "I am your child, and you are my father." Gilyen led Wenlan over to his duca.

"That was a *yataphar*, an adoption," Gyra whispered. "When disasters destroy families, we use the yataphar to build new ones. That way no one is left alone. Gilyen lost all of his family—his parents, his wife, and his children. He will raise this child as his own. When we return to the Pendaram's City, he will join himself to another village."

Gyra turned to Philoah. "How's Gilyen?"

Philoah's eye-rings were still pale. "Gilyen will be all right, but it was close. His crealin nearly ruptured. How is Wenlan?"

Gyra gave a weary smile. "She is young; she will recover faster then Gilyen."

"Well, I don't think I'll ever recover!" David spat in bitterness. "I've never seen anything so horrendous in my entire life."

Gyra's black pupils targeted David. "Such talk from a naharam of Trenara, where mothers kill their own children! I didn't think anything would surprise you here."

"Are you comparing this with abortion?" David asked in a rising voice. "At least abortionists don't expose the carcasses for everyone to see."

Gyra's feathered brows lowered into a scowl. "What difference does that make? It's the killing that matters. What they do with the bodies afterwards is trivial compared to murder. Does the fact that you don't see the mess make it any less evil?

"The mel-naharam kill us because we are at war. They view our existence as a threat to their survival. You have mothers who kill their children because of convenience. That is a far more heinous thing to me."

Hanging his head, David rubbed his weary face. "There's no defense for what my people do. We can be cold and heartless. Massacres are a part of our twisted heritage; I'm just not used to the sight."

Gyra placed a hand on David's shoulder, his red eyes probing. "It would be disastrous if you went to the mel-naharam full of anger and bitterness. Share your grief with me."

Sighing like a deflated balloon, David bowed his head. He felt the three long fingers and thumb rest lightly on his scalp.

"Yavana, give David *sarena*," the phantera whispered.

Sensing the deep comfort of his friend, David released his tears. He let his sorrow flow and rested on Gyra's strong presence. *How do I rid myself of this anger?* David cried out in his mind.

He saw a form, a familiar form. A man hung upon two beams of wood, his tortured body impaled by nails that pierced his hands and feet. The man's skin hung in strips, nearly separated from the flesh, like the skinned phantera. Upon the battered head sat a thorny wreath. Blood dripped down the long spikes. The man's eyes gazed into David's soul. "Remember me," he whispered.

David felt his bitterness and hate slide away. Crying out, the man's head sank lifeless to his chest. A spear appeared and pierced the man's side. Fluid flowed from the wound.

A hooded figure held up a bowl and caught the liquid. Turning, the figure spoke, "Vashua the Provided One shall be poured out, like a bowl of falatirah upon the ground, upon Trenara's ground." The figure poured the bowl's contents onto the ground. The blue-purple liquid stained the soil.

A voice called out, "I am a man of sorrows; those who follow me will know grief, but I will turn their wailing into joy. I myself will comfort them. Fear not! I have known the depths of pain and triumphed over it. I alone can bring glory out of tragedy.

"I have prepared the way for your task. Be bold and do not fear the mel-naharam or the mel-aradelah. I will be with you."

A darkness descended and David felt Gyra's presence recede. Sounds filtered in from outside his mind.

"I have never felt such intensity," Gyra whispered.

"Is he going to come out of it?" asked Philoah.

Shaking his head, David opened his eyes. "Thank you, Gyra. That was an incredible experience. I didn't know your thoughts would be so...vivid."

Gyra snapped his jaw nervously and cocked his head. "My thoughts? I thought they were *your* thoughts."

They stared at each other.

David rubbed his scalp. "If they weren't my thoughts and they weren't your thoughts...whose were they?"

Gyra blinked. "Yavana's. You have a word in English for what we experienced," he said in an even tone. "You saw a *vision*. I had the honor of sharing it."

David gazed out at the valley of slaughter but felt no anger. A soft wind lifted the curls off his forehead. Turning, he faced his friends. Gilyen and his new daughter watched him in silence while Philoah fingered the feathers on his neck.

"Let's return to the Pendaram's City," David said. "It is time I prepared to meet the mel-naharam."

# 5. David's First Panatrel

David's face was raw from the cold dry buffeting wind. Treasar's flashing white bulk flew ahead of him, leading the way.

Yesterday, phantera from nearby villages had flocked to the massacre site. A squadron of ducas, dispatched by Orajar, arrived with empty vests to bear away the corpses. Together, the ducas and villagers quickly removed the dead. Gilyen, his adopted daughter, and Philoah flew on ahead to the Pendaram's City that evening.

Now that it was morning, Gyra and David were heading there as well. David bowed his head. The light reflecting off Arachel's feathers hurt his eyes. *Yavana, how do I prepare for my journey?*

The air grew moist and warmer as they crossed the last mountain and began their descent. David could just make out the city through the dusty haze. The pink landing lawn was more crowded than usual with ducas and delahs. Arachel and Treasar increased the population by two, landing on the pink turf.

"Word travels fast," Gyra noted. "There will be many phantera at the *panatrel*."

David knew the word *panatrel* meant funeral.

"The ceremony is usually performed by the *talaram*, but because the village leader perished with most of his flock, Pendaram Ariphema will be presiding," Gyra explained. "In instances of intense tragedy, such as this, the pendaram himself ministers to his people."

After dismounting, David and Gyra let their ducas depart for the grazing hills. David watched Arachel wing her way toward the forest, still amazed that he owned the magnificent bird.

"Brusaka will be eager to see us," Gyra said.

Following Gyra toward the guesthouse, David asked, "Where will the panatrel take place?"

"Philoah didn't tell you? I thought you would have known that! It will take place at the *Hiya Amada*."

The fire mountain? David scowled. "What is the Hiya Amada? A volcano?"

"Dala, David."

Upon entering the house, Brusaka greeted them with enthusiasm. Philoah emerged from a room and joined them.

After the talk died down, David continued his questions. "I still don't understand. Why will the panatrel be at a volcano?"

Gyra poured a bowl of falatirah to drink. "We place their bodies in the molten lava."

"Why?"

Philoah answered before Gyra could stop him. "To protect them from the mel-naharam. Of course it's a little late for these."

Gyra set the pitcher down hard and looked at Philoah.

"Didn't you tell him?" Philoah asked.

"No, I thought it would be too risky, especially if he ever returns to Trenara!" Gyra raised the feathers on his head.

David's frown deepened. "Tell me what?"

Tilting his head, Philoah stared at his older brother. "David should know. He *is* the vadelah."

Gyra's bill snapped. "You're right. I didn't want to burden him before, but he should know."

"Excuse me! Will someone please address *me*?" David said. Brusaka watched silently with his bright, orange eyes.

Gyra turned to David. "Shalar Gyra. Do you remember the night when I told you about the handcuffs?" He walked over to a shelf and removed a caruk.

David narrowed his eyes. What was Gyra up to? "You showed me your hands could take a lot of heat."

Nodding, Gyra adjusted the setting on the caruk. "I did not tell you everything. It isn't just the scales of our hands and feet that protect us."

Pointing the caruk at the ground, he fired. A patch of floor the size of manhole cover melted to a lava-like liquid. David felt the heat from six feet away.

"You could have done that outside," Philoah chided.

"Dala, but I want David to remember and understand." Gyra turned the laser toward his own chest and fired. The beam vaporized whatever dust was on the surface, but the feathers remained unchanged.

The air grew hotter. David stepped back.

Gyra held the laser on his chest for twice as long as he had done to the floor. He cut the beam. David glanced at the molten hole still glowing in the floor. He really was sweating now.

"Come feel my chest," Gyra instructed.

Drawing near, David stretched out a cautious hand and touched the feathers. He relaxed. They were not even warm. "This is amazing!" David whispered.

"The mel-naharam think so too," Brusaka stated.

David yanked his hand back as if he'd been burned. "No!" he cried, horror and understanding breaking over him. "*That's* why they skinned their victims!" He staggered back against the wall.

"Dala, David," Brusaka spoke in a soft sad voice. "They are after one of Yavana's gifts to us."

Philoah put a hand on David's shoulder.

Gyra spoke again. "We have reason to believe the mel-naharam are fashioning the feathers into coverings for a new fleet of ships."

"Why?" David pulled away from the wall.

Gyra drank his bowl of falatirah and looked at David. "Crullahs and delahs fight with lasers, to borrow an English word. But, as you can see, lasers have no effect on us. If the mels covered a ship with our feathers, it would be very difficult to destroy it."

Shaking his head, David said, "I don't understand. Why don't you use rockets or missiles to shoot them down?"

Gyra scratched the hidden bullet wound on his chest. "We used to fight with missiles. Later, both sides developed the technology to explode an enemy's warhead as it was being fired. It destroyed any ship carrying a missile. So, we advanced to lasers. If a delah is seriously damaged, the enemy might fire small projectiles, but they wisely avoid anything explosive."

Stroking his beard, David said, "I thought delah hulls were pretty tough."

"They are," Philoah added. "And projectiles are generally harmless to them. The only things that can effectively breach the hulls are laser blasts or collisions with other ships."

David scowled. "I don't understand. Why would they want to fire a projectile?"

Gyra and Philoah exchanged glances.

"Don't you see?" Brusaka blundered in. "If a delah is hit by a laser and opens up, a phantera can still survive if he has not been hit by shrapnel."

David stared at Gyra. "You can live in *deep space?*"

Gyra's fleshy eye-rings blushed. "Dala. We close our third eyelids and our noses. We usually go into *pulmar*, a deep sleep."

"Why?" David took a bowl of falatirah from Brusaka.

"Sometimes it is a long time before we are found. We sleep to conserve energy."

Philoah fingered his cloak. "So, the crullahs fire projectiles to kill any phantera that survive a breached hull."

"They're really out to get you guys," David whispered. "I hope what I do will make a difference." Raising his bowl, he said, "Ramara Yavana." The sweet liquid soothed his thirst as it went down.

"Who knows the mind of Yavana?" Brusaka stated in a reverent tone.

That afternoon, David stood at the top of a ramp sloping into the sea outside the council chambers. Brusaka had insisted on giving him a tour of the underwater city.

The black phantera helped him into a tailor-made dry-suit. Pointing to a small box on the back of the suit, Brusaka said, "This machine will draw oxygen straight from the water, like the gills of a loomar, and pump it into your mouthpiece."

After donning a mask and weight belt, David followed his guide down the ramp into the clear lapping water. The phantera gave David a lamp to light the way in the depths. As they submerged, Brusaka placed a hand on David's head to communicate using falarn.

The sea floor dropped away into a dark, blue void. The lamp's brilliant light traveled far underwater, illuminating several large structures. *In the wet season you would need a lamp to see even in the shallows. The cloud cover from the shardreas does not let much light through*, the phantera commented as he pulled David through the water.

Buildings with high domed ceilings rose from the mysterious blue depths. An intricate web of pipes connected the structures.

*The pipes carry fresh air*, Brusaka answered before David could form the question. *The haranda are air-breathing mammals. The domes hold air and provide a place where haranda can rest and sleep, no matter how stormy the seas become.*

Brusaka led David into one of the domed structures. As they entered the air pocket, David found himself in a room ringed with ledges. Platforms floated on the water, some supporting sleeping haranda. A soft, blue light glowed from clear windows set in the roof. Waterproof bags hung on the wall. On the upper ledges rested several low tables, reminding David of the ones in children's Sunday school rooms.

Brusaka continued to use falarn out of courtesy to the sleeping occupants. *This is where they prepare meals and eat. The haranda like to eat things besides raw fish, so we trade melcat and lampar meat in exchange for pagaruna hides.*

*What's a pagaruna?* David asked.

*A large warm-blooded water dalam. In the early dry season, the haranda hunt them with harpoons and call their chelra to help. The hunters drive a pagaruna into a shallow bay during high tide. They kill the animal when the outgoing tide strands it—at least that's how they like to do it.*

*Sometimes things go wrong and they end up trying to kill them in deep water—a dangerous thing to do.*

*I bet!* David replied, noting the mighty harpoons hanging on the walls. *How big is a pagaruna?*

*Bigger than a female melcat! If you lined up two ducas, one behind the other, that would be approximately the size of one pagaruna. The meat they get from a pagaruna will feed three hundred haranda, and the leather is excellent for making duca vests.*

*How smart is a pagaruna?*

*Not very. They may be large, but they are very stupid— even for a dalam. There is no comparison between them and the whales of Trenara.*

David was surprised Brusaka had caught his thought and understood his concern.

Diving again, they watched shimmering fish flit in and out of the buildings, while fantastically shaped crustaceans scurried about on the ocean floor.

A haranda glided by, eyeing them. David felt strange vibrations as a thumping noise came from the haranda.

*She is greeting you, David.*

*Tell her "Hi" for me.*

A similar sound emanated from the phantera. The haranda nodded and swam off. Working his silent black wings, Brusaka led David up a great ridge. The light increased as they rose and Brusaka turned off the lamp. As they crested the top, David caught his breath.

Towering like majestic pines, frilled plants reached up to the silver surface. Rays of sunlight streamed down, illuminating golden patches of sand. A jointed fish burst from the sea floor and lurched away. Clusters of delicate purple leaves and orange branches swayed in the gentle ocean current as small fish darted about.

David glided through an undersea garden of red spiral stems, yellow flowery clusters, and neon-green grasses.

Parrot-colored invertebrates grazed among the plants. A few haranda tended the undersea garden, harvesting strange bulbs and transplanting stems. After visiting a rock and shell garden, David grew tired and they returned to the surface.

"Ramara, Brusaka," he said, removing his mask. "That was wonderful."

The gentle phantera nodded modestly and strode out of the water. David smiled. He knew Brusaka had done more than take him on a mere tour. His friend's real goal was to ease the burden of David's heart—and he'd succeeded. David would never forget that.

Bleak barren landscape rolled beneath the delah as they flew to the funeral site.

"The Hiya Amada is a great volcano situated inland, north of the city," Gyra informed David. "It's only a few hundred miles away—a short trip by delah. Look out the window and you'll see it soon."

Dead cinder cones and the black tongues of old lava flows marred the flat plains. From the midst of the blemished land rose the mighty cone of the Hiya Amada. Her dark shoulders were wrapped in layers of ribbons, once-living flows now solidified into unyielding stone. A flock of ducas hid in the volcano's shadow. Their white feathers were the only "snow" that graced the harsh slopes.

"It's hot down there," Philoah commented. "The ducas are staying in the shade to keep their feet cool."

Staring at the scarred mountain, David asked, "How come there's hardly any smoke?"

"Hiya Amada is not a violent volcano," answered Gyra. "It has lava flows from time to time, but no fierce explosions."

The delah landed on a broad ledge in front of a cavernous entrance.

"Be sure to bring your cloak, David," Philoah cautioned.

David didn't understand why he would need a thick cloak if it was hot outside, but he obeyed. They made their way to the entrance—a gaping natural opening in the volcano's side. Lumpy rocks jutted from the floor like petrified mud monsters. As they traveled the long tunnel, David didn't need his dowel to illuminate the path. A dull red glow lit the far end of the passage—definitely not sunlight. He marveled at the constant wind that drew him further into the heart of the volcano.

The path sloped upward at a steady rate and a low rumble resonated off the hard walls. When they reached the top, the tunnel expanded into a large cavern. The temperature soared.

Mopping his face, David said, "I don't think I can go any farther."

Philoah eyed him. "Time to put on your cloak."

"Are you serious? I'm burning up!"

"Myute, David, you are not burning up yet, but you will be very uncomfortable if you enter the cavern without your cloak."

David shook his head, but put the cloak on. The searing heat diminished. "What's this thing made of?"

Gyra wore a subtle smile. "Wesarel fibers and Brusaka's feathers."

"I didn't know that!" David sputtered. "His feathers looked fine when I saw him last."

Gyra gave a cooing laugh. "We do molt! Brusaka used some feathers from his molt bag."

"Oh," David muttered in English.

They continued into the great vault. The path eased down and broadened out to a large ledge. On it stood a gathering of phantera. The ceiling curved upward in the center, disappearing into the enormous vent. Below the ledge, a fiery lake of lava boiled and churned. Its brilliant red, yellow, and white surface illuminated the great cavern.

Leading them closer to the edge, Gyra whispered, "Isn't it beautiful?"

"I must confess it reminds me of the Lake of Fire in Revelation," David said in a dry voice. He regretted not drinking more water earlier.

Philoah cocked his head. "I suppose it is terrifying to a human. The haranda don't like it either."

"I'm not surprised!" David moved his feet. The ground was hot and his face was roasting.

"Are you still uncomfortable," Philoah asked.

"Dala, dala, *dala!*" Slipping in his melting rubber soles, David danced back to the cooler part of the cave.

Gyra bent down and picked at the gooey rubber left on the ground. "This won't do."

David would have removed his shoes, but the ground was too hot to sit on, let alone rest a socked foot. He hopped to the tunnel, where his shoes cooled quickly.

"We could carry him," Philoah suggested.

"I have a better idea." Using a knife, Gyra cut some strips from his own cloak, wrapping them around David's shoes and lower legs.

"I hate to see you ruin your cloak over this," David whispered.

"Brusaka will give me another one when I return."

"How about my face? I feel like my skin is going to peel off."

Cutting out a square piece of cloak, Gyra made a veil and covered David's face with it, stuffing the excess into the hood.

The assaulting heat faded. Peering through the two holes, David followed Philoah and Gyra back to the ledge. "I feel so stupid!" he muttered in English.

The temperature did not increase as much as he feared. Most of the heat from the molten lava rose toward the ceiling, creating the constant wind of cooler air sucked from the tunnel. Gyra and Philoah made sure David stood near the front of the gathering so he could see.

Pendaram Ariphema waited with his back to the lake. Before him stood Gilyen with his adopted daughter, Wenlan. The bodies of their fellow villagers lay in neat rows to Ariphema's right as the crowd watched from his left. The old phantera bobbed his head at David and his friends. Then he addressed the crowd.

"Dear flock, we have come to Hiya Amada to release our grief, and to inter the bodies of our brothers and sisters within the molten lake.

"We grieve, but not without hope. We cry, but not forever. We wail, but our voices will sing again. Our brothers and sisters are not here. They are with Vashua! They are the blessed! They are free! I say they are the blessed because they heard the Great Revelation before they died. They were briefly allowed the joy of hearing about Vashua's incredible deeds before seeing Him face to face.

"Who will lay these honored ones into the molten lake for safe keeping?"

A robust silver phantera came forward and stood beside Gilyen.

"That's the talaram of Gilyen's new village," Philoah whispered.

"I, Talaram Elaneer, and my village will do it," the phantera said.

"And why do you request this honor?" Ariphema asked.

"Because I have covered Gilyen and Wenlan with my wings. They are the only survivors of the Lamajda Village."

"I accept your request." Lifting his hands, Ariphema proclaimed, "Let us release our grief and our longing for these brothers and sisters who were loved."

A great wailing chorus broke out, resonating through the cavern. Gilyen and Wenlan held each other as they grieved.

David put his hands over his ears, but then removed them, worried the phantera might think he was rude. The crying, weeping assembly moved his heart and he added his own voice. It felt good to grieve.

After several minutes, Ariphema raised his hands and the lamentations died down. "Elaneer, you may begin."

A group of phantera emerged from the crowd and took their places at the head of each of the slain.

Walking solemnly to the foot of the first body, Elaneer said, "Falwen." The wails broke out again.

Elaneer and the phantera who stood at the corpse's head lifted their burden and dropped it into the molten sea. Instantly the cries stopped.

Elaneer approached the next body. "Terooma," he said. Again a chorus of wailing went up, ceasing when the body disappeared into the fluid rock.

The talaram continued down the line. Each body exploded with steam and smoke as the lake enfolded it. The stench of burnt flesh made David queasy.

Gyra seemed to sense his discomfort. "It's not usually like this," he explained. "When they have their feathers, they just slide in without any disturbance."

David nodded, but could not speak. He bent over. The oppressive heat and smell were a potent mixture.

When he finished his task, Elaneer stood beside Gilyen.

David forced himself to straighten up out of respect for the solemn occasion.

Ariphema addressed the assembly. "Now, let us thank Yavana for the gift of life. Let us thank Him for the lives of these blessed brothers and sisters." He looked at Gilyen and Wenlan. "And let us thank Him for those who are living."

Raising his wings and hands, the pendaram broke out in song. The assembly joined him.

David longed to sing, but he didn't know the words or

the tune. For a brief moment he forgot the heat and listened in awe. The song changed to a response.

Ariphema called out, *"Ramara Yavana sa hayan* [Thank you God for life]."

*"Ramara Yavana!"* the assembly thundered back.

David was able to follow the chorus and joined in the responses.

The ceremony climaxed with a deafening, *"Harana Yavana* [Praise God]!" from all in the cavern. The crowd dispersed into babbling groups.

"Is it over?" David asked. The air was quite stuffy under his cloak.

"Dala, David," Gyra replied in a strange distant voice. "We can go outside where it's cooler."

"Just in time!" David mumbled as his vision faded. The last thing he heard was a jarring *thump*.

# 6. The Vadelah's Departure

David rolled over on his bed. A duca trumpeted in the distance as the morning light brightened. The aroma of cooking loomar wafted into his room.

He turned over again. It was two days since the panatrel. The memory of his fainting spell still made him cringe. Gyra and Philoah had to carry him out of the volcano. They feared he might be ill, but the only damage David sustained was a sore jaw and a bruised ego.

With a sigh, David sat up and rubbed his curly hair. Putting on his shoes, he rose and took his new tool belt off a wall peg. The belt was a gift from Mojar, outfitted with all his previous gadgets along with two new ones. He admired the metal cutter and calculator with a conversion program for human units. They would be useful tools on his upcoming journey.

Frowning, he fastened the belt around his waist. The phantera understood the importance of being informed about alien cultures, especially when delivering an important message. Why hadn't they made any real effort to educate him on the mels?

David marched into the dining room.

Gyra bobbed his head in greeting. "Pendaram Ariphema has returned."

Rubbing his eyes, David asked, "When are you guys going to train me, teach me what you know about the mels?"

Gyra's bill snapped in response. "I'm sorry, but we can't tell you any more."

David's stomach twisted. "What do you mean? You can at least tell me what they look like!"

"I'm sorry, David." Gyra picked nervously at the scar beneath his feathers. "We owe you an explanation. Some in the Naharam Alliance (not the phantera) question Rammar's prophecy regarding you. Pendaram Ariphema learned this while attending the Council of Pendarams on Dalena.

"The council was concerned that if we fully assisted you, others might attribute your success to our effective tutoring. They would doubt Yavana's power and His calling in your life."

"Great," David breathed, shaking his head.

The feathers on Gyra's scalp rippled. "Please understand; Pendaram Ariphema pleaded that you be given full instruction. Dal-pendaram Elyara asked, 'Do we believe Rammar's prophecy or not? If David is the vadelah, he will succeed. Although it will be a hardship for the human, the faith of many naharam will be strengthened by his dependence on Yavana for this difficult task.'

"Then they voted. Pendaram Ariphema lost, but he will honor the council's decision."

Gyra's red eyes drove into David. "I believe you are the vadelah. Rammar is never wrong in his prophecies."

David was moved by his friend's convictions. "I wish I had your faith about the matter. I feel like I'm going to my doom."

Placing a gentle hand on David's shoulder, Gyra said, "The council did make one concession to Pendaram Ariphema." A slight smile graced his feathered face. "Pendaram Ariphema arrived this morning...from Thalona."

David scowled. "Thalona?"

"The home world of the *coralana*."

David's hands migrated to his itchy scalp. "Aren't they the ones who carved the tunnels to the doloom...and didn't they make your delah?"

"Dala, their technology is very advanced."

"Can't phantera make technical things?"

Gyra cocked his head. "We can, but we'd rather let the coralana do it. It's their strength and their calling; it brings them great joy to overcome physical challenges with their knowledge and skills."

"You're not intimidated by them?"

"Myute, why should we be? The coralana are builders, we are translators. All naharam are equal in the work of Yavana."

"Amazing," David whispered. "So, why do the phantera live in such primitive environments?"

"We were created to endure harsh climates so we can communicate with many naharam. We feel no need to live with abundant possessions or buildings."

David ran his fingers through his lengthening curly hair. "But back to your point. Why did Pendaram Ariphema visit the coralana?"

The smile returned to Gyra's face. "He was overseeing the construction of a new delah, a very special ship, custom made for a human."

David balked. "For me?"

Gyra gave a laughing coo. "Do you see any other humans around? How did you expect to travel to the three dark worlds?"

"I thought someone would drop me off," David confessed.

Gyra wagged his head. "That would be a sure way to get yourself killed. Any ship carrying a phantera would be reduced to shrapnel before it could land. No, David, you must go alone. Are you ready to see your ship?"

"It's *here*? Where?"

"Parked on the landing lawn. Pendaram Ariphema is waiting for you."

David raced for the door. "I'm on my way!"

Resting on the pink lawn was a white and silver delah with a nose sleeker than the one on Gyra's ship. Another difference was the twin vertical tail fins.

Pendaram Ariphema stood beside the spacecraft, beaming. "We altered the configuration so the mel-naharam won't destroy it on sight. Being curious, they'll scan it. Then they'll be stunned to find a human in it!"

Turning to the door, the pendaram said, "*Toorah barune.*" The white door slid open. Ariphema beckoned David inside. "We will imprint your vocal patterns into the command receiver."

David gazed at all the dials on the instrument panel.

"Don't worry." Ariphema pointed to the main screen. "The computer will tell you what you need to know, and we equipped your ship with two repair robots."

"I'm glad to see this one has a real chair," David said with a light laugh. Sitting down, he relished its perfect fit.

Ariphema opened a narrow panel door. "Your flight suits are in here. They will inflate and apply pressure to your skin, keeping you from passing out during liftoff and abrupt turns."

As he rested in his seat, David stared at the computer monitor. The screen gave information in Ramatera. With a voice command he could direct the delah to any mapped location in the *Cirilla Pala*, the Milky Way Galaxy.

Gyra poked his head into the cabin. "Ready for orientation?"

"David, Pendaram Ariphema would like to see you," came Brusaka's gentle voice.

David sprang out of bed. "I'm not going to keep him waiting for three hours this time."

"And you will not go on an empty stomach. You may have a long day ahead of you," the black phantera said cryptically.

David gave a resigned sigh and followed his host. After a hasty breakfast, Brusaka led him outside.

Phantera and haranda crowded the landing lawn.

"This must be something big," David muttered.

"Dala, David."

Instead of leading him to the council chambers, Brusaka headed for the crowd. The assembly parted to let them through. In the center, Pendaram Ariphema waited with Pendaram Halora and Rammar the Prophet. Philoah and Gyra stood nearby.

Pendaram Ariphema spoke out in a loud voice. "David, human of Trenara, vadelah to the naharam—and mel-naharam—we have a solemn request."

Ariphema, Halora, and Rammar bowed down. It was the first time David had seen any phantera bow. Philoah had told him it was only done on extremely important occasions.

David's cheeks burned as the entire crowd bowed as well, awaiting his reply. "Why do you show me such honor?" he asked Ariphema. "I am but a naharam like you. On Trenara I have no one to cover with my wings."

Ariphema's head remained bowed. "We give you honor because you are the vadelah and you represent Trenara. Trenara is first among planets. We show our recognition of her honored position."

David pondered how to respond. "Rise Pendaram Ariphema, I will hear your request." That sounded impressive.

Ariphema straightened up and the multitude followed his example. "Trenara's Scriptures mention two rituals we would like to participate in. The first is bathing, the second is eating and drinking from Vashua's cup."

*Bathing? What did he mean by bathing?* "Oh, baptism!" David blurted in English. "I would be honored to help you."

"Come." Turning, Ariphema walked further into the crowd.

The group parted, revealing an oval pond on the lawn.

"That wasn't there yesterday!" David whispered to Gyra.

Gyra's red eyes shone. "They dug it last night; Arachel helped."

David stared at the glassy water faithfully reflecting the images around it. Pearly tiles lined the gently sloping bottom.

Ariphema stepped into the shallows. "If you will bathe me, I will bathe the delaram. They will pass it on to those below them until all phantera have been bathed."

Pendaram Halora, ruler of the haranda, wiggled his way through the crowd and into the pond. He offered to pass the rite of baptism on to the haranda.

Placing an arm behind Ariphema's back, David held on to the phantera's bluish hands. "Pendaram Ariphema, I bathe you in the name of Yaram, Vashua, and Naphema!"

The phantera stiffened like a dead bird as the waters closed over him. David worried he might not be able to lift Ariphema, but the phantera popped up easily. Ariphema spread his wings and raised his hands, whooping, "Hoowah! Hoowah!"

A cheer rose from the crowd.

Now David faced the giant bulk of Pendaram Halora. The haranda submerged most of his body until only his head and neck showed. Holding the soft furry face, David spoke the solemn words and baptized Halora. Another cheer went up and Halora howled and swayed his great neck. Both pendaram called their delaram. As the haranda and phantera delaram stepped forward, David felt a tap on his shoulder.

Rammar gazed into his face with laser-orange eyes. "You are to baptize me and your close friends," the old prophet said.

Wading back into the pond, David confided, "This feels so awkward; I feel like you should be blessing me."

Rammar smiled. "The Great Revelation came from you, so it is fitting that you bathe me, but before you leave, I *will* bless you!"

David proceeded to baptize Rammar. Another round of cheering rose up as the revered prophet emerged from the waters. A haranda began a song and the crowd quickly picked it up.

David baptized Gyra and Philoah and stood dripping wet in the shallows. "Come on, Brusaka, you're next."

"*Me?*" Brusaka pointed to his black chest. "The vadelah wants to bathe *me?* But I didn't travel with you!"

David put a hand on his friend's shoulder. "You showed me the underwater city, made sure I was clothed and fed, and gave me the most comfortable bed on Arana." David fingered his cloak. "A part of you travels with me."

Brusaka entered the water in silence. When David finished baptizing his friend, the phantera just stood there, eye-rings blushing bright red. David gave him a big wet hug.

In a daze, Brusaka stepped from the water, muttering, "I was bathed by the vadelah. Harana Yavana! I was bathed by the vadelah!"

Halora inchwormed his way to David. "Vadelah David, must we be bathed in mountain water, or will the ocean suffice? It's getting crowded here."

David noted the mass of bodies filling the pond. "The ocean is fine."

Nodding his horned head, Halora waddled off, bellowing, "Haranda to the sea!"

Ariphema approached David. "We request your help in the eating and drinking of Vashua's cup."

David wrung out his shirt. "We refer to it as *communion* or…Vashua's meal."

Ariphema bobbed his head. "We will call it Vashua's meal, for His remembrance. There is a matter that troubles us. The word *bread* puzzles us. Panagyra has described it, but we have no wheat on Arana." The pendaram held out a plate-shaped piece of material that appeared toasted.

David took it. The disk was slightly pliable with a familiar, yet altered smell. "What is it?"

"We ground some dried *horlah*, mixed it with water and baked it over a fire. After thirty-two different plants and seven hundred and thirty different combinations, we arrived at this. Horlah is a very common plant, available to everyone on Arana. Please, try it."

Tearing off a piece, David nibbled it. Not bad. It was very close to bread. "This will do very well," he said with a nod of approval.

Ariphema gave the horlah bread to a silver phantera, instructing him to make more. Taking a silver bowl from a black phantera, the pendaram held it out to David.

"We do not have grapes on Arana, but we do have many fruits. The fala fruit grows on every planet the phantera colonize. Its juice does not ferment like grapes, but falatirah is mentioned in our prophecies: *'like a bowl of falatirah upon the ground.'*"

Gazing at the swirling purple liquid, David nodded and passed the bowl back to Ariphema. "It is perfect."

The baptisms and spontaneous singing continued for a few hours. Many of the phantera joined the haranda on the beaches to ease the congestion around the pond.

With a full heart, David watched the joyous celebration. *Lord, if I were to die tonight, it would all be worth it. Thank You for using me to bless the phantera and the haranda!*

The stone floor cooled David's knees as he knelt beside his bed. *Lord, I've only had a week of delah instruction, yet I know that it is time. Today is the day I leave this place. Looking back, I can't believe I'm still alive. Looking forward, I have no idea how I'll continue to survive. This I do know: my life is in Your hands.*

His stomach rumbled as he rose and went into the dining room.

Brusaka, Philoah, and Gyra scurried around the table and stood behind it. Three cloth mounds and a leather travel pack rested on the table's smooth surface.

"Uh-oh, do I smell a conspiracy?" David asked in English.

Brusaka's orange eyes shone. "Dala, David!"

Striding up to the table, David asked, "What is this?"

Gyra spoke up. "Since you found Brusaka's cloak so useful, we decided to 'upgrade' our gifts."

David examined the piles: two white shirts, two silvery pants, and a pair of black shoes.

Philoah bobbed his head. "These are made with phantera feathers to keep you comfortable. The white shirts came from Gyra. I didn't have enough feathers of my own, so I acquired a friend's silver ones to make the pants. The shoes are covered and lined with cloth made from Brusaka's feathers. A special material developed by the coralana was used for the soles. They won't melt."

"And the leather pack is made of pagaruna hide," Brusaka added.

Bobbing like a phantera, David said, "Ramara, Gyra, Philoah, and Brusaka. I can truly say that with these gifts, a part of you will travel with me!" He placed the clothes into his new travel pack, along with his Bible. After trying on his new footwear, he eagerly discarded his very worn, partly melted old shoes.

The three jabbered as they served him breakfast.

A pang of melancholy stabbed David. This was probably his last meal with them. He never thought he'd miss Arana so much! "I'm glad I came to Arana, Gyra," he confided. "Although it hasn't always been easy living here."

Philoah's head bobbed like a jackhammer.

David's throat tightened. "But I've come to know and love your naharam."

A somber silence followed. David began to eat, not because he was hungry, but because he needed to be well nourished for whatever lay ahead. After swallowing as much as he could stand, he gathered all his belongings and headed for the door. His three faithful friends accompanied him.

David stepped outside.

The sight took his breath away. Thousands of silent phantera and haranda lined the path leading straight to his delah. The landing lawn was a sea of faces eager to view the vadelah. Sprinkled throughout the multitude were a few visiting aliens. Phantera peered down from the roofs of buildings and the beaches were crammed with haranda.

Blinking back tears, David moved slowly down the street, trying to make eye contact with as many faces as he could. His vision blurred and he wept.

Gyra took David's hand and guided him until his eyes dried.

Halfway to the delah, a female haranda lurched onto

the path. Trembling violently, she cried, "Vadelah! Is there any hope for my son?"

The crowd murmured as David stopped and stared at the aged haranda.

Tears ran around the base of her gray muzzle. "Is there any hope for my son?" she repeated, softer this time.

Her expression of agony held David's gaze by its sheer intensity. "I don't understand," he said.

"I am Hinta. My...son...went mel." She forced the words out.

David bowed his head. There were no mel-phantera, but all other naharam had their mel counterparts. On Arana, when a haranda went mel, he was exiled from the planet. His relatives held a somber panatrel and spoke of him as if he were dead.

But he was worse than dead. He was cut off from Yavana. There would be no reunion with his family on the other side of the grave. He was truly lost. It was a mother's worst nightmare.

Looking up at the grieving haranda, David said, "This is why I am going to the mel-naharam. The Great Revelation is our hope; it has the power to change mels into naharam."

The haranda straightened up. "If you can go to the mel-balahrane, the mel-dijetara, and the mel-honor, why shouldn't I search for my son?"

"Go, and may Naphema guide your way," David answered.

"Ramara, Vadelah David." The haranda bowed. "May Yavana grant you success and bring you back safely."

Moving on, David spied Arachel guarding his delah.

Pendaram Ariphema waited before the ship. At his side stood a large black phantera—Rammar the Prophet.

David stopped before them.

Ariphema held a piece of horlah bread in one hand and a bowl of falatirah in the other. "And now, Vadelah David, we would be honored if you led us in Vashua's meal."

Pulling his Bible out of his travel pack, David opened to 1 Corinthians and read, translating the passage into Ramatera. "For I received from Yavana what I also passed on to you: Vashua on the night He was betrayed took *bread*, and when He gave ramara, He broke it and said, 'This is My body which is for you; do this in remembrance of Me.'"

With reverent trembling hands, David raised the tan horlah bread and tore it in half. He broke a piece off and ate it.

Looking down at his Bible, David continued. "In the same way, after His meal, He took the bowl, saying, 'This is the bowl of the new pharuna [covenant] in My blood; do this, whenever you drink it, in remembrance of Me.'"

Raising up the bowl, David declared, "Ramara, Vashua," and took a sip.

David served Ariphema and Halora. They, in turn, served the delaram. Like the baptisms, the new rite rippled out to encompass the assembly.

With a sad smile, David watched the beautiful ceremony, secretly relishing the delay in his departure.

Rammar's bright eyes caught David. "We are ready, Vadelah David."

With pounding heart, David served Rammar. Turning to his three friends, he said, "I will serve you as well. You have been my *yatala*, my family, here on Arana. I am grateful to Yavana for you and can never repay your kindness. I am honored to have such friends."

He served Brusaka as yellow tears flooded the phantera's orange eyes. Philoah cried before David served him, but Gyra's eyes remained clear until David finished.

"I will miss you dear friend. You're a brother to me!" David cried as he wrapped his arms around Gyra.

Purple rivulets ran down Gyra's neck. "I have no words to describe what I feel for you, David. I would gladly take your place, but Yavana has determined otherwise. I will cry to Yavana for you daily. If we do not meet again in this life, I will look for you in *cerepanya*, Yavana's courts, where we will sing and dance before Him."

Reluctantly, David released Gyra and walked toward his delah. Arachel lowered her head before him. Reaching out, he rubbed her bill. "Be good and wait for me until I return."

Ariphema and Halora raised their hands and flippers over David and pronounced a short blessing over him. Then Rammar came forward.

"It is time for me to bless you, Vadelah David." Closing his eyes, the black phantera raised his blue-purple hands above David's head. He drew in a deep breath and sighed.

"Go in the name of Yavana, bringing the name of Yavana to the mel-naharam.

"Go in the name of Yaram that He may bring forth children for Himself out of the mel-naharam.

"Go in the name of Vashua and declare the mystery of the Restoring One to the mel-naharam.

"Go in the name of Naphema and be filled with His power to overcome the chords that bind the mel-naharam.

"May Yavana sustain you, and your breath not fail you, until you have accomplished all you are called to do!"

Opening his eyes, the old prophet looked at the sky and cried, *"Ramara nal harana sa Yavana* [Thanks and praise to God]!"

*"Ramara nal harana sa Yavana!"* the multitude responded in a mighty roar that shook the air.

Rammar pressed a rolled piece of paper into David's hands. "These are the words of the prophecy I spoke to you concerning the vadelah and the mel-naharam. On the other side are the words from your vision at the massacre. Panagyra said humans easily forget what they hear, so I wrote them out for you."

Bobbing his head, David solemnly took the paper.

Ariphema began a song. The crowd followed with delicate harmonies and counter-melodies. David blushed. This was the formal way the phantera sent off a visiting pendaram!

Stepping into his delah, he glanced around. It was well provisioned with food, water, and medicine. In the rear, three crates held books and information crystals containing Trenara's Scriptures. The phantera had already translated them into Ramatera.

After securing his bag of belongings in a storage panel, he turned to face the singing crowd. *Yavana, bless these dear, gentle naharam. Hear their prayers.*

"*Toorah steen,*" he commanded.

The door slid shut. David donned his flight suit, fastened himself to the chair, and gazed out the windshield. The assembly was still singing. He sighed.

"Farewell, Arana. I will miss you!"

David stared at the control panel. Gyra and Philoah had grilled him thoroughly, but he still feared they might have missed something.

"Delah, take us to the departure zone."

The ship fired up and raised him above the crowd. The cheering multitude jumped and danced.

As the craft turned, the assembly dropped out of sight. Mountains and sky filled the windshield. The delah moved forward, accelerating, as the nose tilted up.

David remembered Gyra trying to explain the concept of *trelemar*. It was one of their most futile conversations. Finally, the phantera picked up a stiff piece of wire and pierced his cloak with it. "Do you see this? The cloak represents time and space; the wire is a delah. When we use trelemar, we do this."

Gyra pulled the wire back behind the gray fabric and popped it up in another section. "It takes no time to travel because in trelemar there is no time or space. The only energy needed is for the initial jump, and it doesn't matter if your destination is four light-years away or four million."

The delah shot into orbit above Arana. Swirls of dense clouds hovered over the blue ocean below. The shardrea season was coming.

"Departure zone reached. Name destination," the computer stated. Words on the screen echoed the information. The ship had reached the area where the atmosphere was thin enough to engage in trelemar travel—one of the requirements for a safe jump.

"Name destination," came the voice again.

David smiled at Ariphema's recorded voice. The pendaram had left his own personal touch in the creation of the delah.

He flinched. Wait a minute, he could ask the delah to take him home to Earth. The phantera would never know.

The temptation grew.

He could see his family, find out what happened to Todd, and live a normal life again. *The mel-naharam will just kill me anyway...*

"Jesus help me!" David cried, as an incredible pressure bore down on his mind.

Suddenly, it was gone.

"I will do what You want, Lord," David vowed, as his resolve hardened. Unrolling the paper Rammar had given him, he read the phantera's prophecy.

*The three dark planets shall receive the vadelah.*
*To the mel-balahrane shine the light without deception.*
*To the mel-dijetara fill the emptiness.*
*To the mel-hanor show no fear and stand your ground.*
*Expose their slavery to passion.*

The mel-balahrane of Wicara were the first on the list. "Set in a course for the planet Wicara," he commanded.

A low humming rose in pitch behind the rear bulkhead as the delah prepared to jump.

Clutching the control stick, David declared, "Enough evil has come from Earth. Now, it's time for something good!"

The stars shimmered, beckoning him.

"Calculations complete," the computer intoned. "Prepare for trelemar."

"Yavana guide me!" David cried as a brilliant white light obliterated the stars.

# 7. The Mel-Balahrane

The window cleared, revealing an unfamiliar pattern of stars and a massive purple nebula. David ran his fingers through his curly hair. The delah rotated and the planet Wicara crept across the windshield. Her dark brown soil and deep oceans gave her a mysterious appearance. Wicara's thin clouds veiled only a few regions. Although water covered half of the visible surface, she was significantly drier than Trenara or Arana.

David consulted the computer. Equatorial temperatures soared uncomfortably high, and large portions of the continents were as dry as the Sahara.

A warning flashed onto the screen. "Two crullahs approaching," the computer said.

The black ominous ships rose from a lower orbit to meet him.

"Crullah Harctel to unknown ship. Identify yourself," came a voice from the speaker. The pilot spoke Ramatera, but with a smooth distinct accent.

"Delah David: I am a human visitor from Trenara." At least they didn't blast him before trying to find out who he was.

After a tense pause, the ship responded. "Crullah Harctel: What are your intentions?"

David's mouth twisted into a smile. What should he say? That he, the vadelah, planned to turn their evil culture on its ear? Did they even have ears?

"Delah David: I have come to visit Wicara and speak with your people."

This time the crullah waited even longer to reply. "Crullah Harctel: Proceed, David of Trenara. May you find what you are looking for."

That was it? No threats? No dramatic chase and capture? Sighing with relief, David consulted his computer regarding population centers. The monitor displayed Wicara's continents and islands, highlighting communities according to their density. He was surprised to find floating cities on the seas.

"Where do I land?" He scratched his beard. The crullahs waiting nearby were probably wondering the same thing.

"Guide me, Vashua." David chose a massive city near the center of the biggest continent.

The delah descended, escorted by the two crullahs. When they reached the lower atmosphere, the crullahs veered off and left him. David didn't know if that was a good sign or not. The last stretch of the flight he flew manually. The delah was easy to maneuver. Spying an impressive charcoal-colored building with a towering dome, David aimed his ship for the paved region beside it. As the delah touched down, David sprang from his seat. He dashed into the closet-sized space that served as a bathroom, shower, and changing room. With racing heart, he stripped off his flight suit and donned the clothes his friends had given him. He pulled back the folding door. A wave of loneliness washed over him, and he fingered Brusaka's cloak.

In the back of the cabin, the cargo containers held the seeds of light for this darkened soil. He popped open a container of books and another of information crystals—the Scriptures in Ramatera. Filling his pocket with the crystals, David stuffed two books into his leather travel-pack. Time for the vadelah's first mission.

"Yavana, prepare the way," David prayed. He faced the door. "Toorah barune." The door slid open.

Wicara's foul heavily incensed breath crept into the cabin. The computer had said the atmosphere was breathable; it failed to say that it stank.

Stepping outside, David closed the door. Brown haze tinged the horizon of the dirty, orange sky, and columns of smoke rose from every building in sight. The air in Los Angeles was pristine by comparison. The clanging of chimes, bells, and gongs—distant and nearby—rode the lethargic breeze. He examined the palatial building before him. Reliefs and statues adorned its gray tiers. Like a Thai temple, the surfaces undulated with figures. The grim faces of a macabre assortment of demons and deities stared down from the roof with expressions of contempt.

Slinging the strap of the pack over his shoulder, David pulled up his hood. Where should he go from here? There wasn't a living thing in sight, at least none he could recognize. He walked toward the looming temple. A row of stone steps rose to its dark recessed doorway. David decided to go around the building rather than use its main entrance. As he neared the back side, a row of obelisks, four feet tall, stood before him like fence posts. Stains streaked the dark granite. He passed between two of the stones. The ground grew black and powdery, smelling of soot. Descending from the back of the building was a smaller, less imposing, set of stairs. Lumps appeared in the blackened soil. Strange yet oddly familiar objects jutted from the ground in places. Something snapped under his foot. Bending down, David took a closer look.

Bones! The closer he drew to the door, the more abundant they became. Whose bones were they? Dalam? Chelra?

Naharam? The vacant eye sockets of a two-foot long skull stared up at the smoky sky. The narrow skull flared like a triceratops's into a hole-pierced bony crest. Drawn by some irresistible unseen hand, David continued. Scattered bones were joined together now. The grizzly progression continued to spinal columns, partial skeletons, and whole skeletons. Their numbers were staggering. Was this the dumping ground for burnt sacrifices?

Reaching the steps, he paused. A freshly roasted skeleton lay partially curled up at the base of the temple. Whatever this creature was, it had four limbs, a long tail, and a bony head-crest. It reminded him of the dinosaur fossils he'd seen in museums. Judging by the ribcage, hipbones, and limbs, he guessed the creature was a slender biped, perhaps a swift runner. Had it been sentient? The jaw appeared frozen open in a silent scream.

Turning away, David faced the temple. His heart skipped a beat. The carvings on the front side had looked down on him with contempt, but these dark figures glared at him with unbridled hatred. Fangs, claws, and talons awaited him. Wings, limbs, and tentacles were poised to attack any who dared approach the back entrance. Odd, he hadn't noticed their fierce postures before. Was it possible they'd moved?

David climbed the stairs, his slow scuffling feet the only sound in the wasteland of silence. The stone carvings appeared to lean forward in increasing malice, but he could see no definite movement. As he reached the door, three dark limbs barred the way. A vicious paw threatened from the right, scaly talons from the left, and a six-fingered hand from above. David was certain the limbs had not been there when he first saw the door. Looking up at the wide-eyed snarling faces, the demonic rage almost made him faint with fear.

"Vashua," he whispered in a faint voice.

Like the opened floodgates of a dam, a surge of strength coursed through him. Anger and resentment at the demonic forces opposing him set his blood on fire. How dare they try to stop the will of Yavana! Straightening up, he glared back at the dark hostile faces.

"I command you in the name of Vashua to move aside and let His messenger enter!" He stepped forward.

Something creaked. The arms slowly withdrew. Stepping into the dark hall, David unclipped his dowel and turned it on. The stone floor rose steeply without steps. A voice, chanting in Ramatera, echoed from the room above and a dim, reddish light lit the far walls. A large chorus echoed the leader in a dead monotonous tone. As David neared the room, he turned off the dowel. Before him stretched a smooth shallow pit with a stone wall at the far end. The wall didn't reach the ceiling, but was high enough to keep David from seeing the assembly—and them from seeing him. He crept across the soft dust in the pit. A doorway led to the larger room, but David couldn't see through it because of the angle. After reaching the wall, David edged his way to the doorway and peered in.

A great dome soared above the cavernous room. Before him stretched another smaller pit and a large stage. Dinosaur-like creatures filled the lower assembly floor. Averaging five feet in height, the blue creatures stood erect on muscular legs, their dainty arms adorned with brass bracelets. Breastplates, anklets, necklaces, and chains glittered on every body. Gold chains were woven through the oval holes of many bony head-crests. Like eyes in the night, jewels winked from the intricate metalwork adorning each attendee. Colorful cloaks flowed regally down their backs, and their long tails ended in a pointed paddle, pierced with rings and jewelry.

As they chanted, the flared head-crests rocked in rhythm to the slow meter. The long deer-like faces never smiled. Their dark eyes gazed into the red flames of the silver firepot on stage.

A black-cloaked creature stood on the platform before the fire. "Speak to us mel-aradelah, spirits of the secret wisdom. Show us how to better serve you. You are our masters. I, High Priestess Jearam, entreat you: enter this room and enter your servant!" The reptile-like being raised her blue hands and closed her eyes.

"Don't let it happen, Yavana," David whispered. "Stop the mel-aradelah."

These must be the mel-balahrane. They were not at all what he expected. He had envisioned scaly ugly creatures, but these were graceful, even elegant. The only light in the cavernous temple came from a flickering firepot. The same hideous carvings haunted the ceiling and walls. Massive columns ringed the circular room, scarred with images of violent creatures rending and devouring one another.

Opening her black eyes, the mel-balahrane high priestess lowered her arms. "The spirits are silent. Something has offended them deeply. We must appease them for the offense."

Pacing before the bowed heads of the assembly, she stopped before a trembling figure in a blue cloak. The high priestess drew a long knife from her jeweled belt. Touching its tip to the forehead of the shaking worshiper, she declared, "You shall serve the mel-aradelah."

"I am honored. My life is theirs to do with as they choose," replied the candidate.

The black-robed priestess marched toward a stone table as the selected mel-balahrane followed with bowed head. Taking a bowl of smoking plant fibers, the high priestess circled the blue-robed worshipper. Then she raised the bowl and faced the flames.

"Spirits of the dark, spirits of the hidden knowledge, spirits of the mighty powers, hear me!" the black-robed creature cried out. "I, Jearam, High Priestess of the Crektul Temple, ask you to accept this daughter of yours for service. She has been purified according to the rite of jamoona smoke."

The high priestess set the bowl onto the polished table. Deep channels cut into its surface glimmered in the firelight. On the floor, silver vases waited, tucked partly under the table's edge. Four black-robed attendants approached from a carved doorway and stood around the oval table. With a tool, Jearam cut away the chains and bonds encircling the trembling creature's torso, exposing the smooth blue skin. The high priestess raised her hands and gazed at her chosen subject. Firelight danced off Jearam's ringed fingers. Closing her eyes, the blue-robed subject trembled feverishly.

Jearam's voice rose in the silent room. "Go and serve the mel-aradelah. Be their faithful servant...forever!"

Before David could blink, the high priestess plunged the knife into her victim's chest. A stifled cry rose from the anguished mel-balahrane as the attendants grabbed her sinking body and dragged it onto the table. The moans ceased after they slit her throat. David felt sick. It was too late to help her—he hadn't anticipated Jearam's actions. After cutting open their victim, the attendants handed her still-beating heart to the high priestess. A wicked satisfied smile spread across Jearam's face. She raised the organ with her soiled hands and dropped it into the firepot. The attendants busied themselves with sorting the various organs and bleeding the carcass. Maroon blood ran into the cut channels and poured into the silver vases beneath the table.

Jearam addressed the assembly. "Tomorrow we will begin the cleansing ritual. Do not come unless you bring an offering." Looking up at the dark carvings on the ceiling, she declared, "Tomorrow the mel-aradelah *will* speak to us!"

The silent crowd began to file out.

Jearam returned to the altar and supervised her assistants. "Mix the organs with yero oil, min, and jazer spice," she instructed. "Place the body in the preparation room. We will burn it tomorrow."

The attendants gathered up the jars of organs and raised the limp body.

"High Priestess Jearam," came a soft voice. One worshiper had stayed behind.

Jearam looked down at her from the raised platform. "Yes, my child?" she asked in a rote tone.

"May I have the honor of washing the altar?"

Eyeing the petitioner, the high priestess said, "You are of the Order of the Red Cloak; you have enough rank to do it. Have you done your daily offerings?"

"Dala, High Priestess."

"Are you current in your temple giving?"

"Dala, High Priestess."

"And you've recited the six prayers to the mel-aradelah?"

"Dala, High Priestess."

"Then you are fit to clean the table." Turning, Jearam departed with the attendants through a carved doorway.

The lone mel-balahrane ascended the platform and walked with ponderous steps toward the bloody altar. Picking up a crystal pitcher, she poured water onto the stained surface.

"Sacred water, cleanse this altar that it may be ready to do the spirits' will," she invoked.

David crept out from the protection of the doorway.

The mel-balahrane poured water a second time. "Sacred water, cleanse this altar that more pleasing sacrifices may be made."

David began to cross the second, shallow pit beyond the wall. His hands and face felt unusually warm as he crept toward the stage.

"Sacred water, cleanse this altar—" Something gave a tremendous *crunch* beneath David's foot. The mel-balahrane's head snapped up. Seeing David, she dropped the ceremonial pitcher and became a statue. The crystal vessel exploded into a million pieces on the stone floor. The mel-balahrane stared at the shards with large black eyes.

"I have been cursed," she said in a faltering voice. Looking up at David again, her crested head trembled. "What *are* you?"

He pulled back his hood. "I am David. I come from Trenara." He stepped onto the platform.

"Trenara!" The creature fell prostrate in worship.

"Stop! Don't do that!" David said sharply.

She cowered before him. "I disappoint you because I have been cursed. My worship is not honorable enough for you!"

"Myute, that is not why I asked you to stop. Only Yavana is worthy of worship."

The mel-balahrane flinched as if she'd been struck. "Do not use that name in here! You will provoke the wrath of the mel-aradelah!"

Reaching down, David pulled her upright. She didn't weigh much and her eyes were nearly the same level as his. "What is your name?" he asked in a gentle voice.

She shivered. "Belrah. A good name until today."

"Belrah, do you love the mel-aradelah?" Why did he ask that? The question had barely entered his mind.

She stared at him with wide black eyes.

"Do you love them?" David pressed again. Perhaps this *was* a good question. "Do you enjoy all the rules they give you? Do you enjoy the sacrifices? Does serving them fulfill you? Are they kind to you?"

Belrah's face betrayed fear mixed with a longing to speak honestly. "I belong to the mel-aradelah—we all do!"

"You still haven't answered my question. Do you *love* the mel-aradelah?"

She clutched her throat.

David suspected Belrah's voice was paralyzed. "Yavana, free her to speak her mind. I ask this in the authority of Vashua!"

"You spoke His name!" Belrah cried, panting. She looked around as if expecting swift demonic retribution.

David had an idea. Raising his hands, he shouted, "Yavana is great, Yavana is powerful! He rules over all the aradelah, His Naphema drives out the mel-aradelah! He brings the truth into the light and frees the captives of the mel-aradelah."

She stared at him with an expression of awe. "I can't believe you are still alive. Don't you fear the mel-aradelah?"

"I fear Yavana more, and He is a *joy* to serve!"

"We are mel, we must serve the mel-aradelah."

"That is a *meno* [lie]," David said with a stern voice. "Now, I ask you for a fourth time, do you *love* the mel-aradelah?"

Belrah trembled, but she forced out an answer. "Do I fear them? Dala! Do I love them? *Myute!*"

"If you could serve Yavana instead of the mel-aradelah, would you?"

"But He is our enemy! He will not help us; we are slaves to the mel-aradelah."

David sighed. "Let me put it this way: if you could serve Yavana, and be accepted by Him, would you?"

"I have never thought about it. What good would it do me?" Her gaze wandered over to the altar.

He saw the distress on her face. "Did you approve of what went on here?"

"I have seen it many times," she answered in a dull voice.

"Did you enjoy it?"

"Myute."

David rubbed his head. "Didn't you have any feelings for that poor victim?"

Anger burned for the first time in Belrah's eyes. "Of course I did! She was my sister!"

# 8. Belrah's Battle

"Your *sister*!" David cried in astonishment. "How can you not weep? Don't mel-balahrane have the ability to weep?"

Belrah flinched. "We do, but it is forbidden to mourn for the sacrifice. Those who do must join them in death. It is hardest when mothers offer their children."

David succumbed to a sudden wave of grief.

"You...are crying," Belrah observed. "Why?"

"I mourn for all those who were sacrificed—for the children, their mothers, and your sister who died needlessly today!"

"Stop, or the spirits will take you," Belrah cautioned.

"They will not take me." David dried his eyes. "No mel-aradelah can. I belong to Vashua."

"David of Trenara, what is your species?"

"My naharam are called humans."

Her lithe body stiffened. "Humans? You are not *mel*-humans?"

"Some of us are mel, but I am not."

"Why did you come here?"

"To bring a message from Vashua."

Circling David, Belrah asked, "Did you come to curse us? To proclaim judgment and disaster on my people?"

"Myute."

"*Myute?*" Backing away, she stared at him with glittering eyes.

"Like I said, I bring a message," David spoke in a gentle voice. "Vashua, who is one with Yavana, has entrusted me with the Great Revelation. Would you like to hear it? It is why I came."

Belrah gazed at the altar and sighed. "Why not? I'm going to die tomorrow. I have failed to complete the cleansing ritual and have shattered the sacred vessel."

"There may be a way to avoid that," David said in earnest. "Let me tell you about Vashua. He came to bring hope to the mels...."

Hours later, Belrah was transformed, the first of her kind to become a balahrane without the *mel* title. Belrah wept when she heard of Vashua's loving sacrifice to pay for her freedom. When David finished, she grieved openly for her sister.

"What shall I do about the altar?" she asked in a hoarse voice.

"Leave it," David instructed. "Let her blood be a sign to the mels."

"But they will only cleanse it and use it again." Tapping the end of her nose with one of her ringed fingers, she narrowed her eyes. "Of course! I know what to do; come help me."

David followed Belrah into a small unlit room. Turning on his dowel, he saw the corpse of Belrah's sister lying on the ground. They carried out the stiffening body and laid it upon the altar.

"If we're going to make a statement, let's make a big one!" Belrah seethed. "All we need are her organs and a foreign flame."

"I have a caruk." Pulling back his cloak, David revealed the laser tool on his belt.

"That should do," she said. "The attendants are done with the organs by now. We are the only ones in the temple."

Trotting out of the room, Belrah reappeared with a large container. "I found some stored phantera organs. This will create quite a stir." She poured the smelly contents onto the altar. Her eyes became slits. "Burn it!"

Aiming his caruk at the grotesque pile, David fired. Smoke rose as flames roared over the entire mess. He cut the beam. The altar was a giant barbecue out of control, its sizzling popping mass charring the stone.

"Can your caruk destroy the altar?" Belrah asked as she stared into the flames.

"Dala." Firing again, he heated the middle of the table until it cracked and crashed to the ground with its gory contents.

"That is good enough," Belrah said. "Come, I will take you to my house." She turned to leave, but paused when she saw the firepot. The balahrane threw her weight against its pedestal. David joined her and together they toppled it into the pit.

"What is this pit used for?" David asked, mopping the sweat from his brow.

"To keep the sacred coals hot and ready for use. That's why I was surprised when I saw you standing on them."

Stepping into the pit, David kicked away the gray dust, revealing the glowing coals beneath.

"They do not harm you?" Belrah asked.

David hopped out. "It's the shoes I wear. They protect me from the heat."

Belrah rocked her head, the balahrane's form of nodding. "Mention those shoes to no one. A jealous mel-balahrane would kill to get a pair of magic shoes."

She eyed the canopy of smoke hovering above them. "Let's go."

As they left through the main entrance, David turned and gazed up at the demonic gargoyles. Magenta fluid ran from the hideous grinning mouths of two serpentine monsters.

"The attendants have fed them the blood of my sister," Belrah said in a cold voice.

Tensing his jaw, David glared at the sinister graven images. "Your time of destruction will come."

Belrah pointed to the delah. "Is this your ship?"

"Dala, is it safe to leave it here?"

"As safe as anywhere on Wicara. There isn't a rock the night patrol doesn't see."

They walked briskly down the empty streets. Crammed between two imperious dwellings, Belrah's elaborate house rose slightly higher than its peers. The balahrane pushed open the ornate silver doors and led him into a small entryway. A decorated stone stairway with a blue carpet rose from the entryway to the rest of the house. Belrah turned to a small shrine carved into a wall beside the door. Within it burned a glass orb of perfumed oil.

The blue balahrane rocked her head. "My house is full of wickedness. I must purify it for Yavana at once."

She seized the orb. Ascending the stairs, they entered a large room. Belrah's ringed fingers poured a pitcher of scented oil onto the square-shaped logs in the hearth. She hurled the burning orb into the fireplace. Flames broke over the logs as the glass shattered. Snatching a black idol from a niche above the hearth, she tossed the grotesque image into the fire. Belrah smiled. Then she scurried about the house, collecting things to destroy. David was amazed at the dozens of shrines, idols, and ritual objects found throughout each room. The fire in the hearth consumed them all.

"Do most mel-balahrane own this many religious objects?" he inquired as Belrah ran by with a curtain. Woven incantations marred every inch of the red fabric.

"Myute, most are not as high ranking." Tearing the silky curtain in half, she stuffed it into the hearth.

After pouring the last of her magic potions into the roaring flames, Belrah crouched down onto the floor. "I hope that is all; I'm exhausted!"

David eyed the innumerable chains, rings, anklets, and stones encircling her lithe body. "Belrah, what does all your jewelry symbolize? Do they represent your high standing?"

"*Clishtip!*" the balahrane swore. "They represent my devotion to the mel-aradelah. The chains symbolize my enslavement to them. I earned the crystals and gems by reciting difficult prayers and serving them." Her weary black eyes turned mournfully to him.

"Don't worry, I'll remove them for you," David reassured. "Lie down and rest."

Unclipping the silvery metal cutters from his belt, David snipped easily through the bonds of copper, brass, silver, and gold. Belrah's blue skin flinched when he touched it. Although she was shaped like a dinosaur, her skin was soft and leathery. Chains, bands, and rings bound her torso and every limb of her body. The reins of an ornate bit and halter attached to her crest. David was relieved when he realized the hooked horn on her forehead wasn't real.

Fingering a chain running from her nose ring to her chest, he asked, "How can you do anything with so many chains restricting your movement?"

"Our suffering shows our devotion to the mel-aradelah," Belrah said in a bitter voice.

A broad band encircling her lower neck bore a Ramatera inscription: *Forever a Slave in Bonds and Chains.* It was the most awkward thing to cut, but David's patient hands conquered it. Belrah's feet consisted of two long forward toes and one short backward toe. David could have called them hooves, for they ended in a tough nail-like substance. The backward toe curved down, giving the species the appearance of walking in high heels.

After vanquishing the bonds, David fingered the silky red cloak. "What does this signify?"

Belrah sighed. "My rank and position."

David put his cutters away. "Do you need it to stay warm or for modesty?"

"We have no modesty customs regarding clothes, but a cloak does keep one warm at night and when we sleep."

"It's not used in worshipping the mel-aradelah?"

"Myute."

"Then keep it." David stretched his stiff legs. "There is one last thing. As a new naharam, Vashua wants me to wash you. It's a simple ceremony, used to demonstrate that your life is linked with Vashua in His death, burial, and resurrection."

"I am ready," she declared. "There is a pond in the back. Will that suffice?"

"Dala."

After her baptism, they ate dinner together. David used his portable tester and determined the food was safe, but that didn't mean he enjoyed the flavor. Apparently, the mel-balahrane preferred foods laden with hot pungent spices.

He conversed with Belrah for hours about their different cultures, recording his findings later in his journal.

> *The mel-balahrane eat four small meals a day and sleep for about six hours. Their average lifespan is forty-five Earth years. A few reach sixty.*
>
> *Public temple meetings are performed in Ramatera so visiting mels can understand, but private rituals are sometimes done in the native language, Wicara....*

Mojar's calculator made time conversions a snap. Each planet had its own measurements of time for days and years. However, most naharam shared the same standard of measurement when they traveled in space. This "space time," or *cipatrel*, was used to convert planetary times. Once David learned the length of Wicara's days in cipatrel units, his calculator converted it into twenty-one hours. He realized he'd better turn in soon if he was going to get any rest.

"Where do I sleep?" he asked.

The balahrane pulled out several large stuffed pillows—much to David's delight—and laid them on the floor.

"We sleep on these," she said.

David awoke. Wicara's red sun was already rising. A glance at his watch confirmed he'd only slept four hours, yet he felt rested. Belrah was preparing the morning meal when he found her.

"Today I will die for defiling the altar unless Yavana intervenes," Belrah said without emotion. She placed a square bread-like material on the table. "Sorry I have no plates or utensils. I threw them in the rubbish because they were inscribed with prayers to the mel-aradelah." Belrah tore the "bread" in half and offered David a piece.

He held it up. "Ramara Yavana."

Raising her portion, Belrah echoed his prayer. After taking a bite, she asked, "David of Trenara, I do not understand why you were hiding in the coal pits."

He forced down a piece of the spicy bread. "When I found the temple, I wandered around to the back and entered through a doorway. The hall led to the coal pits."

Belrah's eyes widened. "You went through the *back* entrance? You're braver than I thought. Didn't the mel-aradelah oppose you?"

"Dala, but Yavana is more powerful."

"What did you do?" Belrah asked, leaning forward.

"I asked Vashua to help. In His name I commanded them to let me through."

"His name was all you used? No potions or spells? No incantations?" The balahrane rocked her head. "Can anyone use His name and fend off the mel-aradelah?"

"Myute, Belrah. You must put yourself under His *authority* to be under His protection, but you did that yesterday when you gave yourself to Yavana. He helps those who do His will."

"Do you mean to say *I* can defy the mel-aradelah just like you?"

"Certainly. Here, I have a gift for you." Opening his travel bag, David gave her a book. "These are Trenara's Scriptures translated into Ramatera. They will tell you more about Yavana and His desires."

A jarring metallic din exploded from downstairs—the rending of hinges and crashing of silver doors.

"It's the temple guards. They've come for me." Belrah shoved the book back to David. "Hide it...and yourself!"

Cramming the book into his pack, David dashed into a nearby room.

A pair of silver-cloaked mel-balahrane burst into the kitchen. They balked when they saw her. "She has no chains!" one of them whispered.

Belrah stared at them, amazed at the sudden calm that permeated her.

"High Priestess Jearam, ruler of Wicara, demands your presence," one of the temple guards announced.

Raising her head, Belrah declared, "I will come, willingly."

David waited a few moments before following. He pulled up his hood and hurried down the stairs. As he stepped into the street, the acrid incense-laden air stung his nostrils and left a bitter taste in his mouth. Without a backward glance, the guards escorted their captive down the street. Several dissonant gongs rang in the distance. David felt very vulnerable as they crossed the open pavement to the temple. The gloating carvings stared down from their perches.

Looking up at them with her neck erect, Belrah spoke in a determined voice. "Stupid statues, Yavana is greater than all of you. He will cast you down!"

David froze as the temple guards turned to her with expressions of horror. They didn't appear to notice him and resumed their pace with eyes averted from the dreaded statues. But David felt a tremor of joy, greatly encouraged by Belrah's boldness.

After the guards disappeared into the temple, David decided he would use the back entrance again. This time when he looked up at the malicious stone faces, he did not feel the same demonic challenge. Leaving his pack in the doorway, he ran up the corridor and crept across the first pit of cooled coals. Struggling to slow his breathing, David peered around the dividing wall.

Mel-balahrane filled the temple, whispering and staring at the desecrated altar. Dread filled their black eyes. Jearam stood before the rekindled firepot and a new black altar.

"Uh oh," David muttered. He wouldn't let them sacrifice Belrah!

The guards led in a white-shrouded figure and backed away.

Gazing down at the still shape standing before her, the high priestess announced, "The mel-aradelah are angry. A strange ship has landed and its pilot has desecrated our altar."

The crowd grew still.

"Because our daughter Belrah was responsible for cleansing the old altar, her blood will consecrate the new one."

Reaching down, Jearam peeled off the shroud and cried, "What is *this*!"

Loud murmuring rumbled through the room as everyone saw Belrah stripped of her chains, rings, and gems.

"Who has robbed you, child!" the high priestess wailed.

"Don't you mean who has freed me?" Belrah replied in a composed voice. "I asked to have them removed."

Jearam's narrow jaw fell open. She finally shut it and asked, "Why?"

"Because I do not wish to serve the mel-aradelah any more. I have chosen to serve Yavana!" Belrah's voice was loud and firm.

The high priestess covered the holes behind her eyes. David guessed they were her ears. A strangled rattling shriek rent the air as Jearam's terrified expression transformed into rage. Aiming a ringed finger at Belrah, she shouted, "You are *unfit* to be sacrificed to the mel-aradelah."

"Then know this too," Belrah replied boldly. "*I* am responsible for the desecration of the altar!"

Jearam's black eyes bulged and a loud hiss burst from her mouth as she trembled. "I can't believe one of our own people has done this atrocity!" She raised her accusing finger again and screamed, "What you have done is *castulshep*, the greatest of all abominations that could ever be done!"

Placing a hand on the hilt of her knife, the high priestess regained some of her composure. "You are mel. You may not choose to serve the mel-aradelah, but they still own you. They will always own you."

Unable to take any more, David stepped forward, shouting, "That's a *meno*!"

Jearam whirled around. "Who dares to call me a liar?" Her eyes widened again when she saw him standing on the glowing coals.

The assembly went as silent as a morgue.

"What are you?" the high priestess demanded.

Hopping onto the platform, David pulled back his hood. "I am David, a human naharam from Trenara."

"Trenara!" The word ripped through the crowd.

Jearam's eyes became shiny, black slivers. "You are a naharam, not a mel?"

"Dala, Jearam."

The black-robed high priestess flinched at the familiar use of her name. "Then you must die," she said with a tone of authority.

"Dala, Jearam," David answered calmly. "We all must die sometime, but what about after that? Don't you fear the flaming blackness of *crulhiya*?"

Jearam trembled. "Our ancestors were mel. We have no choice but to serve the mel-aradelah in this life and the next."

"Myute, Jearam. That is why I'm here. I bring a message that can free you."

"Guards, come take this creature away! What it speaks is castulshep!" Jearam ordered.

Two silver-cloaked guards stepped cautiously toward him.

Locking eyes with the high priestess, David said, "I speak the truth, Jearam. Believe me, my message will penetrate your planet one way or another. If you kill me, then you will not have the honor of being among the first to hear the secrets of Trenara." David prayed she would take the bait.

The high priestess fingered the handle of her knife. "You are willing to *die* for this message?"

"Dala."

"Very well, let us hear it. Then I will decide how to kill you."

Taking a deep breath, David started with the fall of Trenara's first naharam. He spoke for over two hours without interruption, amazed Jearam let him talk for so long. But when he came to the resurrection of Vashua her patience came to an abrupt end.

"Enough!" she cried. "I have never heard such a dangerous meno before." The high priestess turned to the temple guards. "Take them both away to the torture room."

"Myute, Jearam!" Belrah shouted. "If the mel-aradelah are so powerful, then let *them* punish us!"

The black-robed high priestess glared at Belrah, but the unchained balahrane pressed her attack further. Pointing her bare finger at the high priestess, Belrah declared, "If you touch us, then everyone will know that the mel-aradelah are weak, unable to punish those who defy them. If this is so, then why should we serve them?"

Jearam's tail trembled as she hissed. She must have known Belrah was right. And if the mel-aradelah appeared weak in the sight of the people, the status of the high priestess would also be affected. The worshipers watched in silence as the ruler of Wicara pondered her decision.

Placing a palm on the handle of her jeweled knife, the black-robed high priestess said, "Very well, we will call on the mel-aradelah to deal with you."

The guards withdrew at the flick of her wrist.

Lifting her proud head, she eyed David and Belrah. "The spirits will make an example of you!"

## 9. Yavana's War

The high priestess turned to the firepot, threw in a handful of pungent incense, and began her incantations. David looked at Belrah to see her response. His friend's eyes were as hard as polished black stones. They showed no fear, only grim determination.

Finishing her chants, Jearam raised her hands. "And now, mighty mel-aradelah, keeper of the dark secrets and terrible powers, avenge yourselves on these who would defy you! Let all mel-balahrane know that you alone shall be our masters!"

A foul wind stirred within the dark temple. The smoke from the incense molded into grotesque and obscene forms, incarnations of fear, rage, lust, and death.

*Shine the light*...came a prodding silent voice.

David remembered the prophecy. Should he light his dowel?

*Shine the light without deception.*

Yavana's light! He felt Naphema's power pouring through him, eager to do battle with crulhiya's legions. Raising his hands, David sang one of the phantera's new songs.

> *Yavana the mighty!*
> *Yavana the righteous!*
> *Yavana the loving!*
> *In You there is light!*

> *Yaram is our Father*
> *Vashua our Sacrifice*
> *Naphema our Counselor*
> *In You there is safety*

More words came to David's mouth, words he had never sung before.

> *Break the chains of the mel-aradelah!*
> *Tear down their dark strongholds!*
> *Come display your awesome power,*
> *For the sake of Your great Name!*

The boiling canopy of demonic shapes descended like a great net.

"We are covered by the blood of Vashua!" David shouted to the lowering dark cloud. He raised his arm like a lightning rod. "In the power and authority of Vashua's name, we command you to leave! This is Yavana's war!"

A fierce, white light exploded across the ceiling as demonic shrieks burst through the air. The stone floor awakened like a great lethargic beast. With a wail, the naked apparitions dissipated like smoke in a windstorm, but the ground's tremors increased. Panicking, some of the mel-bal-ahrane stampeded for the main entrance. They returned, screaming. The foundations shuddered so violently, the firepot toppled into the coal pit, plunging the temple into darkness. Cries and wails of panic rent the air, but no one could move. Like an earthquake, the shaking slowed to a rolling motion and subsided. The great room grew quiet except for a few voices calling out to loved ones. Turning his dowel on high, David unfolded its stand and set it down. The temple looked less menacing in the white light. All the carvings had disintegrated into the fine rubble littering the floor. A cloud of chalky dust hovered in the air.

Taking in the scene with a slack jaw, the high priestess wailed. "It will take many sacrifices to restore the temple!"

A red-cloaked male pressed his way to the platform's edge. Bowing before David, he said, "I would like to be Yavana's servant."

"Fool!" Jearam retorted in a hoarse voice. "Don't you know that such a statement will disqualify you from being a sacrifice?"

"Then I want to be Yavana's servant too!" cried a young female.

"Yavana, I'm your servant," came another voice.

David tried not to smile at Jearam's blunder. The temple rapidly divided as bitter arguments broke out.

Turning to David, Belrah whispered. "We'd better leave while we have the chance."

David didn't think they could get through the crowd without making a greater stir, so he left his dowel, picked up Belrah, and ran across the coal pits.

"Stop them!" Jearam cried. "Don't let them escape. They're running out the—"

David looked back to see who might pursue him. The high priestess clutched her jeweled throat. Her mouth moved, but made no sound. Stepping out at the back of the coal pits, David set Belrah down and they ran down the long corridor.

"Wait!" David stopped to retrieve his travel pack.

Stepping through the doorway, Belrah said, "What is this?" David joined her.

Shattered rock covered the stairs and ground. They picked their way down and headed for the boundary stones.

"Look!" Belrah cried, seizing his arm.

Staring back at the temple, he saw that the evil carvings were gone. "So that's what all those rocks were."

"It also explains why those who tried to flee were turned back." Belrah rocked her bony crest. "They were afraid of being crushed."

A growing crowd gathered outside the temple.

"Where to now?" David asked.

"I know just the place." She led him down several narrow streets and up to a door. Since mel-balahrane did not knock, Belrah opened the brass door and shut it as soon as David was inside. An elaborate stone stairway rose up in front of them. Belrah rang a small bell and waited.

"Why is hardly anyone out on the streets?" David whispered.

Belrah hissed. "Have you any idea how long it takes to complete a house prayer and our temple obligations? We spend most of our lives in our houses or our temples. Each year the requirements increase.

"The only way to get out of them is to enlist. Warriors have all their obligations waived and receive special prayers from the high priestess. Of course, once you join, you're in for life."

"Who are you?" called a mel-balahrane from the top of the stairs. Her eyes went big when they locked onto David. "And *what* are you?"

Rocking her head, Belrah answered, "Don't you recognize me, Sintwar? It's Belrah."

"Belrah? *Belrah!* What happened to your chains, your rings, your jewels?" Sintwar ran down the stairs, her blue cloak rustling.

"Sintwar, this is Vadelah David, a human naharam from Trenara."

"Trenara!" Sintwar lowered herself to the ground.

"Do not worship me!" David cried as he raised the melbalahrane to her feet.

Mounting the stairs, Belrah stated, "We have much to talk about and little time to do it. Tell me, Sintwar, do you remember the time you said you wanted a way out? When you complained about all the prayers and rituals? Vadelah David knows something that will make your head-crest tingle!"

David found Sintwar to be an eager convert. He and Belrah assisted her in cleansing the house and then gathered around the table for a meal.

"I can't tell you what this means to me to be free of all that rubbish," the newest balahrane stated. "I would have jumped at this opportunity long ago if I'd known it were possible. There are many others who would be eager to hear the Great Revelation."

Rocking her head, Belrah said, "Many at the temple asked to serve Yavana. The others will kill me if I return, but you can reach the seekers."

"Me?" Sintwar squeaked in surprise. "I know hardly anything!"

"Just tell them what you *do* know," David encouraged Sintwar. "I will leave you two with this." He withdrew a book from his bag.

Opening it, Sintwar asked, "What is this?"

"Trenara's Scriptures," Belrah whispered.

Sintwar gave a soft cry of delight. "If only we had access to an encoder, then we could store this in an information crystal."

David pulled out a small clear object.

Sintwar trilled. "You have a *crystal*! Don't tell me you have Trenara's Scriptures encoded on it. It's too good to be true!"

"Dala!" David answered.

"Yavana is a wise God!" Sintwar gave a joyful squeal.

Looking at David, Belrah stated, "We don't have access to an encoder, but we can send pre-encoded messages all over the planet."

"And they will not be able to trace it to us until the damage is done!" Sintwar crowed, as her bare crest trembled. "I'll get started right away!" She glided out of the room.

"Yavana sent you to the right people in the right city," Belrah observed. "You destroyed Wicara's highest temple and confronted the highest of the high priestesses—"

"With Yavana's help," David interrupted.

"And escaped her wrath," Belrah finished. "You also befriended two high-ranking balahrane who have access to a vast communication network. After we send the message throughout Wicara, what should we do?"

Tapping the book, David said, "Learn what you can from the Scriptures, and send a few balahrane to the phantera on Arana."

Belrah gawked at him. "The phantera will kill us before we can land!"

"Myute, tell them Vadelah David sent you to discuss the Great Revelation. They will help you understand this book and assist you in making a translation for your culture."

Hissing softly, Belrah asked, "Why should they do this for us? We have been at war with them from the beginning."

David held her with his eyes, determined to drive home his point. "The blood of Vashua makes you brothers and sisters. Family members should not kill each other. The phantera understand this and will not harm you *if* you come in peace."

A sad smile graced Belrah's face. "It is strange that an alien should be a more trusted friend than my own kind."

"Dala, Vashua experienced the same thing."

Placing a blue hand on her book, she vowed, "I shall have to read this. Ramara, Vadelah David, for risking your life and bringing the Great Revelation to us. What has Yavana called you to do now?"

"I'm to go to the mel-dijetara and the mel-hanor. They, too, must hear the message."

A shiver traveled down Belrah's slender frame. "*Yavana hamoth Vadelah David.* You will need much strength to accomplish that!"

The balahrane stiffened, her eyes strangely focused. "Vadelah David, it is time for you to go! They will be searching for you, trying to stamp out the seeds of light. Leave now while they are confused!" Her deep eyes turned toward him. "Yavana has told me to warn you."

"Then I will go, but first I will bless you." David blinked. Where did that idea come from?

Placing a hand on the balahrane's warm forehead, he said, "Yavana will be your light, Yavana will be your shield, Yavana will be your comforter. Stand firm in His love and power. Though you see the blood of His servants spilled, stand firm!"

Leaving the two books on the table, David slung his pack over his shoulder and descended the stairs. He pushed open the silver doors and stepped into the street. The roads remained void of life until he rounded the final corner. There he spied the great crowd gathered around the ruined temple. Some mel-balahrane shouted in anger while others wailed over the scattered rubble. A few spoke with animated gestures to a group of silver-cloaked temple guards and city security officers. Two more officers guarded his delah. David drew back from the corner. Was he too late?

A ringed hand grabbed his mouth as a voice hissed, "Say nothing! I don't want to harm you."

David froze, heart racing.

The hand relaxed and withdrew. "I want to know more about Yavana," said the barely audible voice.

Reaching cautiously into his pocket, David retrieved some remaining crystals. "Here," he whispered, pressing them into the creature's four-digit hand. "Send this information to everyone you can think of."

"What's on them?"

"Trenara's Scriptures."

After a long pause, the red-robed mel-balahrane stepped in front of him. "I will help you to your ship."

The delah's guards faced the temple.

"Nobody can figure out what happened," one guard said. "The high priestess and half the assembly have lost their voices, and most of those who still have them won't tell us anything!"

"I have a bad feeling about this," the second guard muttered.

David's red-cloaked friend walked around the delah, greeting the guards in a loud voice. "Do you want to know what *really* happened? I'll tell you. I was there! First, there was..."

"*Toorah barune,*" David whispered.

The door slid open quietly. David stepped inside and spied the open crate. Grabbing some books and a bag full of crystals, he placed them on the dark soil outside the door.

"*Toorah steen,*" he breathed.

The door slid shut with more noise than when it opened.

One of the guards stiffened. "What was that?"

"You're missing the important part!" the storyteller lamented.

"Wait a moment." The guard crept around the ship. "What are *these*?" Picking up one of the books, he opened it to the first page. "Look at this! It says these are Scriptures from Trenara!"

"Let me see!" the second guard cried, as he snatched another book. "These should be taken to High Priestess Jearam!"

The balahrane in the red cloak spoke in a low voice, "If you take them to her, you will never see them again."

The first guard looked up. "Why?"

"Because she is jealous for her position, and these books can bring about her ruin."

The two guards stared at each other.

"I really think we should at least hand them over to the city officials," the second guard said.

The first guard examined an information crystal. "Myute! Do you know how much the rival sects will pay to have a copy of Trenara's Scriptures? We'll be rich!"

David finished changing into his flight suit and leaped into his seat. "Delah, get us out of here!"

"Please be more specific," came a voice.

"Take us to the departure zone, now!"

The engines fired up and the ship erupted from the surface.

"What do we do?" the second guard cried. "They will kill us for letting the ship escape!"

The red-cloaked balahrane smiled. "I will tell them you were attacked and couldn't move. You became disoriented and went home."

The first guard fingered his dagger. "In exchange for what?"

"Just one of the books. Sell the rest." He smiled again.

Gathering their prizes in haste, the three scattered before anyone could report them.

Four hours of sleep were not enough. Exhausted, David leaned back and closed his eyes. He'd just rest for a moment.

"Five crullahs approaching from deep space," intoned the computer.

David lurched awake. "Can we trelemar before they reach firing range?"

"Myute," answered the voice.

"Can we outrun them?"

"Myute. Estimated arrival in four *ciplets*."

*That's only five minutes! Yavana, what do I do now?*

David watched and prayed as the screen counted down the time.

Laser beams streaked past the windshield.

Seizing the control stick, David zigzagged his way to deeper space. He wasn't a fighter pilot! How could he survive against Wicara's warriors? His heart beat against his ribcage like a wild bird.

"Departure zone reached," the computer announced. "Name destination."

"Plot a coarse to Trenara," he blurted without thinking. Nothing happened.

"Delah, why aren't we jumping?"

"Trelemar jump is not recommended during maneuvering. Acceleration makes for inaccurate calculations. Resulting jump could be fatal."

David could have kicked himself for forgetting. He screamed as a laser grazed his wingtip.

The crullahs closed in.

"Vashua, help me!" David whispered as he swung his delah to face them.

The black ships approached in formation with two in the front, three in back. One of the rear crullahs fired.

David closed his eyes as a blinding flash filled the windshield. Debris clattered against his ship. He looked up. Only three crullahs remained. They peeled off and circled him.

"What happened? Delah, scan for communication between enemy ships."

"Crullah Lagora: I was told to protect it, not destroy it."

"Crullah Silnay: We keep getting conflicting reports. Do we kill it or protect it?"

"Crullah Lagora: You can't bring back the dead! Let it go and wait until we receive clear instructions."

David steadied his ship.

"Prepare for trelemar," the computer called.

"Finally!" David cried as the white light enveloped his delah.

# 10. An Empty Race

The flash cleared revealing Trenara's stars. The delah banked toward the planet.

"Five crullahs approaching from low orbit," came the computer's voice.

"What!" David protested. Did those nasty ships infest the whole universe?

"Ten more crullahs have trelemared into scanning range," the voice continued. "Seventeen *cipras* until firing range."

He had less than seventeen seconds to escape. "Get us out of here!" David shouted.

"Please be more specific."

"Take us to..." he had to think of a safe place other than Arana. He couldn't return until he was finished. "Take us to Dalena!"

The back bulkhead rumbled as the mysterious equipment prepared for the jump. "Calculations complete. Prepare for trelemar."

Like vultures to a kill, the dark shapes sped toward him. The nearest fired. The laser beams rotated, slicing closer to his ship with each burst. They vanished behind a white light.

Dalena appeared, a shining gem among the stars. A few deserts and barren peaks scarred her otherwise lush tearel-covered continents. Golden islands dotted her vast blue seas.

Unbuckling his seatbelts, David floated over to an oblong panel in the wall. He pressed a button and a berth slid out. With a sigh, David flipped into the bunk and strapped himself in. Zero gravity enabled him to do many amusing acrobatics with little effort.

Just as he was relaxing into a nice sleep, a voice cut through the serene cabin. "Twelve delahs approaching."

David moaned.

"Delah Ranjar to unknown ship, please identify yourself."

David blew out his breath. "Delah David to Delah Ranjar, I am David, a human from Trenara—"

"The vadelah!" a voice cut in.

"Dala," David said with an irritated smile.

"Delah Ranjar: What are your intentions?"

"Delah David: I just want to get a little sleep before I travel to the mel-dijetara."

"Delah Ranjar: We will be honored to guard the vadelah while he rests."


Five hours later, David awoke still feeling groggy and miserable. Zero gravity had a way of making him nauseated. Feeling desperate, he took a shower. The warm soothing spray helped him feel better, but it took a while to master the water vacuum. Towels would have been softer on his skin.

When he finished, he turned on the dehumidifier to remove the extra water vapor. So much for a simple shower.

After changing, he opened the food panel. He grabbed a container of falatirah, some cooked horlah, and dried fala fruit. Turning to look out the window, his heart nearly seized.

Delahs hovered outside, some close enough to see their occupants. The computer showed an armada of thirty surrounding his ship.

"I'm like a freak in a side-show," David mumbled as he downed his food. *What time is it anyway? Not that it really matters out here.*

Consulting the computer, he assessed his ship's condition.

"Minor laser damage was sustained by left wingtip," the computer informed him. "Do you wish the external robot to repair it?"

Swallowing the last of his breakfast, David said, "I guess so."

"Please restate your answer in Ramatera."

"Dala!" he said irritably.

An external compartment opened and a tethered machine floated out to the damaged wingtip.

He sighed. *Lord, it wouldn't be wise if I continued my mission in such a sour mood. Forgive me. Let me use this time to thank You for what You did on Wicara....*

By the time the robot finished repairing the delah's wing, David's perspective had been corrected as well. It was amazing what a little session of thanksgiving could accomplish. Invigorated, he buckled himself into his seat.

The phantera eyed him from their spaceships.

"Delah David: Ramara, Ranjar, for guarding my ship. I will be leaving now."

"Delah Ranjar: Yavana hamoth David! We will remember you when we speak to Yavana."

David smiled. "Delah, set in a course for the planet Cruskada." Retrieving the rolled piece of paper from a compartment on the instrument panel, David reread it and slid it back in. Rammar's writing comforted him.

The humming behind the rear bulkhead grew as a voice said, "Calculations complete. Prepare for trelemar."

The bright flash still startled David. When it ended, he waited for his eyes to adjust.

And waited. Galaxies glimmered faintly in the distance, but few celestial beacons shone in the wasteland of darkness. Consulting the computer, he found Cruskada's location in the Cirilla Pala.

"So, we're on the edge of the Milky Way Galaxy," he noted in English.

Turning, the delah faced the gray planet. Cruskada's surface was barren of oceans, ice caps, and plant life. On the night side, billions of tiny lights sparkled.

"Ten crullahs approaching," announced the computer. "Five from deep space and five from lower orbit."

With a few crisp maneuvers, they surrounded his ship.

"Crullah Ah-602-722295-375 to unidentified spacecraft. Identify yourself." The voice was concise but lacked tonal inflections.

"Delah David: I am a visitor from Trenara." He thought it best not to announce his status as a naharam.

"Crullah Ah-602-722295-375: Follow me to the Visitor Arrival Center." The crullah directly in front of David spun around and descended toward the planet's surface.

"Delah, follow descending crullah," David instructed. His view screen showed the other nine crullahs escorting him in tight formation.

The delah had no problems tracking the lead crullah. By now David was familiar with the creaks and rattles as his ship bounced through the thickening atmosphere. He glanced at the surface scanner reports.

Interlocking webs of geometric shapes covered the cement-colored planet. Much of Cruskada's soil lay entombed beneath buildings and pavement while rivers ran like trapped rats within a maze of engineered canals.

Fantastic buildings rose and spread out like mushrooms, seeming to defy gravity, as they cast great shadows on the grid-patterned streets below.

Golden land vehicles raced along tracks, while metallic-red air vehicles buzzed from building to building like dragonflies. Smaller drones of various shapes and colors darted about and patrolled the traffic.

Leveling out, the lead crullah flew into a hole in the side of a colossal building. The semicircular opening frowned ominously like a dark mouth. David cringed as the techno-monster swallowed his delah. *This must be what Jonah felt like when he saw the whale.*

Cool lights illuminated the artificial cavern. Blue, green, and red lines traversed the charcoal-gray floor, neatly marking off areas. The crullah landed and David set his delah down beside it.

*Vashua, guide me.* Unbuckling himself, David grabbed his restocked pack and tool belt. He hesitated, and then placed his caruk in the delah's tool panel. The mel-dijetara would certainly confiscate the laser if he brought it. It would be no match against the mels' weapons and he didn't want them to think he was an aggressor.

"Toorah barune." The door slid open. Cruskada's stale air smelled like a file cabinet of old musty papers. All around him machines droned, whined, and roared, echoing off the hard floor and walls.

David stepped out, his shoes gripping the matte-finished pavement. With a soft whir, a pigeon-sized machine with three rotor blades darted up and hovered about him. He suspected it was armed with a camera and a laser weapon.

Several insect creatures with horizontal banana-shaped bodies scurried toward David on six legs.

"*Toorah steen*," David commanded. The door sealed behind him.

The six-foot-long creatures surrounded him, polished bodies gleaming blue-gray, brown, or khaki. Their compound eyes glittered with iridescent colors.

A brown one thrust forward. "David from Trenara, you will do exactly as told or you will be incinerated." The creature pointed with all four hands to the armed hovering drone.

"I understand," David answered.

"You are to come with me to the Alien Processing Center."

The tentacles twitched at the end of the creature's up-curved tail. It spun around and pattered toward a doorway. David followed, well aware of the humming drone shadowing him. The brown insect activated a door in the wall and gestured for David to enter. Once they were inside, the door snapped shut like the blade of a guillotine. The room shot upward. David fell to the floor, pinned momentarily by the acceleration. He noticed the drone had attached itself to the ceiling, its propellers still whirling. The elevator's transparent walls flickered as they passed each lit level. His escort tapped a foot impatiently. In less than ten seconds, the ride ended with a stomach-lifting stop. The door slid open.

David rose cautiously. He glanced up and down a crowded corridor that stretched seemingly forever. The floor was divided into two moving walkways, each traveling in opposite directions. David stepped quickly onto the rumbling floor. It moved far faster than any escalator and he nearly lost his footing.

Although the walkway traveled at a brisk pace, his escort scurried on ahead. David hurried to keep up. Clearing his throat, he said, "I'm David. My species are called *humans*. Who are you?"

The creature glanced at him before pointing its dolphin-like snout down the hallway again. "I am Gah-675-850853-750-Cah."

David blinked. "That's your name?"

"Myute. Mel-dijetara have no names. It is inefficient. We use numbers and letters to identify ourselves."

Grimacing, David replied, "I'm sorry. I don't think I can remember all those numbers."

"Apologies are unnecessary. You may call me Gah-675."

"I think I can handle that. Are you male or female?"

"Male!" the mel-dijetara snapped.

David glanced at all the other insects rushing by. "Have your people seen humans before?"

"Myute. I hear the mel-hanor have visited Trenara, but I don't know the details."

Like cars on a freeway, the great insects scurried down the busy hall. Gah-675 stayed on the right side of the corridor. Another group of five passed them on the left, moving single file, each neatly spaced behind the other. The gray and white walls of the corridor were immaculate but monotonous.

David marched over the rubbery floor ever mindful of the menacing purring drone behind him. "So, what do you do, Gah-675?"

"I escort new species and visitors to the Alien Processing Center."

David would hate to work in this windowless catacomb. "Do you like your job?"

"That is irrelevant," the creature replied in a methodical voice.

"It is? Where I come from, people try to get jobs they enjoy. They work better when they find pleasure in their labor."

The insect raised his long snout. "The mel-dijetara work for Cruskada's glory. The whole universe stands in awe of our technological wonders. Our scientists are quickly unlocking the secrets of the universe."

David frowned at his horizontal escort. "But what about you? What are your goals in life?"

"To complete my job as quickly as possible."

"Balute?" asked David.

"To make Cruskada an efficient planet. We must always have the best technology in the Cirilla Pala."

David lowered his brows. "Balute?"

The mel-dijetara paused. "Your question is...irrelevant."

"No, it's not! What good is technology by itself? What is the purpose behind gaining knowledge?"

Gah-675 rubbed his long nose with a hand before resuming his hurried pace.

A sparrow-sized drone buzzed past David's ear, startling him before it zipped down the corridor.

"Here is your destination," the mel-dijetara stated. He hopped off the walkway and stood beside a doorway.

David scrambled off barely in time. Looking at Gah-675's compound eyes, he asked, "Do you feel it?"

"Feel what?"

David shook his head. "The terrible emptiness."

The numbered gray door slid open and Gah-675 directed him to enter. Once David stepped inside, the door closed, separating him from Gah-675. Flitting up to the ceiling, the ever-present drone secured itself.

"Come further in and place your bag on the table," another toneless voice called. "If you resist interrogation, you will be incinerated."

Shiny instruments, polished tables, complex machines, and orderly desks crowded the large room. A mel-dijetara crept out from behind a u-shaped desk.

Setting his bag on the table, David announced, "I'm David—"

"The human visitor from Trenara."

"You know that already?"

"We value efficiency on Cruskada," the blue-gray creature said crisply.

"So I've noticed."

"Do you have any weapons or dangerous articles to declare before we begin?"

David wore a slight smirk. Would the mel-dijetara consider the Scriptures dangerous? No, they would label them irrelevant. "I have a caruk. No, wait a minute, I left it in my ship."

Opening David's pack, the mel-dijetara sorted through the contents. David looked down at his shiny, blue flight suit. In his rush to exit the delah, he had forgotten to change.

"So, what's your na—uh, number?" David began.

"Dah-378-905054-428-Cah." The mel-dijetara examined David's dried vegetables.

Wincing, David asked, "Can I call you Dah-378? I have a hard time remembering so many numbers."

"Dala." The creature reached for one of the crystals. "What are these?"

"They contain…information about Trenara's history."

"A crude culture, I'm sure," the mel-dijetara muttered. "You can't be too advanced if your memory won't store a twelve-digit number." He picked up another crystal.

"They're all identical," David explained.

A khaki mel-dijetara pattered into the room and addressed David. "Strip off your clothing for a scan."

David's cheeks grew warm. *Come on, this is just like a visit to the doctor—sort of,* he reassured himself.

His examiner tapped the floor impatiently with a jointed leg. "Another species for the files."

"Do you treat all your patients this way?" David asked.

"Patients? I am a scientist, not a doctor! I take bodies apart. Doctors put them together, if it's worth the effort."

Sweat broke out on David's forehead. "Is that why you're here? To take me apart?"

"Not yet. I only have orders to scan you. It's disappointing. I can't wait to open you up and see what makes you work. Sometimes the best inspiration for our machines comes from studying organs. One day we will remake life itself, creating the perfect species."

"I can hardly wait," David mumbled. "Then what will happen to you and the rest of us inferior species?"

"We will pass away, but our work will live on!" the scientist gushed.

"A lot of good that will do you, or the rest of us. What's the point?" David asked. "Suppose you made a perfect species. Where would you go from there? Would you try to create an even *more* perfect species?"

The scientist stomped a foot. "You are babbling nonsense. The mel-dijetara are the keepers of the secrets of the universe. One day we will know everything."

David cocked his head. "What if you *did* know how everything worked? Where would you find fulfillment then?"

Ignoring David's barb, the scientist beckoned David to stand on a platform. A metallic wall rose from the floor around him until he could no longer see over it. The wall hummed and David's naked flesh tingled. A purple light swept his body. Millions of long shafts, each the diameter of a needle came out of the wall. The silvery shafts stopped when they touched his skin. Closing his eyes, David felt them cover his eyelids. The shafts went rigid. He couldn't move. Something like needles stabbed his leg, abdomen, and arm simultaneously. Before he could cry out, a mild electric jolt traveled through his skin. The shafts retreated back into the wall, leaving him panting. He could find no wounds where he'd been jabbed.

As the wall receded into the floor, the scientist typed on a hand-held computer board. "Body scan is complete. Samples of bone, skin, blood, muscle, and intestinal contents are being processed. You may get dressed now."

Leaving his computer board with Dah-378, the scientist pattered out of the room. David pulled his flight suit on in haste.

Dah-378 called David over to his desk. "Now we begin your interrogation. Since you don't have a number, we will use your awkward name."

The creature typed faster than any human secretary. Each hand consisted of four jointed fingers and two thumbs. The four hands danced on a console with corresponding upper and lower keyboards.

As Dah-378 questioned him, the upper arms typed in David's answers while the lower arms recorded his belongings and physical make-up.

David began to feel very intimidated. *Yavana, help me!* he prayed in silence.

The mel-dijetara stopped. "Let's have a look at those crystals."

Depositing a crystal into a decoder, he faced the screen. "What is this? *In the beginning Yavana created*...oh no. This is worse than the mel-balahrane's jabbering about spirits. I thought it would describe Trenara's technology, your greatest feats of engineering!"

As an idea flickered in his mind, David broke into a sly smile. "But it does. The greatest feat of engineering on Trenara was when Yavana made humans."

"The concept of Yavana is unnecessary and irrelevant!" the creature snapped. "Spirits and incantations are useless. They don't help build complex machines or unlock the secrets of the universe. Time shouldn't be squandered on illusions that have no bearing on the real world. There's no benefit in spiritual discussions!"

"I wouldn't be so confident about that."

Dah-378 shook his head and gathered the remaining crystals. "I will send these out to the Department of History for them to analyze."

"Wait!" David cried. "Why don't you send just one?

They're all alike. You can keep one here and send the others to...different departments. The information would be examined more fully that way."

Running a segmented finger down his dolphin snout, the mel-dijetara said, "That would be acceptable."

David released a silent sigh.

Dah-378 sliced a dried vegetable, placed a sample into a clear container, and deposited it in a machine. As the machine whined, he returned to his computer. The mel-dije-tara's nose nearly touched the screen. "This tearel is from Arana! Now you've got my nose itching with worry. Did you visit Arana?"

Panic stabbed at David. "Dala, I've been to Wicara too."

Swiveling his head to stare at David, Dah-378 ran a finger down his snout. "You have? Which was more dangerous?"

"My life was threatened on both planets." A melcat did chase him on Arana.

"Are you an enemy or an ally?"

"The choice is yours," David answered with a sad smile.

Flailing all four hands, Dah-378 shouted, "How can I do my reports if you refuse to fit into a category?"

"On Trenara we have that problem all the time."

"*Clishtip*! How aggravating."

"Tell me, Dah-378, do you enjoy your job?"

"That is irrelevant—and I'm supposed to be questioning you. Now, where did you get your ship?"

"It was given to me as a gift from...another alien."

Dah-378's compound eyes shifted color as he turned his head. "I suspected humans were too inferior to make such a vessel on their own. What drew you to Cruskada?"

"Yavana."

"No spiritual jargon!"

David rubbed his scalp. "I just wanted to talk to the mel-dijetara."

Dah-378's hand paused above the keyboard. "You came to learn from our vast knowledge?"

"Actually I came to share my knowledge."

The creature stomped his six legs independently. "Is this a joke? You have no technology to share with us. Even your ship was easily captured by our crullahs. People come to Cruskada to *learn*. They come for our advanced technology, our amazing inventions, and our deadly weapons!" Dah-378 made a sneezing sound and composed himself. "Now, what did you come for?"

Leaning closer David said, "I came for your hearts."

"What would you want our organs for? A sacrifice? *Clishtip*! The mel-balahrane weaken their own population through their detrimental rituals. Did they send you here? It's bad enough we have to trade with them for metals."

"I don't want your organs!" Squeezing his curly head with his hands, David prayed silently to avoid further ridicule. *Yavana, help me.*

Releasing his head, he looked up.

"Let me try again," David ventured. "When you finish working, and you go to sleep—"

"Sleep is a waste of time. We take medicine to avoid it." Dah-378's four tail tentacles twitched.

"*Listen*!" David blurted in frustration. "Do you *feel the emptiness*? Do you look around, even after your best day of work, and sense there must be something better? When you face death, do you wonder if your life was worth anything? Do you feel like a tiny irrelevant piece of hardware in a giant useless machine?"

"My feelings are irrelevant. Are all humans this troublesome? You're worse than the mel-balahrane by a factor of ten!" snapped the mel-dijetara.

David resisted the urge to lapse into a few choice English words.

"What is the reason you came to Cruskada?" the mel-dijetara stated in a toneless voice.

Crossing his arms, David replied, "Put this down: 'I came to Cruskada to fill the emptiness.'"

The mel-dijetara typed it in. "And how did you intend to 'fill the emptiness'?"

"By bringing *real* purpose to your miserable lives."

"You'll have to be more specific than that!"

"Do you have a lot of space on your form?" A faint smile grew on David's face.

"I can use as many pages as needed to finish the interrogation."

"Good. Get ready to type because I intend to fill a lot of space!"

# 11. Dah the Inefficient

Not knowing how much time he'd have, David spoke as fast as he could. He laid down the basics of the Great Revelation first, building quickly to encompass the privileges and moral responsibilities of a naharam.

From time to time, Dah-378 asked questions for clarification of David's points, and after the first four pages, the mel ceased complaining about spiritual issues. His jointed fingers had no trouble keeping up with David's fast monologue.

"So, humans don't make the pursuit of knowledge, efficiency, and group cooperation their highest goals?" the mel-dijetara asked with twitching tentacles.

"Some do, but not most of them. The naharam find that kind of thinking empty, incomplete, without meaning." Pacing, David thought of a crude illustration.

"You make crullahs with specific purposes in mind—to travel through space and to fight. A crullah that can't do those two things is defective. Naharam were made to fulfill specific purposes too."

"To pursue knowledge, be efficient, and cooperate with the group," the mel-dijetara recited.

"That is only a small part, Dah-378. Those are like the scanner, communications equipment, and cabin lights of a crullah. They're nice to have, but not essential. If your ship's weapons don't work and the trelemar equipment malfunctions, what good is your crullah?"

"It would be useless, needing repair!"

"Dala, and that is how Yavana sees us when we don't do what we're designed to do."

"Everything comes back to Yavana! You're saying all my hard work and studies are meaningless?"

David peered into those compound eyes. "Without Yavana, yes. What is the purpose of studying the universe when you ignore its maker? Suppose you made some great scientific discovery. How long would the thrill last? Would it comfort you when you were lonely? Others might remember your fame long after you died, but what good would that be for you?

"We were made to have a relationship with Yavana, the creator of all the secrets of the universe. Without Him, our lives are like a crullah without a pilot, without guidance and purpose.

"Don't you feel the futility of your life? Doesn't the emptiness gnaw at you?"

The mel-dijetara scratched his nose in silence.

David winced, "I can't read your face, you'll have to tell me what you're thinking."

"I am reflecting on your information," Dah-378 responded.

"And?" David prompted.

"It scares me."

"Well, I have an empty feeling gnawing inside of me right now—I'm hungry!"

Dah-378 ordered food for David. The "meal" consisted of a square-shaped piece of spongy matter.

After testing it with Mojar's instrument, David determined it was not poisonous. He bit into it.

"*Boosah*!" David cried. This was worse than Aunt Diana's health food. "How can you eat this awful stuff?"

"Taste is irrelevant. The meal square is efficiently processed and will replenish the body's needs," Dah-378 recited like a computer.

Picking up a chunk of dried horlah, David offered the vegetable to his questioner. "Try this."

The mel-dijetara reached hesitantly for the piece. "I have never consumed anything from another planet. Why are you offering it to me?"

"Because out of my own inefficient life, I want to give you something."

Breaking off a morsel, Dah-378 tasted it. He tasted another morsel, and another. "It's difficult for me to give an accurate assessment of this food. I will have to try more."

Chuckling, David gave him another vegetable. "You ought to eat real food more often."

Dah-378 paused. "It does satisfy in a unique way. I have read about off-world foods, but to actually taste one is quite...exhilarating!"

David grinned. "There are so many things the mel-dijetara are missing in life, things that would bring you great joy."

"Like knowing Yavana?" Dah-378 asked, rubbing his nose.

"Dala."

The mel-dijetara clasped all four of his hands together. "Is it really possible to have a relationship with Yavana, the First Engineer?"

"It is His desire, Dah-378. Through Vashua, He has made a way."

The exchange of words and ideas increased ten-fold over the next few hours.

"The mel-dijetara are superior to all known life-forms," Dah-378 stated, tapping a jointed toe. "The despicable mel-balahrane are preoccupied with burdensome rituals and superstitions. Unfortunately, we depend on them for valuable minerals and metals. They keep their mines well hidden.

"The mel-balahrane trade raw materials for food, medicine and crullahs. We grow great quantities of plants in our underground gardens, process them into meal squares, and ship them to Wicara. They season the food as they please."

"What about the mel-hanor?" David asked.

Dah-378 stuck out his black tongue. "We despise them too. They are *extremely* primitive and inefficient but love to raid other planets. They bring us valuable metals and phantera hides in exchange for crullahs, a few machines, and some medicines.

"The mel-balahrane advise the mel-hanor on the timing and locations of their raids in exchange for the organs of the victims.

"What about the coralana?" David asked.

Dah-378 raised his long nose. "We view them as inferior because they are distracted by spiritual things." Dah-378 trained his compound eyes on David. "Do humans have the same emptiness on Trenara?"

"Dala, many feel as you do. Only Yavana can fill them."

Rotating his head down, the mel-dijetara ran a finger along his nose. "If I continue as I am, I can predict the path of my life. I will be deactivated in three circuits. Since I am not a prominent scientist or inventor, my life will have counted as little. No one will remember me; no one will miss me.

"But if I pursue Yavana, who knows what would happen? My life would be...unpredictable, different. How the thought makes my nose itch!"

David nodded. "You must look at both options and choose. Do you want a safe but meaningless life, or will you risk the unknown with its possibilities of pain, fear, and joy?"

Dah-378 shook his head. "My entire species has been mel since the beginning. How can I change that now? We were bred and genetically manipulated to be what we are today. Even if I did pursue Yavana, what difference could I make?"

Glancing at the complicated instruments around him, David asked, "Doesn't a good engineer know the abilities and needs of his machines, the right fuel, the right maintenance?"

"Dala." The mel-dijetara rotated his head to look at David.

"Then isn't it logical to expect that Yavana would know your needs?"

"That would be reasonable."

"If Yavana is the First Engineer, the maker of everything, then don't worry about how to change your world. Just do what He asks, and you *will* make a difference."

"Dala, I accept!"

The dijetara's conversion was quick and methodical, yet David sensed it was real. He fingered his beard. "You will find that many of Yavana's desires are contrary to Cruskada's system."

"Like the disassembly plants for mel-dijetara who are past their prime?"

"He definitely doesn't approve of those!" David said firmly.

The dijetara ran a finger down his nose, fidgeting his jointed legs. "If Yavana thinks they are wrong, then I won't go to one when my time is up. Not only that, I'll try to keep others from going! I always hated those plants. I wonder how long we'd live if we didn't have them? Perhaps I will be the first to find out!"

David nodded. "It would be just one of many firsts for your people."

Dah-378 removed his finger from his snout. "Do you know what's amazing? I thought I loved my people, but now that I've chosen to serve Yavana first, I love my people more, not less! My rote sense of duty has been replaced with a passion to help them. Others must hear of this teaching!"

The dijetara's tail tentacles twitched. "My mind feels like it's been caught in a trelemar explosion! The thought that Yavana would care so much for the individual makes me feel significant.

"Significance: the one thing every mel-dijetara longs for, but rarely mentions out loud."

A message flashed on the screen. "*Clishtip!* It is the Inter-Planetary Communications Department," Dah-378 exclaimed as a report scrolled up. "There's been a major disturbance in the social order of Wicara. The mel-bal-ahrane are fighting among themselves: 658 dead, 975 wounded.

"The disturbance was caused by a new religion, brought by a human from Trenara. It is spreading rapidly across the planet. Every major city has reported problems."

Dah-378 stopped and looked at David. "You did make an impact, didn't you?"

David winced. "I just wish so many hadn't been killed."

Dah-378 batted at the air with three hands. "Don't worry. If you make a dent in their sacrificial system, you will have saved many more lives than have been lost. *Clishtip!* They kill millions each circuit!"

The dijetara glanced back at his monitor. "They want me to escort you to the Alien Research Department for disassembly." He ran two fingers down his snout.

"You mean they want to kill me, take me apart, and study me."

"Correct." Dah-378 scratched his snout vigorously and lurched back from his computer. "I've had enough of 'Dah-378-905054-428-Cah, the Efficient.' It's time for 'Dah the *Inefficient!*' Cruskada's methodical system of scheduled death and meaningless life is about to be sabotaged!"

Scowling, David asked, "What are you going to do?"

"I'll destroy your records, return you to your ship, transmit the information on your crystals to millions of workers, and stop the crullah patrols from hindering your escape. *That* should make me known throughout Cruskada!"

"You plan on doing all of that?" David marveled.

"Dala, it will be a start. I will do far more, as Yavana guides me! In the things that matter, I will be efficient."

Leaning forward, Dah typed furiously. High up on the wall, a small door slid open. The drone flitted through it.

As the door slid shut, David asked, "What happened?"

"I just sent the drone on an errand." Dah continued to type. "There! This will keep them occupied."

"What will happen to you?"

"I will be very busy for a while. By the time they send an inspector to investigate my sudden drop in 'productivity,' I will be gone."

"Where will you go?" David wondered if Dah could survive outside his world.

"I will wander Cruskada as a naharam, wrecking havoc on this empty system, and telling others of your message!"

"Won't the authorities send someone to find you?"

Rotating his head toward David, Dah declared, "We pride ourselves in being a civilized culture. We do not have soldiers on our streets. The only place anyone will look for me is my office. If they *do* search for me, it will be like trying to find a broken kelion connector on a moving celitron array!"

Dah gestured to the items on the table. "Do you need these?"

"Just my tools. You can have the rest; I brought them to leave here." David strapped on his tool belt.

After popping more vegetables into his long mouth, Dah packed the Scriptures and crystals into a case and slung it around his body. He held up the computer board. "This contains all the results of your scan. The knowledge of the mel-dijetara is the pride of the mel-dijetara. Today, I will worship it no longer."

Tossing the computer board into the air, Dah blasted it with a caruk.

"Yavana, may all of Cruskada's knowledge be turned to serve You!" Dah declared.

Picking up his water pouch, David removed the stopper and approached Dah. "We're pressed for time, so I'll make this fast."

After a quick explanation, he baptized Dah, pouring water on his blue-gray head. It was the best he could do for now. Dah passed David his pack.

"Let's go!" Dah urged. The door opened, and they scrambled onto the moving walkway.

"Where will you be going from here?" Dah asked.

"To Morsala, home of the mel-hanor."

Extending his black tongue again, Dah declared, "*Boosah*! They are an ugly hairy species."

David wondered what Dah thought of humans.

Swiveling his head around, Dah asked, "Are you going to tell them about Yavana too?"

"That's my mission."

Dah led David back a different way. Except for the shuffling of multiple feet, the halls remained silent. The mel-dijetara never talked in the corridors, never acknowledging each other's presence.

*This is worse than people in an elevator*, David thought.

Dah scratched his long snout and swiveled his head as if seeing the impersonal isolation for the first time. "They hurry to complete as many tasks as possible just to have their name on the Honored Worker Roster. This is so empty, so meaningless. It must stop!" he spoke in a soft, yet passionate, voice. "My people are dead, but Yavana can fill them with life!"

When they reached the giant hanger, David's heart froze. A team of thirty mel-dijetara swarmed over his delah like ants on a dead bird. Each tail tentacle grasped an instrument. The mels held computer boards with one pair of hands and typed away with the other.

"What do we do?" David whispered in a panic.

Curling his tail tentacles, Dah replied, "Follow me and say nothing. No one will suspect." Racing up to the delah, Dah shouted, "Emergency Privileges! The human from Trenara must be released to leave on an urgent errand."

Most of the group withdrew and darted away, but a dark brown creature approached Dah.

"I am Bah-206-375163-702-Hah, level-two manager of New Technologies Research Department. Who is assuming command of this project?"

"Sah-213-522037-505-Bah, level-four director of Inter-Naharam Intelligence," Dah said with an air of authority.

The dark brown mel-dijetara typed the number into his computer board and glanced at David. "What a handicapped creature! With only two arms, two legs, and a frail upright frame, it could never amount to any threat. No wonder they decided to let it go." Wagging his snout, the mel departed.

David opened the delah's door and looked back at Dah. "Ramara for your help. When you've established a solid group of filled dijetara, send some to Arana. The phantera will be happy to help you, but be sure to tell them Vadelah David sent you. Do you think you can remember all that?"

"Vadelah David, *I'm* the one who can remember twelve-digit numbers. Now go! Soon we will both see whether Yavana can take care of His inventions."

David gave Dah the remaining bags of crystals, knowing now that the mel-hanor didn't have the technology to use them.

As the door whispered shut, David leaped into his seat and shouted out commands.

"Delah, take us to the departure zone."

He barely had time to fasten his seatbelts before the ship shot out of the hanger. As the delah climbed, David selected an uninhabited planet where he could rest, a place of no interest to the mels or the naharam. Watching his scanners, David realized the beauty of Dah's simple plan. The mel-dijetara didn't openly lie to each other, so they never questioned Dah's information. Due to genetic manipulation, all bore identical features, making it impossible to distinguish an individual by sight. All mel-dijetara were blue-gray, khaki, or dark brown. Only their number identified them. A mel-dijetara who forgot his number would be declared defective and disassembled. The thought of a mel-dijetara *deliberately* lying about his number was not foreseen in the system. It was unheard of, unthinkable.

David smiled. Dah would be almost impossible to find. As the atmosphere thinned, the delah neared the departure zone—the vacuum of space where his ship could safely teleport.

"Ten crullahs approaching from deep space," the computer announced.

*       *       *

Back in his office, Dah the Inefficient typed furiously, his fingers a blur of activity. "Yavana, I can't remember being so excited over a project. Vadelah David was right; there is much my people have missed!"

Using his Emergency Access Code, Dah burst into several departments of Cruskada's orderly system. He issued a multitude of bogus orders and requests. By the time he was done, Cruskada's leaders would be chasing their own tentacles.

"Yes, I really am enjoying this!" Dah said, tapping his six feet in rapid succession. "You *did* make me for a secret special mission! Ramara Yavana!"

With apprehension, David watched as the crullahs approached. "Delah, scan for communications," he ordered.

"Crullah Pah-527-765546-735: I am receiving a priority message. We are instructed to let the delah leave."

"Crullah Fah-663-328437-933: Can you verify that?"

"Crullah Pah-527-765546-735: I already did. Break off pursuit." Banking sharply, the black shapes returned the way they came.

"Departure zone reached. Prepare for trelemar," the computer announced.

David cheered as the white light engulfed the nearly starless night. Arriving in orbit around the gaseous planet Estrolar, David stared at its swirling dark green atmosphere. Estrolar was a frozen lifeless sphere. Five battered moons traveled within the rocky debris of her rings. No one would look for him here.

Feeling more exhausted than after a final exam, David ate a real meal of dried loomar, cooked plumos, and cold falatirah. He still had a headache from Cruskada's stale air. With a groan of relief, David strapped himself into his berth and fell asleep.

\*    \*    \*

*Where am I?* David bolted upright, awake.

The green swirling surface of Estrolar enveloped the windshield. With a heavy sigh, David stretched, remembering the last few days. Today he faced the scariest of the three species—the fierce mel-hanor. No one had anything good to say about the meat-eating hairy beasts. His experiences on Wicara and Cruskada had been vastly different from anything he'd expected. Perhaps the mel-hanor would be easy converts and he could get out of there ASAP. Feeling an uncomfortable tightness in his stomach, David ate breakfast. The dread of anticipation just might kill him first.

Breaking into a nervous sweat, he muttered, "I'd better take a shower."

As the warm water massaged his skin, the tension beneath remained. Deep inside, where the water couldn't soothe, he was terrified. Why? He believed the prophecy Rammar had given him, but the prophecy only spoke of his encounters with the three mel-naharam. It mentioned nothing afterwards. There was a very real chance he was going to die on Morsala.

David finished vacuuming his skin and flipped on the dehumidifier. With shaking hands, he pulled on his flight suit. Perhaps he should eat again?

"No!" David spoke firmly. That would be stalling. He combed his fingers through his damp hair. *I need to pray.*

Jittery, he glided over to his chair and buckled himself in. Floating around the cabin would be too distracting. David tried to pray, but his mind wandered. He wanted to flee to Trenara, climb into bed, and hide from everyone for a month.

*I could go to Trenara...*

"Yavana, clear my mind," David pleaded. "I feel like Jonah again; I don't want to go to Nineveh; I don't want to die; I'm terrified of the mel-hanor!" He paused. Did the Ninevites kill Jonah? No. Perhaps there was hope.

Images of the slaughtered phantera on Arana exploded into his mind. The gentle villagers had found no protection from the mel-hanor. David's chest ached. It wasn't just death he feared, it was torture, and the mel-hanor reveled in torture. What was it he'd heard in his vision? If only he had the memory of a phantera!

He found Rammar's paper, thankful the phantera prophet had consulted Gyra and recorded David's vision. Reading aloud from Rammar's graceful script, David struggled to keep his voice steady.

"Fear not! I have known the depths of pain and triumphed over it…. Be bold…"

Squeezing the paper between his trembling fingers, David prayed, "Yavana, if You are leading me to suffer, I will go. Please give me the strength to endure it!"

This was his "Gethsemane," where his dreams had to die, where his will had to submit to the Hand that led him into the darkness. He said good-bye to Earth, his friends, and his hope for a family.

A strange peace descended on him. He would go, but he would not go alone. He was never alone. There was One who had gone before him, and He would be David's guide and strength.

Turning the paper over, David read Rammar's prophecy again. "To the mel-hanor show no fear and stand your ground. Expose their slavery to passion."

David rolled up the paper and slid it back into the compartment. "Delah, take us to the planet Morsala." He half expected the computer to protest.

"Calculations complete. Prepare for trelemar."

"Ramara Yavana for *hayan* [life]!" David cried as the light enfolded him.

# 12. Fear and Depravity

Once more, David was surprised. Morsala nearly matched Trenara in mass, water distribution, and climate. The planet hung before a backdrop crowded with stars. Emerald continents and cobalt seas shimmered before him. David drank in her beauty like a condemned man enjoying his last sunrise.

"Two crullahs approaching from lower orbit," the computer informed.

Only two? "Delah, scan for communications."

The dark shapes fired a few warning shots. David was tempted to flee.

*"Stand your ground,"* he could hear Rammar saying. Removing his hand from the control stick, David waited.

"Crullah Nerak to unknown spacecraft. Identify yourself before we blast you into oblivion!" the harsh voice growled.

*Yavana, make my life count.* "Delah David: I am a human from Trenara."

"Crullah Nerak: The same that visited Wicara and Cruskada?"

They knew! Panic dug its nails into his heart.

*Show no fear!* came the silent command.

If he lied, it would certainly show fear, but if he told the truth, now *that* would be bold. "Delah David: I am the same naharam who visited those planets. I intend to visit yours too."

"Crullah Nerak: We will fight you!"

"Delah David: Destroy me now and you will forever wonder why I came. You can kill me, but I will not fight you."

"Crullah Aktor: I say we slice off a wing with our lasers. Then he'll run." A black ship fired a few shots.

"Crullah Nerak: Stop firing; he's not budging! Let him land. He may be more amusing on the ground."

"Crullah Aktor: But someone else will find him first and have all the fun."

"Crullah Nerak: Whoever finds him will be certain to boast about his death. It will make a more entertaining tale than if we simply blast him. Let's go to Wicara like we planned. I want to find out when the next raid will be. I heard another opportunity is coming."

"Crullah Aktor: I'm with you. That last one on Arana was the best blood-fest! I'll race you to Wicara's visitor station!"

Both crullahs winked out of sight.

David's stomach felt like taut elastic. "Yavana, please protect the phantera!"

As his delah descended, he searched the surface for cities. Dah the Inefficient was right about the mel-hanor being primitive. A few empty stadiums were the only significant structures on the planet.

"Delah, scan for mel-hanor life signs."

The computer showed dots scattered all over the continents. Only the very arid northern deserts remained clear. Where should he land? Spying an area with a moderate concentration of mel-hanor and animal life, David pressed his finger against the screen.

"Delah, take us to indicated area."

His palms sweated as the ship bumped through the thickening atmosphere. Soon the delah swooped over the abundant green vegetation. An occasional odd-colored tree reminded him that this was an alien world. Regardless of the inhabitants, Morsala's appearance was more inviting than smoke-filled Wicara or cement-gray Cruskada. He landed in a clearing. This time David changed out of his flight suit and hung it up. He didn't anticipate needing it again. As he fastened his tool belt, David pondered taking his caruk. It could be useful.

"No," he spoke aloud to strengthen his resolve. "This is not the time to fight. I came to bring peace and—if necessary—to die." Unclipping his caruk, he placed it in the tool panel. David donned Brusaka's heavy cloak. "Vashua, guide me through the valley of the shadow of death. Help me to fear no evil." Fingering the cloak's soft dark material, he whispered, *"Toorah barune."*

The door slid open and a gentle light filtered in. Earthy smells filled the cabin, accompanied by the soft coos, peeps, and ticks of the indigenous forest creatures. David crammed his pack with provisions and books. The mel-hanor had no use for crystals. He was fortunate they were literate. The soil crunched beneath David's feet as he stepped into the sunlight. It was a good thing Morsala wasn't the first planet he had visited. Her deceptively peaceful environment would have tempted him to lower his guard.

*"Toorah steen,"* he said in a subdued voice.

The delah's door slid shut. Would he ever see his ship's interior again? Walking across the blue-green turf, he followed the sloping ground down to a ravine. Clumps of trees and scattered shrubs hampered his field of view.

Where were the mel-hanor? His instruments had indicated a large group scattered around the area. Perhaps they were watching, waiting...

Reaching the edge of the ravine, he froze. On the dry streambed below, two lion-like creatures sat on their rumps, each with a short tail like a cropped Doberman. Their brown muscular backs tensed as they faced downstream. Were these mel-hanor? David was content to watch them before attempting contact.

Clattering stones echoed from downstream and the figures exchanged brief words. The tan one bounded up the opposite side of the ravine on all fours. His short fur revealed the hard muscles just beneath his skin. The darker brown beast crawled up behind another bush and peered further down the ravine. He bore a long canine muzzle, but his low forehead, rounded ears, and slanted eyes gave him a feline appearance. The sound of a large galloping creature grew louder. Slowing to a trot, an elk-sized dalam lumbered into view. Roan sides heaving, head drooping, the split-toed animal stumbled over the rocky streambed as it approached them. It was a lampar from Arana.

The dark hunter tensed as the tired beast came near. Like a panther, he sprang into the air releasing a chilling roar. The lampar screamed as the predator latched onto its back. Black claws from all four paws pierced the bucking animal's muscles. Dazed in disbelief, David watched the bellowing tormented dalam struggle to shake off its attacker. The tan hunter leaped from hiding, urging on his companion. David didn't understand the words. At that point he didn't want to. Snarling, the dark wolf-lion bit his victim repeatedly, not to kill it, but to torment it. David wanted to run, to close his eyes to the violent scene before him, but he remained frozen—watching in stunned silence.

The exhausted lampar collapsed, each breath a wail. Its bulging eyes rolled as the wolf-lion growled into the lampar's ear. The predator sliced the skin with his many claws. Every cut was methodical, designed to bring a response. The vicious creature gloated over the cries of his prey, making each consecutive wound deeper than the last. Using a massive thumb-claw, he slit open the heaving belly. David thought he had seen the worst. He was wrong. As the dying animal wallowed in the dirt, its tormentor inflicted upon it a final act of depravation.

At last David found the strength to turn away. Kneeling down, he covered his ears to block out the sounds of the obscene act below.

This was the mel-hanor. This was the depraved species he was going to speak to about Yavana's love. He gagged.

"Yavana, I can't do it. I have no love for these...monsters! They're worse than animals! They won't listen to me; they're too evil, too cruel! They'll kill me like that poor lampar in the ravine."

Gradually, his nausea decreased. A Scripture came to mind. *But God demonstrates His own love toward us, in that while we were yet sinners, Christ died for us.*[1]

David released a shuddering sigh. "I'm going to need Your strength to love them, because I can't do it on my own!"

The two mel-hanor chatted and laughed in their rough tongue as they sat on the dead lampar. Another clattering echoed from down the ravine. The two mel-hanor scattered up opposite slopes and hid. A second lampar staggered into view, obviously pregnant. Her long blue tongue hung out of her mouth as she wheezed. The tan mel-hanor crouched down, preparing to make his kill.

Something in David snapped. He wouldn't tolerate the torture of another dalam—especially a pregnant one. Ignoring the possible consequences of his actions, David ran down the hill, yelling and waving his hands. Rallying its strength, the dalam bolted up the side of the ravine, unharmed. The lampar was not the only one surprised by his actions. Conversing in low tones, the hunters rose upright and sauntered toward David.

The dark mel-hanor licked the bloodstains on his muzzle. "Hasket, what is it?" he asked in rough Ramatera. "I've never seen a dalam like it before."

His tan companion growled. "They didn't announce any new dalam or chelra for the hunt."

The dark mel-hanor's nose twitched and he laughed.

---

[1]Romans 5:8 NASB

"The puny thing doesn't appear to be much of a challenge. Look at those dull claws on its bony limbs."

"Well, it scared away my prey. Let's see how it responds to a mel-hanor!" Hasket raised the tan fur on his back, barred his teeth, and charged David.

*Stand your ground.*

Remaining still, David faced his attacker. So, this was how he was to die. Perhaps the mel-hanor would wonder who he was, read his books, and turn to Yavana. His blood might not be shed in vain.

*Wham!* The creature knocked him flat. David felt the sharp nails pressing against his flesh as powerful forearms squeezed the breath out of his chest. He fought to keep from screaming.

The second mel-hanor spoke to Hasket. "The thing didn't even run. It must be an incredibly stupid dalam."

"I...am...a naharam," David forced out.

"It's a naharam!" the dark mel-hanor shouted. "Don't kill it—yet. Let's find out where it's from. Perhaps there's a new planet for us to raid."

Hasket wrinkled his muzzle. "It sure doesn't put up much of a fight. I would have preferred the lampar, Shektul."

The iron grip relaxed. Filling his lungs, David silently thanked God.

"So, you are a naharam," his captor stated. "What brings you here to chase off my prey?"

"And where are you from?" added Shektul, the dark mel-hanor.

"I am David, a male human naharam from Trenara."

"Trenara!" Shektul roared. The two mel-hanor glanced at each other.

Hasket growled. "I thought he looked weird. Smells funny too."

Wiping more of the blood off his muzzle, Shektul cocked his head. "Some of our mels have gone to Trenara.

They've been bringing back great game. There's one called a *horse*—a real favorite. They're fast, beautiful, and great screamers."

"But how do they taste?" Hasket asked.

"Better than lampar!" Like a ravenous tiger, Shektul's black-ringed eyes stared down at David. "So, what brings a naharam to Morsala. Did you come to fight us?" The skin on his muzzle rippled, baring his teeth.

"Myute," David replied in a quiet firm voice. "I came to bring a message."

"How disappointing." Dropping his fierce posturing, Shektul sniffed David. "Why do I smell phantera on you? Have you been to Dalena?"

David remembered his clothes. "Myute, I have been to Arana."

Hasket narrowed his feline eyes. "I fail to see anything interesting about him. Let's kill him."

"Myute, Hasket, I'm still curious. If you kill him now, he won't be able to answer any questions." Shektul turned to David. "You say you will not fight us and you bring a message?"

"Dala, I came to talk, not to fight." David looked straight into Shektul's golden eyes.

"He already sounds like the mel-balahrane," Hasket growled. "I bet he's full of weird ideas."

Shektul circled David. "Look at it this way, Hasket. This naharam is a pathetic skinny little creature. Our cubs could kill him."

"Now there's a thought!" Hasket showed his teeth in a wicked grin.

"Listen!" Shektul growled. "Try to see it from the naharam's point of view. If you were as weak and ugly as he is, would you want to land on Morsala?"

"So he wants to die," Hasket replied. "We can help him; killing is our specialty."

Shektul snorted. "I never heard of a naharam seeking death by torture." Sitting down, he scratched behind his ear. "He did say he brought a message." The dark mel-hanor looked down at his right paw and rubbed his claws together. Extending the five-inch claw on his thumb, he gazed at David.

"Human from Trenara, did you know about the mel-hanor before you landed here?"

"My name is David. I have known about you for quite some time now. I sought you out."

Raising his paw until the long curved claw hovered inches from David's neck, Shektul asked, "Do you know what the mel-hanor do to their victims?"

"Dala, I saw you kill the dalam." David stared into his opponent's eyes.

"I mean *before* you arrived on Morsala."

The claw slowly grazed the skin of David's neck. He didn't flinch but kept his eyes locked onto Shektul's. "I saw what you did to the phantera on Arana. I helped gather their skinned bloody bodies. I closed their eyes and wept at their panatrel."

The claw stopped and pressed against David's windpipe. The needle tip pricked his skin. David remained rigid. He was determined to die well, not like a coward.

"So, you saw what we did on Arana?" Shektul asked in an amused voice. "I was on that raid. It was the most fun I've had in a long, long time. You should have seen us in action! What I did to the dalam was cub's play compared to the fun we had with the phantera." He seemed to wait for a response.

The claw pressed harder.

"This is better than I thought," Hasket whispered. "We'll torture him in his mind and then in his body."

Shektul kept his golden eyes riveted to David. "You must hate us for what we did. I bet you came here out of guilt, wanting to join your dead friends!"

David didn't blink. "Myute."

"Myute? Which statement do you disagree with?" Shektul cocked his head, but kept his eyes on David.

"I do not wish to die." Memories of David's vision filled his mind until he no longer saw the glaring eyes in front of him. Instead, he beheld a battered human face. David's stoic expression melted. "I do not hate you, I give you shalar. You may kill me, but another will be sent to take my place."

A second claw pressed against his belly; its sharp point pricked his skin. "So, you know all about us, yet you are willing to die for this message, even at the hands of the mel-hanor?" Shektul's face came back into focus.

"Dala, it would be an honor," David replied.

Shektul withdrew his claws as if he'd been stung. "*Clishtip!* I've never seen a naharam like this! Are all humans like you?"

David shook his head. "Myute." He had not expected the mel-hanor to release him.

"Why did you stop?" Hasket asked Shektul in a disappointed tone.

"Because I am curious about this weak naharam. If you are still annoyed because he scared off your lampar, then you can have my turn at the hunt tomorrow."

Hasket wrinkled his furry brow. "You're serious?"

"Dala."

"Your loss!" Hasket taunted.

"Why don't you go up the canyon and see if you can find some more game," Shektul suggested. "I'm going to keep this human—to amuse myself."

# 13. A Slave of Slaves

Hasket bounded off in search of more game. David felt as helpless as a piece of steak while Shektul's golden eyes examined him.

"I don't suppose those skinny limbs of yours can carry my dalam," Shektul stated in a hard voice.

David eyed the dead lampar's massive bulk. "Well, not in one trip. Do you have a cart?"

Shektul snorted. "Mel-hanor don't use carts to carry their food! I guess I'll have to get my carrying hide. Come!"

"Wait," David said. "There is a pack of books I left up on the hill. I will bring them." After climbing up the ravine's side, he returned with his pack. "Now I am ready."

Shektul's muzzle wrinkled, showing a few teeth. "I will examine your pack first." Dumping the contents onto the ground, the mel-hanor pawed through them. "What are these?" he asked, holding up David's extra shirts and underwear.

"Those are my spare clothes. I wear them for warmth and modesty."

"Modesty. Now *there's* a useless word on Morsala. What are these books?"

"They contain the message I bring to the mel-hanor."

Shektul leafed through one of the books. "Looks like a long message. I doubt if you could find a mel-hanor who'd sit still and listen to even part of it."

"I can give a shorter version. What you see are Trenara's Scriptures."

"It must take a long time to read through all these books."

David laughed. The sound startled both of them.

"Shalar David. I didn't mean to surprise you. The books are identical, not multiple volumes. I brought many copies of the Scriptures to give to the mel-hanor." Gathering up his belongings, David stuffed them into the pack.

"Let me be clear about something," Shektul stated with a low growl. "If you wish to survive this day, you will do what I say or I will kill you. I gave Hasket my place in the hunt tomorrow in exchange for your life. That makes you my *lastor*. Do you understand?"

"Myute, Shektul, I have not heard the word *lastor* before. Please tell me what it means."

"You are mine, like the phantera own their ducas and lampar."

So, he was Shektul's slave. David could think of a worse fate. Rubbing the scratch on his neck, he said, "I understand. I will do what you ask as long as it doesn't violate my conscience."

Shektul's muzzle rippled again. "You are a pitiful weak naharam, but you are very brave. Now come."

David followed his captor down the ravine. It opened up to a larger dry riverbed. They passed another pair of mel-hanor standing beside a battered dead dalam. The hunters howled at Shektul, who returned the greeting.

"What is that creature with you?" one called.

"It's a human from Trenara. He's my lastor," Shektul answered.

"Is it a mel?" asked the other hunter.

"Myute. He's a naharam."

The first hunter bared his teeth. "A naharam? Why don't you kill him?"

"I intend to take my time enjoying him." Shektul smiled, flashing his fangs, as the two hunters howled and laughed.

When they were alone again, Shektul spoke. "You say

you are willing to die for your message. If you can tell me a short version, I will hear it now."

*Yavana, what was I supposed to expose about the mel-hanor? Their slavery to passion? And how do I do that?* David got an idea.

Looking up at Shektul, he asked, "When you were a...cub, did you kill dalam like the one today?"

Shektul chuckled. "I ask you to tell me your message, and you ask me a question! Perhaps Hasket was right; I should kill you."

"Great messages sometimes require preparation for the listener."

"Very well, but if I sense you are stalling, I will kill you." The mel-hanor sighed. "When I was a cub, my mother started me off with small dalam—flightless birds and small mammals. I can still hear her say, 'Be sure to make them scream before you eat them.'"

David was glad Shektul didn't see him flinch. "And when you grew older, you killed bigger dalam?"

Shektul smiled, showing his fierce teeth. "Dala, I needed something more exciting. The dalam I killed became larger and larger. When they no longer thrilled me, I went on to hunting chelra and finally naharam."

"And then?" David pressed.

"And then I grew more skilled in inflicting pain. It took more and more to make the hunt exciting. I began to physically 'humiliate' my victims. I became as you see me now."

Feeling sick, David continued. "And now where will you go? Are you still not satisfied?"

The mel-hanor was silent for a moment. "No, I am not. Perhaps if I killed more naharam at the same time, or bigger naharam—"

"Then your lust for blood would increase still more," David finished.

Shektul trained his feline eyes on David. "Are there mel-humans on Trenara?"

"Dala, some are responsible for exterminating thousands of humans, but it never satisfies them. They, like you, are lastors."

"The mel-hanor are lastors to no one!" Shektul snarled. "We do as we please!"

"You are lastors to the worst master of the universe, your selfish passions."

If looks could kill, Shektul's would have. But David continued his explanation. "When you serve your passions, you're never happy for long. Your passions grow, demanding more and more to satisfy them. And the more you feed them, the more they control you."

"But if I don't follow my passions, I'll be bored! What else is there to do?"

Wearing a wry expression, David asked, "Do you think I was bored when I first met you?"

Shektul laughed. "No, but I bet you were terrified. I would have been if *I* were you!" His golden eyes rested on David. "And yet when you saw us, you didn't run in fear. It is my curiosity that saved you."

David pressed his fingers against his smiling lips. It was a lot more than Shektul's curiosity that had protected him. He remembered his discussion with Philoah about *myudel*, the Ramatera word for boredom and lack of purpose.

"Shektul, you think following your passions will keep you from myudel, but the real cause of myudel is lack of purpose. Just look at the word *myudel*. It comes from *myute* and *del*—'No message.' You have no purpose because you haven't heard my message."

Snorting, Shektul retorted, "And your message will keep me from boredom?"

"Myute, *doing* what my message requires will keep you from boredom!"

"Are you done with your preparation?"

"Dala, I think you are ready to listen. My message has the power to free you from being a lastor to your passions, and to banish the myudel in your life."

They walked at a snail's pace, pausing often, as Shektul let David talk uninterrupted for about an hour. The mel-hanor showed no emotion, but David was certain he was listening.

As they drew near to a canyon, Shektul interrupted him.

"That's enough for now! I will hear more later…if you please me."

Caves dotted the towering walls of the canyon, inhabited by a community of mel-hanor. Cubs frolicked in the stream that chattered across the canyon floor.

David was surprised to see small animals tethered outside some of the caves.

"Those are for the cubs," Shektul informed him. "They practice their killing skills on small dalam before eating them."

David pitied the doomed creatures, but his heart grieved more for the playful cubs taught to embrace evil at such a young age.

Shektul turned into one of the lower caves.

David followed. The interior walls were whitewashed rock, and fur carpeted the floor. Worried that his soles might damage the soft pelts, David asked if he should remove his shoes.

"What?" the mel-hanor snapped. "You mean humans clothe their feet too? I thought they looked funny. Is this another modesty thing?"

"Myute, our feet are tender so we wear shoes to protect them."

"You humans are pathetic," Shektul mumbled. "Take them off if you wish, but don't worry about the hides. I'm always getting new ones."

If Shektul didn't worry, David wouldn't either.

The mel-hanor went to a basin and washed the remaining blood off his muzzle.

David's throat itched. Rubbing it, he felt dried blood. The nail scratch was getting irritated.

"Lastor, get me that white hide hanging on the wall," Shektul commanded.

Handing the soft fleece to his master, David noticed it had a familiar smell and feel. As Shektul dried his face with it, David asked, "What kind of animal did that pelt come from?"

The mel-hanor sniffed it like a dog. "One of the imported dalam. *Sheep*—that's what they call it. They were a dud for hunting, too slow and dumb. We give them to our cubs instead."

Shektul removed a belt from the wall. "Grab that coil of rope hanging above your head and the rolled-up carrying hide beneath it."

David did as he was instructed.

"Carry this too." Shektul dropped the leather belt over David's shoulders. Then he picked up another rolled hide. "Now, we return to my kill."

At least the mel-hanor wasn't going to let the meat go to waste.

When they returned to the dead lampar, David unrolled the carrying hide. Leather straps and fasteners punctuated its stained surface. He wondered how Shektul would dress his kill without a knife.

But the mel-hanor had no need for knives. His sharp skilled claws dressed the beast faster than any human counterpart. It was a gory process, but not as bad as the killing itself. Shektul piled most of the butchered pieces onto the carrying hide and folded the edges over the meat. The rest of the flesh he wrapped to carry himself. Using the rope, he attached the leather belt to David's carrying hide.

Shektul held the belt out to David. "Here, pull this back to the cave."

David looked up at him. "You've got to be kidding."

"Are you defying me?" The mel-hanor gave an ominous growl.

"Myute, Shektul, I'm telling you I'm not strong enough to drag that whole load back to the cave."

The mel-hanor scowled. "Are you really so weak? Just try it."

Fastening the belt about his waist, David leaned forward. He pulled with all his might, but the massive burden refused to budge. David stopped, panting.

Raising his claws, Shektul snarled, "If you don't bring that dalam back to the cave, I will kill you."

"Then kill me!" David shot back in exasperation. "There's no way I can drag this back unless you let me do it in more than one trip."

"That will take too long!" Shektul sulked. "How much *can* you take?"

"I don't know; let's find out." Removing his belt, David opened the hide. "Where will we put the stuff I can't carry?"

Shektul unrolled his bundle.

David transferred hunks of meat onto Shektul's mound until some pieces balanced precariously, threatening to slide into the dirt. Although most of the carrying hide was empty now, the remaining meat was still an impossibly large load.

David cleared his tight throat. "It's still too much. What do I do now?"

Marching angrily over to the carrying hide, Shektul bent over and sliced a piece off with his claw.

David raised his eyebrows but said nothing. After placing more chunks of meat onto the new piece of hide, he pulled on the rope to see if he could budge the carrying hide. Nope.

On the fifth try, David finally found a weight he could drag.

Shektul gave up threatening him. Wagging his head as he eyed the smaller load, he grumbled, "You humans are so weak! How do you get anything done?"

"Some are much stronger than me," David replied.

The mel-hanor wrapped up the remaining meat and added it to his previous bundle, lifting it all with ease.

"If Yavana really did send you, why didn't He pick someone stronger?"

Leaning into his belt, David grunted and replied, "I don't understand everything Yavana does!" The carrying hide slid over the stones more easily than he'd expected. "Our Scriptures do say that Yavana's strength is made perfect in our weaknesses."

Shektul cocked his furry head. "A strange saying. I don't understand; explain it."

David paused in his pulling. "Do you have any dangerous dalam on Morsala."

"Another question for an answer!" Shektul retorted. "Well, we have the *skatolar*. It's a savage dalam, a challenge to hunt."

"Suppose Yavana told a big warrior to slay a skatolar, and he did. Most mels would say the warrior killed it with his own strength and skill."

Shektul's ear flicked. "Dala."

"But what if Yavana sent a small weak cub to kill a skatolar?" David asked.

Shektul raised a furry brow. "You have not seen a skatolar."

"It doesn't matter. If this cub were to kill a skatolar, and claimed he did it by Yavana's power, it would be different, wouldn't it?"

"Dala, lastor, it would cause quite a stir!"

"Precisely! Perhaps that is why I was chosen. If I survive long enough for Yavana's message to take root, it will not be because of my strength, but because of Yavana's strength." Resuming his labor, David dragged his burden down the ravine.

Shektul's eyes studied him. "Yavana must want to gain a lot of glory for Himself. He sure chose a weak messenger!"

David was wishing God had made him a little stronger long before they reached the village. He entered the canyon with sweat pouring down his face and blisters under his belt. Seeing his struggle, the villagers gathered around to watch. They teased and jeered when he stumbled, but David got up and continued without a word. Shektul saw the small crowd harassing David, but neither encouraged, nor dissuaded his fellow mel-honor.

At last, David paused outside the cave and turned to Shektul. "And where would you like me to place it, master?" He smiled in satisfaction.

The crowd ceased their taunting and murmured instead.

Dropping his massive load, Shektul roared, "Unwrap the hides and carry the flesh back to the meat locker."

Heads in the crowd nodded. David opened the hides. His sweaty smile created a stir among the spectators. Grabbing a large haunch, he staggered into the cave.

The meat locker was a closet hewn from stone with a wooden door and shelves. David suspected it was cooled artificially. By the time he finished bringing in all the meat, most of the crowd had dispersed.

"Go wash the carrying hides in the stream and place them on the rocks to dry," Shektul ordered.

Gathering up the bloody hides, David waded into the cool waters. He bent down to wash the skins. Something surfaced beside him. A cub played in the water, watching him. Smiling, David grabbed a handful of sand and scrubbed a hide.

The cub swam closer. "You are weak, naharam," he taunted.

"Dala, I will never be as strong as a mel-hanor." Still smiling, he continued to scrub.

The cub frowned and drew closer. "Being weak doesn't bother you?"

"Sometimes it does, but I am not ashamed of it." David worked another stain.

"You are strange and ugly, naharam! Why aren't you ashamed of your weak body?"

David restrained his chuckle. "Yavana made me as I am; I cannot change that. Even though I am weak, I can still do many things."

Pulling himself erect, the cub declared, "The mel-hanor are strong. We have no need for Yavana."

David's hands stopped. He looked at the cub. "Are you strong enough to live forever?"

The cub hesitated. "Myute, no one is."

Turning away, David resumed his scrubbing.

The cub moved around to face David. "Why do you ask that, naharam?"

"Because if you are not strong enough to keep death away, then I think you need Yavana."

"But Yavana has forsaken us!"

"Myute, it is the mel-hanor who have forsaken Yavana. I was sent to call the mels back to Him."

The cub gazed at the flowing water.

"Haltek!" A female mel-hanor called.

"I've got to go. It's time for me to kill and eat." The cub bounded away.

David focused on scrubbing the hide. He hummed loudly to drown out the screams of a dying dalam.

# 14. The Way of the Mel-Hanor

When David finished his washing, he rung out the hides, spread them on the rocks to dry, and returned to Shektul's cave.

Stepping into the entrance, he stopped. Low groans met his ears. A pair of groans.

David turned around and walked out in disgust. Lowering his weary frame against the cold stone wall, he bowed his head. "Lord, they're so perverted," he said in English. "Help me to love them, to see beyond their—"

"Naharam, who are you talking to?"

Flinching, David looked up at the cub he'd met in the stream. "I was talking to Yavana."

The cub's dark brown eyes blinked. "What language were you using?"

"English. It's one of the languages of Trenara." David was grateful for the momentary distraction.

Haltek's brown eyes scowled. "Humans speak more than one language on Trenara?"

"Dala! We have thousands. Different areas of Trenara use different languages."

"So, you all speak Ramatera when you travel?"

Chuckling, David said, "Myute, I am the only human who speaks Ramatera. Trenara has no unifying language."

The cub snorted. "How do you talk to your own kind when you travel?"

"It is difficult. We try to find someone who speaks our language and the language of the area."

"Someone who is a bridge, like a phantera?"

"Dala, but we have no phantera." David noticed a red

smear on the cub's face. "You have blood on your muzzle."

"*Clishtip!* I thought I got it all off." The cub licked his paw-like hand and rubbed the soiled fur. "Did you hear my dalam scream?"

"Yes," David said wearily.

His response was not lost on the cub. "Don't they kill and eat dalam on Trenara?"

"Dala, but we usually don't torture them."

The cub continued to wet his fur. "Why?"

"Yavana cares about the dalam He made. They were given to us for food, but out of respect for Yavana we try to kill them quickly and mercifully."

"But then you don't have the fun of watching them suffer."

David marveled at the cub's callused response. "Most of my kind take no pleasure in the suffering of others."

The cub was silent for a moment. "What do you find pleasurable?"

"Many things! Exploring forests, swimming, playing games with my friends, but the thing I enjoy most is worshipping Yavana. There is no pleasure as great as that."

Pointing into the cave, the cub asked, "Is it better than having sex with females?"

David wanted to scream. The cub's casual use of intimate language was like a bucket of cold water in his face. Shektul was right. Modesty was a useless word on Morsala!

Composing himself, David stated, "Sex brings pleasure for a moment, but it is meaningless without commitment." Mel-hanor did get pregnant didn't they? He hoped he wasn't mistaken.

The cub eyed David. "Morsala is a lot different from Trenara, isn't it?"

"In some ways, but they have a lot in common, too. Morsala looks more like Trenara than any other planet I've been to.

"This canyon reminds me of a place where my father used to take me. I was just a...cub back then. We would creep around the bushes and stalk a dalam called *deer*. It was fun to see how close we could get before it leaped away.

"Sometimes we'd climb the steep walls, just like the ones you have here. When we reached the top, we'd howl and listen to the echoes. Then we'd throw small stones and count until they hit the bottom.

"One time we hiked a hill in the evening and watched the sun set. Even though we didn't say a word, I felt a closeness that was—" The cub stared at him with a blank expression. "What's wrong? Doesn't your father do things like that with you?"

"Myute," the cub said in a subdued voice. "I don't know who my father is."

David felt the knife of compassion slice into his heart. "Does your mother know who he is?"

"Myute."

The knife slid deeper. "I'm sorry to hear that."

Furrowing his brow, Haltek said, "Why? No cub knows who his father is. The males mate with different females every day. It's the way of the mel-hanor. Isn't it the same on Trenara?"

The soft tread of feet interrupted them as a female emerged from Shektul's cave.

"Naharam! Why are you crying?" the cub exclaimed.

"I weep because Morsala is so far from where Yavana wants her to be. I am grieved at how poor and broken her mel-naharam are—and they don't even know it."

Shektul's husky voice growled from the cave. "*Clishtip!* I threaten your life, and you are like stone, but a cub comes along and you cry like one newly born!"

The cub fled and joined some juveniles.

Shektul stood with folded arms. "I don't know what to make of you, lastor. You are very strange."

David wiped his eyes.

The mel-hanor sighed. "I am having some friends visit tonight and I want you to serve them."

"Dala, Shektul." David rubbed his running nose. If only he had a tissue.

Scowling, the mel-hanor grumbled, "Go to the stream and take a bath. You've been stinky ever since you dragged that pitifully small load to the cave."

"Dala, Shektul." David got up and left.


Keeping a firm grip on the serving platter, David smiled as he served raw meat to Shektul's guests. He drew several comments about his demeanor. Although the visitors teased David from time to time, they did not threaten him, for he belonged to Shektul.

The guests swapped stories of wild hunts, each trying to out-do the other in gore. The mel-hanor had a very macabre sense of humor. They laughed at the story of one unfortunate hunter who was gored by a horned dalam. The conversation progressed downhill from there.

"Tell us about this ugly lastor of yours!" requested a guest.

Shektul smiled as he spoke of David's courage and willingness to die for a message, but he neglected to say what that message was.

One of the older guests pointed to David. "He is brave. You ought to get him a female for tonight. I know where to find one."

"No!" David protested.

The room went deathly silent.

"He defies you, Shektul," a younger mel whispered.

Shektul gazed at David. "My lastor has told me he will do whatever I ask so long as it does not violate his conscience. For some reason he finds females objectionable."

"Is it because they are mel-hanor?" an older guest asked David. "You shouldn't turn one down until you've tried one."

That brought a round of howls and laughs.

"Perhaps he thinks human females are better," the older mel continued. "Why don't you try one of ours and tell us how they compare?"

"I have never...had a female," David stated.

Shektul's furry brows rose. "Never?"

A young mel laughed. "He is so ugly and skinny even his own kind won't have him!"

This brought an even louder round of laughter.

David's cheeks burned.

A different mel-hanor pointed to David's face and asked why it was turning red.

"I am embarrassed." David wagged his head. "You have mistaken a great strength for a weakness."

"Do all naharam on Trenara avoid females?" Shektul asked in a hushed voice.

"Myute, we take females, but we practice *dalaphar*, staying faithful for life."

"Dalaphar? How dull!" the young mel-hanor complained. "Who wants to see the same female day after day?"

"You don't understand." With a burst of inspiration, David turned to the younger mel-hanor. "Don't you like a challenge?"

The mel raised an eyebrow. "Dala!"

"Then what could be more challenging than keeping the same female interested in you, and only you, circuit after circuit?"

The mel-hanor raised his other eyebrow.

David rearranged the pieces on his meat platter. "Of course, that does depend on whether you have the ability to *keep* a female interested in you."

The older mel-hanor roared in laughter. "Now *there's* a thought! But how do I keep interest in her?"

Raising his finger, David replied, "That, too, is a challenge. The female has a part to play, but you can spark interest yourself by a very simple technique." He paused for dramatic effect before continuing in a soft voice. "Talk to her. Ask her questions. How does she feel? What does she want? What does she like? What does she hate?"

The mel-hanor eyed each other and turned back to him.

David lowered his voice further. "And then you have an even more challenging task."

"What's that?" the old mel-hanor whispered.

"*Listen to her!*" David shouted.

The effect shocked all the guests, and Shektul beamed at his lastor's boldness. The guests fell into laughing and teasing each other over David's prank. They practiced his delivery so they could retell the story, verbatim, for weeks to come. Unfortunately, the mel-hanor were more interested in the delivery of the message than its content.

When the guests finally left, David picked up the bones and scraps. Shektul glanced at his lastor every now and then, apparently puzzled that his slave would do chores without being told.

"I have no more work for you tonight, lastor."

Looking around, David asked, "Where do I sleep?"

Shektul scratched the back of his furry neck. "You are my first lastor. Clishtip! I guess I'll have to care for you until I decide to kill you." He pointed to a worn hide. "You can have that for a bed."

David unrolled the hairy hide onto the hard floor. It was better than sleeping on the platform of a doloom, but he longed for Brusaka's bed.

Before Shektul retired, he flashed David a fierce look and said, "Don't even think of escaping tonight—or any night. I am a light sleeper, and I will hunt you down and kill you."

"Dala, Shektul," David answered in a weary voice.

\* \* \*

Sitting beside the stream in the early morning, David wrote in his journal.

*The first few days, I lost count of the times I was threatened. Shektul has never carried them out, but they hang over my head like a dark cloud.*

*He really has no need to threaten me. I'm determined to keep my promise in hope of changing him. It appears to be working. The more I've proven my trustworthiness, the more freedoms I've been allowed.*

*I finally persuaded Shektul to let me search for edible vegetables in the forest. Morsala is filled with wonderful things to eat!*

*Shektul watched in amusement when I first tried to cook some meat. I skewered the pieces on a thin branch and roasted them over a fire. The problem was that the branch kept catching on fire. It finally broke, spilling the meat into the coals. Shektul laughed and shook his head as I fished the chunks out with a stick, burning my fingers on the hot meat. But I learned. The next time I covered the stick with meat so it wouldn't burn.*

*I've been ordered to take a bath each morning, and sometimes in the afternoon too. It's one of my favorite "chores." I talk often with that curious cub, Haltek. He's young and impressionable. Haltek's questions make me laugh as often as they make me weep. My furry friend often seeks me out to talk. I sense I'm meeting a deep need in him—the need for a father.*

*I now have a little fan club among the cubs, but the bond between Haltek and myself is the deepest.*

*Shektul goes hunting every few days, and I help bring back the meat. He doesn't insist I accompany him on his hunts, much to my relief!*

*After being sore the first few times, I've learned to gage how much I can drag back to the cave. What a workout!*

*I'm learning all I can about mel-hanor culture. Each morning they apply a black greasy eyeliner to enhance their fierce appearance. The cosmetic causes eye infections from time to time, but they wouldn't think of stopping the practice.*

*Their native language, Morsala, is quite guttural, sounding like a cross between an angry cat and a growling wolf.*

*The mel-hanor have one ruler, a* kunah, *who reins unopposed for an entire circuit. At the end of the circuit, all strong mel-hanor compete in feats of endurance. Older mel-hanor act as judges and anyone who dares to challenge their decisions is torn apart by their colleagues.*

*During the initial competitions, the players wear mitts on their paws to avoid injury. If blood is spilled, both players are disqualified.*

*The games are held in large stadiums where the females, the cubs, and the elderly watch. When a mel-hanor loses, he joins those seated to cheer for his comrades. It's considered shameful to be among the first to sit with the females and cubs.*

*Once the final contenders are chosen, there is a four-day preparation time. The contestants exercise and groom themselves to look their best.*

*On the fifth day, the chosen two are flown by crullah to the largest stadium on Morsala. They parade around the arena, exult in the cheers of the crowd, and remove their mitts. Then they fight to the death. The victor rules unopposed for the next circuit. If both die in the contest, the selection process is repeated.*

*Overall, I find the lack of stability in the mel-hanor's politics and family life depressing.*

*In spite of my continued survival, I'm certain my death is imminent. Someday Shektul will find fault with me and it will all be over, so I carefully sow the seeds of light every day, knowing I may never have another chance.*

David looked up as a female left the cave. They still visited Shektul once or twice a day.

His master came out and folded his hairy arms. "Is it true that you know who your father is?"

"Dala." David closed his book and returned it to his leather pack.

"Clishtip! Do you ever see him?"

"Of course. My parents have been together for over twenty-two circuits."

Shektul's mouth moved but no sound came out. Eventually he found his tongue. "And they enjoy being with each other? Still?"

"Very much!" David answered with a grin. "When they are apart, they miss each other terribly."

The mel-hanor wagged his head. "Go inside and prepare breakfast."

Later that day, David was taking inventory of the hides in the cave when Shektul called him outside. His master held a leather tether.

At the other end was a sheep.

"I have brought food for my lastor. I can't have you looking so skinny and sickly. You need to learn how to hunt and make yourself strong to serve me better." Shektul gave the leather line to David. "Here, kill it and enjoy."

David was not sure how to respond. He had never killed anything larger than a fish, but he wasn't about to offend his master. "Ramara, Shektul."

The mel-hanor folded his strong arms and waited. "Well?"

"I'm sorry, I've never killed a dalam this size before."

Shektul frowned. "It is cub's work. Do you mean you can't even do that?"

"Well...do you have a knife?" David eyed the placid sheep.

Wagging his head, Shektul cried, "I don't believe it. I bring you a dalam from your home world and you can't kill it without a tool! How do humans eat on your planet?"

David tried to explain agricultural methods on Trenara, but Shektul only wrinkled his brows.

"Enough! I will get you something to kill it with." Shektul disappeared into the cave, sputtering, "Weak, sickly wimpy human. What will I do with him? Such a helpless creature!" He returned with a three-foot metal blade.

"What is that?" David asked as he took the silvery object.

"It's a spearhead. We use it when hunting the mighty skatolar. Don't tell me it isn't good enough to kill a sheep!"

"Myute, it should be...fine." David's hands sweat on the cold blade.

"Now what?" Shektul asked with crossed arms.

"I'm trying to figure out the best way to use it. Such a wonderful gift should be killed...respectfully."

Throwing up his arms, Shektul snorted. "Kill it any way you like; it doesn't matter. You can eat it alive for all I care."

David straddled the sheep, grasped its head with one hand, and held the knife with the other. "Ramara Yavana for this food. Help me to kill it mercifully."

He slit its throat.

"That's pathetic," Shektul observed. "It didn't even cry. I don't understand you, human." Shaking his furry head, he retreated into the cave.

David looked down at the vacant eyes. "Sorry," he whispered.

# 15. A Lastor's Devotion

David's hand wrote in graceful Ramatera script as he sat beside the stream. The pages of his journal glowed in the afternoon light. Shektul had left early in the morning to go hunting so David wrote while awaiting his return.

> *Since my first, awful experience, Shektul has brought me more small dalam. I have learned to play the butcher—much to his amusement. Shektul has shown me how to cure hides so now I have a better bed.*
>
> *After much prodding, I joined the cubs in their small animal hunts. Shektul's hunting partner, Hasket, was so amused he gave me a cub's bow and a quiver of arrows. I felt like a kid. With a lot of practice (and encouragement from Haltek) I have been able to add more food to my master's table.*
>
> *But the adults still look down on me for my weaknesses and tease me frequently. They like to hear me talk, but don't take "the skinny naharam" seriously.*

A distant groan met his ears. David looked up.

Shektul staggered as he returned. Was he drunk?

"Lastor!"

Uh-oh. Something was wrong. Was that blood on Shektul's side? Running to his tottering master, David put an arm around him. "Easy, Shektul. The wound is deep."

The villagers watched as David supported the wavering mel-hanor.

"*Clishtip!* Everyone sees me," Shektul swore. "They will talk about how the mighty Shektul had to be helped home by a human!"

"I'm sorry," David whispered.

"I suppose it doesn't matter now." The mel-hanor groaned. "That stupid dalam gored me, and now I will get an infection and die...if I don't bleed to death first!"

Guiding Shektul into the cave, David lowered him onto a pile of hides. He poured a bowl of water and dipped a small cloth into it.

"*Ayeen!*" the mel cried as David dabbed the wound.

"Hold still," David spoke firmly.

"Hasket was right. I should have killed you. Now you will torment me as I die."

"Nonsense," chided David. "Now, hold still!"

"*Ayeen!* It hurts. I can feel the black flames of crul-hiya already."

"I pray you will never see those flames!" David said with determination. "Now, where can I get help? Is there a healer around?"

"Myute. We buy medicines from the mel-dijetara, but we have to treat ourselves. There are no mel-hanor healers." He winced as David pressed a clean spare shirt against the wound.

"I've got to apply pressure to stop this bleeding. Why won't any of your friends help?"

"It is not our way. We take care of...ourselves. *Ayeen.* I'm going to vomit."

David kept pressure on the wound as Shektul retched. As soon as the mel-hanor was finished, David rolled up the soiled hide with one hand and shoved it aside. He held the bloody shirt in place until his arms grew numb. The leather belt hanging from the wall caught his eye. David grabbed it and a skin full of driya. The fermented drink was a favorite among the mel-hanor and loaded with alcohol. Peeling away the dressing, he poured some driya onto the wound.

Shektul bolted upright. "*Ayeen!* You're torturing me!"

"Lie down!" David ordered. "I am trying to disinfect the wound." He wrapped the belt around Shektul's waist, tightened it over the dressing, and settled the mel-hanor back onto the skins.

Leaning over Shektul's face, he asked, "Can you breathe all right?"

The mel-hanor nodded.

"I'll be right back. I'm going to get some materials."

Racing from the cave, David spied Haltek. "Do you still have those gibtel fishing claws and sinew lines? I'll trade you lampar meat for them."

Haltek bounded off eagerly, returning with the claws and fishing line. David paid him a generous hunk of lampar.

The cub's eyes widened. "Why do you give me so much, naharam?"

"Out of ramara for your help."

"Are you going fishing?"

"Myute, I am trying to save Shektul's life."

Haltek frowned. "Balute? If your master dies, you will be free of him. You could escape!"

"I didn't come here to escape. I came to tell your people that Yavana can free you from your passions. If I have to remain a lastor to bring you freedom, so be it."

"I don't understand you, naharam." The cub walked away, sulking.

Stripping off his shirt, David heated an iron bowl of water. He fastened the line to the pre-drilled hole of a small claw. When the water boiled, David threw in the shirt, fishing line and remaining hooks. After twenty minutes, he poured out the water, hung the shirt up to dry, and returned to his patient.

There was no soap so David washed his hands with driya. Then he soaked the claws and line in the alcoholic drink. All was ready.

He undid the belt around Shektul's waist.

"Now what are you doing?" the mel-hanor asked. "Can't you let me die in peace? I thought you didn't believe in torturing your victims."

"You're not my *victim*, you're my patient. I'm going to try to close your wound."

"How?" Shektul asked with a wary look.

"On Trenara, healers sew up wounds...like you sew two hides together."

"How many times have you done this?"

David grimaced. "Never."

"This *is* a form of Trenara torture. As your master I order you to stop and let me die!"

"Myute, Shektul, I can't. It would violate my conscience." He peeled away the bloody shirt.

"*Ayeen!* Stubborn useless lastor. I should have killed you. I'd kill you now if—*ayee, ayee, ayee!* What are you doing?"

"Putting driya on the wound to disinfect it before I sew you up. Here drink some to numb the pain."

David poured the fermented drink into the mel-hanor's eager mouth. Placing a small hide into his master's hand, he said, "Put this in your mouth and bite on it. It will help you feel better."

Wincing, David started his first stitch.

The mel-hanor chewed the hide to shreds and David had to find another one. Twenty minutes and five hides later David was through. He poured more driya on the wound and covered it with a rolled-up pair of spare pants.

Tightening the belt in place, he said, "There, get some rest."

Shektul watched with narrowed eyes. "You will let me die in peace now?"

"Myute, I will ask Yavana to restore you to health quickly."

"Even if it means I will shred you like a hide as soon as I can?" Shektul growled.

"So be it." David picked up the soiled shirt and left.

David's thin pale hand crawled across the page as he wrote in the late morning light.

*These last, few days have nearly killed me. I've been constantly boiling dressings, washing Shektul's wound, feeding him, coaxing him to drink water, and changing the soiled hides beneath him. On top of that, I've had to hunt to keep the meat locker full.*

*The villagers ask if Shektul is still alive, but that's all. Haltek only watches me, shaking his head in silence.*

*To add to my misery, Shektul has contracted a high fever. I pour tepid water on him and rub him down regularly to keep him cool. It helps, but the sickly sweet smell coming from his wet hide makes me gag.*

*This morning, Shektul confided he's scared. He said, "I'm lost. Crulhiya's flames will soon roast me in the dark pit."*

*Yavana, don't let him die! Please, spare him! Every time I see his heaving chest, my heart goes out to him. The last two days Shektul has eaten only small bites. I've eaten nothing.*

On the seventh day of his ordeal, David awoke with a start. Shektul lay beside him on the furry hide, so still. Panicking, David sat up and felt the mel-hanor's chest. It was warm, but not hot as it rose and fell. Shektul was sleeping. Gone was the sickly smell that had permeated his damp fur.

Carefully, David changed the dressing. The angry swelling around the wound was gone; the oozing pus had ceased. Taking the dry shirt he'd used on the wound, David went out to the stream. It seemed like ages since he'd bathed.

While he washed himself, an elderly mel-hanor picked up the shirt and smelled it. "Shektul still lives," he said, eyeing David. "You have kept him alive for a long time with your tortures. We want to learn your skill."

David caught his breath. "I haven't been torturing him. I've been trying to save him."

The mel-hanor snorted. "You're his lastor, yet you're trying to save him? You're either unbelievably stupid, or lying about your torturing skills!" He trotted off with a growling chuckle.

So, the whole village thought he was torturing Shektul! David bowed his head. Why wouldn't they help one of their own kind? But he knew the answer. It was "the way of the mel-hanor."

Returning to the cave, he found Shektul awake. David looked down at his weak master. "Are you hungry?"

"Dala, and feeling better."

David fetched some meat and a bowl of water. He dropped the pieces into Shektul's waiting mouth.

"Soon...I will be...strong enough...to kill you...for tormenting me," the mel-hanor said between gulps.

"If you wish," David responded without emotion.

"Lean over now and I will slit your throat."

"Myute, Shektul. You may not kill me until you can take care of yourself." David dropped another piece of meat into his master's mouth.

"Then I will...have to get better soon."

\*   \*   \*

As David watched, Shektul staggered into the meat locker and shook his head. Every shelf was stocked. It was all small game, but it was meat. David's master had improved quickly. Each day the mel-hanor swore he would kill David "tomorrow." The wound kept him from making any sudden movements, but he had been able to stand briefly the past few days.

Shektul shuffled outside for the first time since his illness. He eyed the washed pelts hanging up to dry. "Crazy naharam," he muttered.

The villagers jabbered excitedly when they saw Shektul. David knew they expected his master to be dead. When Shektul had screamed from David's treatments on the first day, they assumed the human was slicing him up. But instead of a battered dying mel-hanor, they saw a mending well-groomed Shektul with a large scar on his side.

"Shektul, tell us what happened!" asked a mel-hanor.

David wondered what his master would do. But his master only glared at the villagers before hobbling back into his cave.

The following day, David beat the dust out of a floor hide while Shektul bathed in the stream.

A large crowd gathered around his master. One of the elders stepped forward. "What form of torture did the naharam use on you? We'd like to know. We also want to know if you are going to punish him."

Emerging from the stream, Shektul shook himself gingerly. He was still sore, but obviously recovering. The mel-hanor pointed to his scar. "He poured driya on my wound. Then he sewed me up like we sew two hides together."

Several furry heads nodded. "That would be a painful torture," one muttered.

"And?" the elder prodded.

"Isn't that enough?" Shektul snarled. "Lastor!"

David walked up. On the edge of the crowd, he spied Haltek with a tethered sheep.

Shektul's eyes were slits. "Come here, lastor! These mel-hanor want to know about my torture. I told them how you poured driya on me and sewed me up like two hides. You should have left me to die. Today, I will kill you."

David was about to respond in anger when a thought struck him. Was Shektul upset because he secretly wanted his lastor to escape? Did the big mel-hanor somehow care for him? But with the pressure of the crowd, he had no doubt that Shektul would kill him.

David's face burned. After all his hard labor, something rose up inside. "But Shektul, you didn't tell them everything. Before you kill me, at least tell them everything."

"Is this true?" the elder asked Shektul.

David put his hands on his hips. "Of course it is! I will tell you what I did. After I sewed Shektul up, I took one of my shirts and covered his wound. Each day I poured driya on the wound to keep it free from infection, and changed the dressing.

"I fed him meat and gave him water to drink. When the meat locker was low, I went out and hunted game for him.

"Every day I bathed him in water and rubbed him down. I slept beside him and pleaded with Yavana to spare his life.

"When he soiled his hides, I washed them in the stream. I did everything I could to make him healthy. Those long days when his fever soared, I ate nothing as I fed him bits of meat. I bathed him to keep his temperature from killing him and wept by his side."

David sighed as he met those surprised furry faces. "That is how I tortured Shektul."

He turned to his glaring master. "This is how I treated you. If it pleases you to kill me, then do so in whatever way you wish!"

Kneeling to the ground, David bowed his head, praying his master would kill him quickly out of rage.

Shektul bared his teeth and growled. He looked around at the nodding heads of the villagers and then at David's kneeling form. Raising his claws, he roared.

A movement caught his eye.

Spinning toward Haltek, he saw the tethered sheep and fell upon the dalam with a vengeance. The animal disintegrated beneath his slashing claws.

Panting, Shektul stared down at the wide-eyed cub. "I will pay you for it later. I just needed to vent my anger." With blood splattered all over his fur, he held his aching side and hurried into the cave.

David was still kneeling on the ground when Haltek approached him.

"I have never seen Shektul so angry," the cub whispered. "I don't understand why he didn't kill you."

Sighing, David stood up. How many more times must he face death before it took him?

The crowd spoke in hushed voices and dispersed, but an elder mel-hanor approached David. His gray muzzle twitched. "You saved your master's life when you could have let him die. You chose to stay when you could have escaped. Today, you would have let him kill you without protest. Is there no brain in your skull, naharam?"

Rubbing his forehead, David replied, "I have a brain, but I am lastor to a purpose that is greater than my life. I know how you think, and I don't expect you to understand."

"Does Yavana want you to remain a lastor?" Haltek asked.

David smiled wryly. "I think He does for a little while longer. For a moment, I thought my service was finished."

"You do not fear death?" Haltek's alert eyes watched him.

"At times I do, but I know I will go to cerepanya, to Yavana's courts. Vashua Himself will welcome me. Cerepanya is my real home, not Trenara or any other planet."

The elder mel-hanor shuffled off in silence.

David noticed the bloodied end of Haltek's leash. Turning, he saw the remains of the sheep. Boosah! Shektul *had* been mad. Pointing to the scattered remains, he asked, "What about your dalam?"

"Shektul will buy me a new one," the cub said in a low voice. "The meat belongs to him."

David gathered up the gory pieces. "This poor sheep reminds me of Vashua," he said under his breath.

"How is that?" Haltek asked.

David examined the bloody strips. It would take a while to remove all the sand and dirt. "On Trenara, Vashua is referred to as a *lamb*, a young sheep..." David talked as he washed the pieces. *How ironic that a sheep from Trenara would find its way to Morsala for this conversation to take place.*

Haltek listened, his deep brown eyes attentive to every word. Apparently, David's stand for his convictions had made a profound impression on the cub. Haltek continued listening long after the last piece of meat was washed and wrapped up in the tattered hide.

"Lastor, come bring in the meat!" Shektul called.

"Wait outside the door," David instructed Haltek. "I want to give you something." He brought Shektul his meat.

His master didn't bother to inspect it. Taking the whole hide, the mel-hanor sat down and began eating.

David removed a book from his bag and met Haltek at the door. "These are Trenara's Scriptures translated roughly into Ramatera. They will tell you more of what we were talking about." He opened the book to the Gospel of John. "Start reading here."

Haltek laid the fragment of his leather tether in the book to mark the place. "Ramara, David," he whispered and ran off.

The cub had called him *David*, not *naharam*. Was it just a slip of the tongue? David wondered.

David listened to the chattering stream as he wrote in his journal.

*It has been quite a while since the incident with the sheep, and Shektul mentioned it for the first time today. Since that tense event, he's never threatened to kill me and his demeanor has softened considerably.*

*He continues to see females, but not as often. Although I'm still called "lastor," there is a tone of affection in his voice.*

*I was deeply honored when Haltek asked me to be his hunting partner. The mel-hanor hunt in pairs with someone of the same sex. A hunting buddy is the closest the mel-hanor get to friendship.*

*Haltek questions me daily about the Scriptures. We have great discussions when we go hunting. He appears to be an eager pupil, but I'm not certain if he's really serious.*

*Tomorrow we hunt in the western hills. I've never been there before. Haltek says the adults rarely venture there so we will have a better chance of catching something large.*

*I am looking forward to it.*

# 16. The Cub's Hunt

"Come on, David, we hunt with a group today," Haltek called.

David turned to his master. "May I?" He always asked for permission before leaving.

Shektul waved him off with a paw.

"I'm coming!" David shouted as he ran. He knew that if the cubs brought down a large dalam, it would elevate their status, bringing them closer to adulthood. A mel-hanor had to earn the status of adulthood by killing a large dalam on his own, so the cubs were eager to practice.

They traveled in a group of eight, counting David. One of them pointed to a set of tracks on the ground. "Lampar! Lampar!" he jabbered.

The tracks were fresh enough to pursue and their quarry led them up a high ridge. An older cub hesitated.

"What is it?" David asked.

"We're nearing skatolar territory," the tan cub whispered. "Sometimes they travel through here."

But the others were determined to go on. Cubs were encouraged to take dangerous risks when hunting. It was the way of the mel-hanor. After spotting fresh lampar droppings, the cubs readied their arrows and spears. They closed in on their quarry. Entering a narrow box canyon, they spied the lampar grazing beside a bush. Silently they fanned out to encircle their prey. Haltek scaled the canyon wall, ready to leap onto the lampar's back.

Before they could surround their target, the lampar bolted, galloping further into the canyon. Growling and yelling, the cubs gave chase. David could never keep up.

Their prey leaped through a narrow opening between two canyon walls. A large slab of rock had fallen from above, creating a natural bridge. Haltek climbed onto the bridge while his peers ran by below.

The lampar screamed. At first David thought one of the cubs had attacked it, but the furry hunters stopped and stared at each other with large eyes. Like a rocket, the lampar burst through the opening, nearly trampling the cubs. The whites of its eyes flashed as it flew by. Caught off-guard, the cubs fumed in anger.

"How could we let it escape so easily?"

"Clishtip! It ran right through us!"

A deep rumbling growl made the ground vibrate. Lumbering out of the opening on four massive legs, came a hairy monster, the size of a small house. David watched in awe. This was a skatolar. The gray creature resembled a bear, a very large bear. The black horn rising between its small eyes seemed to pierce the sky.

Squealing, the cubs scattered, each eager to save his own hide.

The mighty beast spied David with its yellow eyes. David knew he couldn't outrun the towering behemoth, and there was no time to hide. Standing his ground, he raised his puny bow and waited for his adversary to come within range.

His pulse pounding through his body, he prayed. *I'm going to die in the paws of this nasty dalam. Yavana, please complete your work on Morsala. Send someone else to finish...what is that ranting Haltek saying?*

The cub danced on the bridge of stone. "You skatolar! How dare you attack one of Yavana's servants! I defy you in the name of Vashua! Yavana give me strength to slay this skatolar, just as You helped David slay the *lion* and the *bear*!"

Before David could stop him, the cub leaped onto the monster's back. The skatolar turned, but could not see his tiny attacker. While the creature was distracted, David dove behind a bush and peered out.

Haltek jabbed his tiny spear into the skatolar's back. The beast let out a deafening roar but could not reach its tormentor. Its terrible mouth opened, displaying teeth the size of stalactites. David smelled its foul breath. This was worse than a melcat. If only he had his caruk! Running along the creature's back like a tiny flea, Haltek reached the head and paused beside a large ear. The skatolar lowered its head and tried to brush off the pesky cub with a massive paw, but Haltek nimbly crawled into the monster's ear.

Then the skatolar really roared. Shaking its head, it clawed at the ear. The angry roar rose to a grating shriek of torment as the giant bear dropped to the ground, thrashing. Rolling onto its back, it convulsed as fluid poured from its ear. The flailing limbs slowed; the twitching ceased. The monster lay still. Emerging from the bush, David joined the other trembling cubs.

"Haltek is a skatolar slayer," a cub whispered.

"Myute, he *was* a skatolar slayer," another corrected.

"He did it to save the naharam," the first cub said in a low voice. "Who can take the horn? If Haltek is dead, then doesn't it go to his hunting partner?"

Walking up to the fallen beast, David touched it. "But what happened to Haltek?"

"Look!" a cub shouted.

Out of the ear popped a spear followed by Haltek's head. As the cubs cheered, David helped the slime-covered hanor emerge from his dead opponent.

Wiping his fir, the conquering cub sat on the ground. "The ear was just large enough for me to crawl into. It was dark, but I stabbed and stabbed with my spear and slashed with my claws. I felt the skatolar's head swinging back and forth, but I pressed further in."

"You killed it so fast," one of the cubs commented.

"I didn't kill it for pleasure," Haltek explained. "I wanted to save David."

Mounting the creature's head, Haltek took his spear and sawed into the horn. Ten minutes later, he kicked it free. The cubs howled and cheered as Haltek leaped off the skatolar and danced around. Eventually, the laughter died down.

"This could feed the village for a long time," a cub said.

An older cub grinned. "They will be stunned; we must go tell them!"

"A cub has killed a skatolar!" another cried.

The others rallied behind the cry and ran out of the canyon toward the village. It took four of the cubs to carry the massive horn. David would have been left behind, but Haltek made sure they waited for his naharam hunting partner.

"What were you saying before you jumped onto the skatolar's back," David asked, panting to keep up.

Haltek gave a sly smile. "Naphema moved me and gave me words to speak."

David stopped in his tracks. "What? Then I *did* hear you call on Yavana, and use Vashua's name!"

"Dala."

"Haltek, are you a naharam?"

"Dala, David. Does that make you my father?"

David's mouth fell open. "Yaram is your father. I am your brother!" He embraced his beloved student and wept.

The other cubs looked on curiously as Haltek's eyes watered too.

When they finished, David asked, "What were you shouting about David?"

"I read about a human named David who used to protect sheep from vicious dalams called *lions* and *bears*."

"You've been reading from the *Old Pharuna*?" David was surprised his student was studying the Old Testament on his own.

"Dala, it's full of exciting battles. I didn't think humans knew how to fight until I read about your wars."

David sighed. "We know how to fight all right. We know it too well." Pausing beside a stream, David looked at the rushing water and trembled. "Haltek, I don't know what will happen when we get back. Would you like me to bathe you like the ancient vadelahs bathed Vashua's followers?"

The hanor's brown eyes lit up. "Would you? I read about those bathings! Can you explain them to me?"

David waded into the chilly stream. "The water represents when Vashua was put in the ground after He died. When you go into the water, it represents your old self dying with Vashua and being buried. When you come out of the water, it represents your new self, raised with Vashua."

Haltek waded in. "I'm ready!"

Being a cub, he was easy to baptize. David would not have been able to lift a full-grown hanor unassisted. As Haltek came out of the stream, he raised his fists and roared.

A few of the impatient cubs ran ahead, eager to break the news of Haltek's hunt. By the time David and Haltek arrived, the whole village had turned out.

Shektul stood frowning with his arms crossed. "Lastor, what's this cub's talk about Haltek killing a skatolar? What *really* happened?"

"He did kill a skatolar," David replied.

Shektul wagged his head. "Myute, David! They are playing a game with you. If you saw a skatolar—"

"See and believe!" Haltek roared as his companions held up the eight-foot horn. *That* made an impact.

"Let me see!" cried the village elder. He sniffed the long dark horn and felt its smooth surface. "This is fresh and it's definitely from a skatolar." He backed away as others examined it.

Staring at David, Shektul muttered, "*Myute.*"

Haltek invited everyone to see the skatolar and the entire village clamored to go. David stayed with the slower part of the crowd as they headed back to the canyon.

Wearing a puzzled frown, Shektul kept glancing his way. Something was going on in that mel-hanor's furry skull, but what?

When they reached the giant hulk, the villagers jabbered with excitement. The mel-hanor elder approached Shektul and asked, "Do you think the human could have done it?"

Shektul snorted loudly. "*Him?* Myute! He can't even kill a sheep without a tool, and even then it is difficult for him! He's such a weak—" Shektul stopped. The light of understanding flashed across his face.

Climbing onto the muzzle of his trophy, Haltek raised his hands. The villagers grew silent. Every ear twitched forward. With vigor, Haltek told his story, complete with hand motions and a recitation of his battle cry.

When he finished, the village elder climbed to join him on the slain beast. Raising a paw, the old mel-hanor announced, "I recognize Haltek as an adult. Let us bring him females to complete his rite!"

"Myute!" Haltek shouted.

The elder raised an eyebrow and smiled. "Very well, then let us bring males—"

"Myute!" Haltek interrupted.

Twitching his gray muzzle, the elder sputtered, "But, but...that is the way of the mel-hanor!"

"I am not a mel-hanor," Haltek declared.

The crowd fell silent. Only a slight breeze whispered through the canyon.

Standing tall, Haltek cried out, "I am a naharam. I serve Yavana. I will take no female except through dalaphar. I will know my cubs and they will know that I, Haltek, slayer of the skatolar, am their father."

David didn't know if the village was going to follow Haltek, or kill him.

Before anyone could respond, Shektul bounded onto the skatolar. "Mel-hanor hear me!" he shouted. "When the naharam David came to live with me, he told me Yavana had sent him to bring us a message. I laughed and asked, 'Why would Yavana send such an ugly skinny weak thing to us? Why not send us a mighty warrior?'"

Laughing and chuckling, several mel-hanor nodded.

Shektul rubbed his scar. "But David said that Yavana's strength is revealed in our weakness...or something like that."

"Not too bad," David muttered.

Shektul continued. "I asked my lastor to explain what he meant. He said if Yavana told a mighty warrior to kill a skatolar, everyone would say the warrior did it by his great strength and cunning.

"But if Yavana told a *cub* to kill a skatolar, and he did, then everyone would see the power of Yavana!"

Pointing his muscular arm at David, Shektul declared, "This naharam prophesied that a cub would slay a skatolar, and it happened. Can anyone doubt that Yavana has sent him?"

David was about to protest but he stopped. He remembered there were occasions in the Bible when people prophesied without realizing it.

Looking at the confused crowd, the elderly mel-hanor said, "The skatolar will rot if we talk about this now. Let's butcher it first. Later, we will hear what the human naharam has to say."

The crowd agreed and tore into the great carcass. The body heat would spoil the meat if it wasn't cooled quickly.

David was amazed at how much the mel-hanor could carry. Like ants at a picnic, they labored under enormous slabs of meat.

Shektul grunted under his load. "*Clishtip*, lastor, you picked a big skatolar!"

The local meat lockers filled up fast. Messengers galloped off to invite two more villages to share in the spoils. With the combined labors of three whole villages, the carcass was picked clean by evening.

Haltek gave David a tooth as a memento.

By mutual agreement, David's speech was postponed until the next morning. The mel-hanor had the rest of the day to gorge themselves on skatolar and ponder the day's strange events.

The next morning, David arose to pray and do his chores. The mel-hanor slept more than humans, and David was usually the first one up in the village. After bathing in the stream, he changed his clothes and served Shektul.

David heard the jabbering of a large crowd outside the cave before Shektul had finished his morning meal.

Haltek poked his head into the entrance. "Shektul, they are asking to see your lastor, David." Now that he was an "adult," Haltek could interrupt Shektul without fear.

"Tell them we will be out soon," replied the dark mel-hanor.

Haltek disappeared, shouting Shektul's words.

"Now is your chance to tell your message to open ears," Shektul said with a grin.

Kneeling on a hide, David bowed his head and prayed silently, fervently, for wisdom. As he ended, he said, "Ramara Yavana for this day. Give Your lastor boldness to speak Your truth, no matter the cost."

Shektul raised an eyebrow, but said nothing.

David stood. "Let's go." He walked out of the cave and into a mob.

"Let him through!" the gray-muzzled elder shouted. "Move away and let him through!"

Many mel-hanor had come from the nearby villages. They pressed in to get a look, and a whiff, of David. This unruly group had no discipline compared to the assembly in Arana's council chambers.

Shektul bellowed from behind David. "Get out of the way! Let us through!" His loud voice achieved the desired response as mel-hanor scurried aside.

The elder stood on a boulder beside the creek. He beckoned David to come up and raised his paws to quiet the crowd. "Mel-hanor, we have seen how a cub has become a skatolar slayer. We have heard from Shektul how this naharam prophesied about this amazing feat on the day he arrived. We have also seen how this strange human has acted while among us. Shektul says this naharam claims to be sent from Yavana.

"Now, we will hear this human. We will listen to his message and judge it for ourselves. I personally can't think of anything Yavana would want to tell us mels, but I am curious. Be still now, so we can hear this message."

All murmuring ceased as the elder hopped down, leaving David alone on the rock.

Gazing out at the expectant furry faces, David wondered how long they would let him talk before they killed him. He might as well give his all. "Mel-hanor of Morsala," he began in a clear voice. "As most of you know, I come from Trenara. On my planet we have humans and mel-humans. But the mels on my planet do not always stay mel. Sometimes they become naharam."

A murmuring arose, but subsided as he continued.

"You may wonder, 'How can a mel become a naharam?' I will tell you. When Trenara's first naharam rebelled, death, sickness, and suffering entered the universe."

"And freedom from Yavana's rule!" a voice cried out, but it was hushed by the rest of the crowd.

David took a deep breath. "Yavana is righteous. He must execute judgment on evil. But, He is also merciful and loving. He loves His naharam...even the mels.

"How can He satisfy these two parts of His nature? How can He love His creation and punish the evil in it at the same time? This is the message I bring to you."

Pausing, David collected his thoughts. Not a cough, sneeze, or whisper came from the crowd.

"Yavana had a plan. He sent Vashua to become a naharam. Vashua laid aside all His rank and privileges and became a lastor. He served the humans, living as one among them.

"He depended on Naphema to empower Him. Vashua lived the way Yavana wanted us to live, and He showed us love. When mel-humans asked to speak with Him, He never turned them away, but welcomed them."

"But what about Yavana's need to punish evil?" came a voice.

David held up a hand. "When Vashua had been on Trenara for thirty-three circuits, His own people grew angry with Him. His enemies seized Him. They took Vashua and beat Him. He was flogged with leather thongs studded with sharp pieces of bone, metal, and glass. The whip sliced open His skin like a mel-honor's claws.

"They wove a crown out of thorny tearel and placed it upon His head. He was spit on, mocked, and laughed at in His misery. Beaten and exhausted, He was marched up a hill. When Vashua reached the top, they laid Him on two intersecting beams of wood."

David stretched out his hands to demonstrate. "They took His hands and drove metal spikes through them, fastening them to the beam. Another spike pinned His feet.

"Then they set the whole thing upright, like a tree, and let Him hang. He had to pull himself up for each breath as His battered chest muscles failed. It was designed to be a slow torturous death, and His enemies taunted Him as He hung in agony.

"But before He died, He uttered a request to Yavana. What do think that was?"

"Shred them, Yavana!" shouted a mel-hanor.

"Slay them slowly, painfully!" another called.

"May the fires of crulhiya consume them alive!" cried a third.

David held up his hand again. "That is what *we* would say, but not Vashua. He cried out to Yavana and said, '*Yaram*, give them shalar. They don't know what they are doing.'"

"But what about Yavana's need to punish evil?" a mel repeated the earlier question.

Smiling wryly, David asked, "Do you remember when Shektul said he was going to kill me?"

Many in the crowd murmured and nodded.

"But what happened? He didn't want to kill me, so he shredded Haltek's sheep instead. In a similar way, Yaram took all the mel-deeds we have ever done and laid them on Vashua. Then, using the mel-humans, He 'shredded' Vashua."

Many in the crowd blinked and stared at him with large eyes.

"Vashua opened the way to Yaram by taking our punishment. And to prove that Vashua's sacrifice was enough to take away all of our mel-ness, Naphema raised Him from the dead three days later. Vashua went back to cerepanya where Yaram exalted Him. Now Vashua calls all naharam and mel-naharam to follow Him and learn His ways.

"There are two doorways set before you, mel-hanor. Over one is written 'Lastor to Passions,' over the other 'Lastor to Yavana.' You must choose which you will enter.

"I say to you, as one who has followed Vashua for a long time, that you will never find fulfillment, or real lasting adventure, until you take Yavana as your master."

David stepped down. He was finished and his body was shaking.

The gathering burst into loud babbling. Some spoke for David, others were skeptical. A few talked of shredding him.

A strong, clawed hand wrapped around David's arm, pulling him back. "Hurry!" Shektul urged as he dragged David back toward the cave.

Some of the mel-hanor argued so vehemently, they stole the crowd's attention from David.

Once inside the cave, Shektul spoke in a stern voice. "As my lastor, you will do exactly as I say. Grab your travel pack and your sleeping hide. Then follow me."

David snatched up his gear. Shektul led David into the meat locker. Holding a container of spice in his paw, he sprinkled the shelves and floor. Then he picked up a wide floorboard and moved it aside, exposing a deep hole.

"Step inside," the mel-hanor ordered.

Peering into the dark hole, David lowered himself down. He felt the ground under his feet. The light dimmed and went out as Shektul closed the meat locker's door.

"Move over," Shektul said.

David heard the board slide back into place.

"Now come," his master called in a low voice.

"Wait, I can't see!" David whispered.

A clawed hand grasped his wrist firmly and led him down the unseen path.

"They will be looking for you soon." Shektul's voice was barely audible. "I covered our scent with a strong spice. They might not think to look under the floorboards."

Feeling the cool tunnel wall with his free hand, David asked, "Where are we going?"

"To a place where you will be safe for a while, if Yavana has mercy on us."

# 17. An Unexpected Release

David thought his eyes were playing tricks on him, but then he recognized the faint outlines of the tunnel walls. They emerged from behind a large bush.

"This way," Shektul instructed, stepping into a shallow stream.

They waded through the water, following its course to hide their scent. The mel-hanor stopped when they reached a branch arching over the water. Grasping the low limb with his claws, he swung himself up. He pulled David up after him. They traveled along the branches of the dense forest. Shektul moved through the trees with ease.

"When I was a cub, we used to play 'Predators and Prey.' I was often the 'prey.' I climbed boughs over streams, using them to cut off my scent. Traveling in the trees, I avoided leaving a trail. When I was on a hard surface, I always doubled back on my trail."

David took hold of another branch. "Were you successful?"

"They only caught me three times. After that, they never found me."

The trees crowded close together, making their long intertwining branches easy to negotiate.

Shektul paused beside the trunk of a large, red-leafed tree. "Do you see this? It's a croto tree. The bark and leaves give off a strong odor that will mask our scents. Whenever you enter or exit the tree canopy, do it on a croto tree or on a branch above a stream."

They continued in the trees until they reached a rocky out-cropping. Shektul leaped from a branch onto the top of the natural fortress. David followed his master.

"We should be safe here." The mel-hanor sniffed the wind, rotated his ears, and scanned the forest for any sign of pursuit. His taut muscles relaxed and he sat down. "I must confess, David, I am ashamed."

"You? Ashamed? Balute?"

"Because a cub beat me to becoming a naharam. I had the honor of hearing the message before anyone else on Morsala, yet I did nothing."

David looked Shektul square in the face. "Do you want to be a naharam?"

Turning away, Shektul stared at the ground. "Dala, David. I have for quite a while, but my pride prevented me. Whoever heard of a master becoming a student of his lastor?

"But I don't care anymore. A cub has shamed me. Haltek has more courage than ten mel-hanor." He looked up at David with burning golden eyes. "And you have more courage than a hundred! You knew who we were, and yet you still sought us out."

"Myute, I am not so brave, but Yavana is able to make a weak human like me stand and face great adversity."

Shektul gazed up at the sky. "His strength revealed in your weakness," he whispered.

"Dala, Shektul."

"Show me how to become a naharam."

*I spent the rest of the day teaching and praying with my master. Confession of sins is a foreign idea on Morsala, but Shektul has grasped it. He spent a long time practicing this lost art.*

*We talked until the stars came out and missed the evening meal—something unheard of among the mel-hanor. It only underscores my master's commitment.*

Looking up from his writing, David saw Shektul climb across the rocks, carrying a medium-sized dalam. Only a few claw marks marred the dead beast.

After starting a fire, David cooked some meat while his master ate his portion raw.

"I should return to the village," the hanor said licking his muzzle.

"Do you think it's safe?"

"Myute, but I need to know what's going on. I will return quickly, if Yavana is merciful."

David fretted and prayed all day. Toward evening, he spied Shektul leaping through the trees with a small group behind him. His master was leading a pursuing band right to David's hiding place! Wait, wasn't that Haltek at the end? Who were the others?

As Shektul landed on the rock, he shouted, "Don't worry, these are other naharam."

David greeted the new brothers and embraced Haltek.

Shektul grinned. "Your message has created quite a stir among the villages. They are equally divided into four groups: those who want to follow you, those who want to shred you, those who haven't decided and those who don't care."

"At least that's how it seems," Haltek added. "I think there are more who wish to follow, but they are afraid."

Shektul nodded. "Some of them searched my cave, shredded my hides, and stole my meat. The opposition is forming a search party for you, David. We may have little time before they kill you. Tell us all you know about Yavana and being a naharam. We want to be able to spread this knowledge across Morsala."

Opening his pack, David passed out the Ramatera Scriptures. He made sure Shektul had one of them.

"This is a rough translation of Trenara's Scriptures," David explained. "Once you are firmly rooted in Morsala's soil, send a few of your people to Arana. The phantera will help make an accurate translation into Morsala. Be sure to tell them Vadelah David sent you."

"It will feel strange to ask the phantera for help," Shektul said with a frown. "Are you sure they won't kill us for shredding their people?"

"They won't harm you if you tell them I sent you. Besides, they know I'm here and will be expecting you."

"It sounds like an ambush to me," growled a pale-colored disciple.

"Not at all," countered Shektul. "David said we should send *a few* of our people. If it were an ambush, they would want many to come. But that is not my current concern. Right now, we must use David while we still have him."

As was his habit, David got up before the others. He wrote in the soft, dawn light.

> *I've spent the past three days cramming information into those furry skulls. With Haltek's help, I baptized Shektul, and my former master assisted with the rest of the baptisms. Each day holds a sense of urgency as I feel an unseen noose tightening around us.*

A shout startled David.

"*Clishtip!* I knew I should have shredded him," Shektul bellowed. "Up! Everyone up! We've been betrayed!"

For a moment, David feared his master had turned on him.

But the mel-hanor wasn't looking at him.

"What is it, Shektul?" David whispered.

Shektul waved his arms. "Count your students!"

David looked around. Arkut, the pale-colored student was missing—the same one who thought the phantera would ambush visiting hanor.

"Quick, we may have a little time yet!" Shektul called the hanor together.

Placing all the books back into David's leather pack, the group followed Shektul. He led them into a stream which wove through a canyon and joined a roaring river. Snagging a low bough, they traveled through the trees.

Shektul led them to a place where a great fallen snag spanned the canyon, forming a natural bridge.

"With the rivers so full, this is the only place we can cross for miles," Shektul informed David.

The hanor all bounded across the massive trunk like cubs and waited on the other side.

David stared down at the foaming thundering water, and menacing boulders. *If I fall, I'm dead.*

"Come on, David," Haltek called. "Yavana will give you the strength!"

David got down and crawled on all fours. "Your grace is sufficient," he whispered over and over.

When he reached the other side, Shektul cocked his head. "I didn't know humans could crawl like that. You looked like a strange dalam."

"Thanks for the encouragement!" David muttered, standing up.

Traveling on the ground, David looked around at the peaceful woods. Sunlight filtered through the trees in long glorious shafts, spotlighting patches of grass and under-growth. Dank logs and blossoms scented the cool air. In the trees above, hidden creatures called to one another as woolly clouds crept across the powder-blue sky.

It would be a good day to die.

As they pressed through the bushes, Shektul motioned them to stop. Creeping up, David joined his master. Before him spread a small clearing. His delah rested undisturbed, glowing in the warm light. Encircling the ship stood a large group of armed warriors.

"What do we do now?" whispered one of the hanor. "They're too many for us."

Shektul lowered his brow. "We will fight them. If Yavana can help a cub slay a skatolar, then—"

"Myute!" David interrupted. "My time here is finished. As it is, many of you may be killed for what you know. I can't let you die for me. You must survive so the message can spread to others."

Before Shektul could protest, David sprinted into the clearing. Shouting and waving his hands, he tried to distract the group so they wouldn't see his hanor brothers hiding in the brush.

"Here I am! Come and kill me. I'm the one you want!"

Shektul was beside himself. "David! Wait! As your master I order you to come back. *Clishtip!* You stubborn lastor!"

He tried to follow David, but Haltek and the others restrained him.

Shektul wailed.

David continued to run until he reached the middle of the group. Kneeling down, he bowed his head.

"Here I am," he said, panting. "I'm the one you want."

He waited for the growls, the slow rending claws, and the searing pain of torn skin. A clawed paw grasped his shoulder.

"Take me now, Yavana. I have completed Your task," David whispered.

"Human naharam, why do you talk like this?" came a gentle voice.

David looked up. These furry faces were different. They lacked the customary black eyeliner. He was amazed at how regal they looked without it.

"It's a good thing we found him first," another warrior commented.

"Who are you?" David asked.

"We are naharam. We heard you speak at the canyon village. When we learned that some of the mels were searching for you, we came to guard your ship. We thought you might need it."

Surprising the hanor with an embrace, David wept.

"What are they doing to him?" Haltek asked.

"I don't know, but it must be awful," another hanor answered. "I can hear him wailing from here."

Shektul paused in his sobbing and looked up. "David does not cry under torture. *I* ought to know!"

"Look!" Haltek whispered. "David's yelling to us, calling us to come out."

The group galloped from the brush, ready to attack.

"It's all right!" David shouted. "They're hanor too!"

"*Ramara Yavana*!" Haltek muttered, pulling himself upright. "And to think we almost fought them! It's a good thing David went ahead."

The two groups merged and talked excitedly.

"Why don't you wear eyeliner?" Shektul asked one of the warriors.

"We want to show the mels that we are different. A naharam has no need to look fierce among his own people."

Shektul nodded. "I will stop wearing it too."

Turning to David, he said, "Now is your chance to go. The mels will find us soon, and you are right, your time on Morsala is through." He embraced David.

With watery eyes, Shektul gazed into David's face. "I release you from being my lastor. As Vashua released me from a debt I couldn't pay, so I release you from a debt you cannot pay."

"Ramara, Shektul." David rubbed his eyes. "I'm curious. What was the debt I would have had to pay?"

Shektul smiled. "You would have had to kill a lampar. You and I know you're too weak and puny to do that!"

David laughed. "Someday I might surprise you, Shektul!"

"Dala! If a cub can slay a skatolar, perhaps you can bring down a lampar!" Shektul roared. He grew serious. "I have wanted to release you since the time you nursed me back to health. I didn't because if I had freed you, another might have killed you or made you his lastor. With me, I knew you wouldn't be treated badly."

"Ramara, Shektul, for looking out for me." David squeezed Shektul's muscular shoulder.

He said farewell to all of his students, saving Haltek for last.

Placing both hands on the growing hanor's shoulders, David said, "You, Haltek, have the honor of being the first naharam among your kind. Honor Yavana in all your ways and continue to seek Him diligently. You have been like a son to me. Now, I leave you as a brother."

The furry face quivered as Haltek responded. "You were the father I never had. I can't repay you for showing me Yavana's love, opening my mind to His wonderful Scriptures. May Vashua bring you safely to your people and guard your life until we meet in cerepanya."

They embraced and Haltek howled with wet eyes.

David stroked the furry head. "Perhaps we will meet again before cerepanya. Who knows the mind of Yavana?"

Nodding, Haltek released him.

A scout ran up and joined the group. "The mels are approaching the bridge. It won't be long before they cross it."

Taking the books from his travel pack, David left them with the gathered hanor.

"It is time," Shektul said with a sigh.

To honor David, the hanor stood in two lines, forming a path to the delah's door.

Overwhelmed with emotion, David walked toward his ship. He couldn't believe he was leaving Morsala alive—in one piece. *Ramara, Yavana, for giving the mel-hanor the Great Revelation and for sparing my life.*

He faced the metal door. "*Toorah barune*," he called in a choked voice. The door slid open. He never expected to see the inside of his delah again, yet here he was.

Entering the ship, David called out, "I have a few more crates of books to give you. Come, take them."

With eager paws, the hanor removed the crates. They jabbered excitedly.

David faced the beloved furry faces one last time. "I love you all. May Yavana guide you and protect you."

With surprising reluctance, he shut the door. He watched through the window as Shektul and his group sprinted into the woods, galloping on all fours.

David changed into his flight suit and belted himself into his chair. Launching the delah to an altitude of five hundred feet, he hovered to spy on the mels. Shektul and his group guarded one end of the log bridge, while the mels prepared to cross it.

"This won't do," David muttered.

He had to keep the mels from slaughtering the naharam. He didn't want to harm the mels; that would only fuel their hatred. Using the ship's lasers, David fired a few warning shots across the bridge. The mels beat a hasty retreat as the naharam jumped and cavorted like kids on a winning team.

David trained his lasers on the bridge. He blasted it. The great trunk shattered in the middle and crashed into the violent river below. The mels leaped and clawed at the air toward his ship.

"Delah, take us to the departure zone. Plot a course to Arana." *How good it feels to say that!*

The delah accelerated, leaving the green forests of Morsala behind. The blue sky gave way to black.

"Two crullahs approaching from deep space," the computer announced.

*I knew it was too easy.* David was ready to fight now. He had given his message and saw no use in being martyred in space.

"Crullah Hasket: You're mine, little human! Today you are my enemy."

"Delah David: I'm sorry to hear that. Shektul will be disappointed. Besides, I enjoyed the bow and arrows you gave me."

"Crullah Hasket: I did it out of amusement, but you amuse me no longer! You have filled the mel-hanor with cub's thoughts and threaten to take away Morsala's freedom."

"Delah David: You give me credit for a lot of things. I didn't know a weak human could threaten your entire planet so easily. Don't you think the credit should go to Yavana for this mighty work?"

"Crullahs approaching firing range," the computer chimed.

"Crullah Hasket: I will shred you!"

The two crullahs dove at David, one behind the other.

David gripped his control stick. "Delah, can we reach the departure zone before they open fire?"

Lasers blazed from the first crullah. Jerking the control stick to one side, David turned to avoid his attacker.

"Myute," came the computer's voice.

"Thanks a heap!" David snapped in English. More shots streaked by as he flew erratically to avoid them.

"Yavana, I am no warrior. Help me!" David cried. Morsala wasn't going to let him go without a fight. Pulling hard to one side, David spun his delah to face his attacker. He fired furiously without aiming.

"Crullah Hasket: You call that shooting? I will show you how to shoot!"

"Break his pride, Yavana!" David yelled.

Hasket's crullah came in fast, lasers flashing. David prayed, closed his eyes, and fired. The delah shook as it took a few hits.

"Ayeeen! No! No! *Clishtip*!" screamed a voice.

Looking up, David saw he had damaged the crullah, but not destroyed it.

"Delah David: Give up, Hasket. I have no quarrel with you. Yavana's hand is mighty, but He'd rather see you turn than be crushed."

Hasket responded with a few guttural words in his native tongue before switching to the trade language. He swore with gusto, but David understood little profanity in Ramatera. "Clishtip!" snarled the mel-honor. "I'll send you to crulhiya if it means going there myself!"

David prepared to fire. What was that flashing blue light on his screen? *Weapons system offline.*

Hasket barreled toward him, screaming obscenities.

Clutching his control stick, David pressed the firing trigger. Nothing.

The crullah fired and exploded into light. Blinded, David held up his hands to shield his eyes. The delah shook and tumbled as it was pelted with shrapnel from the exploding ship. The light faded leaving a cloud of floating debris.

David had no time to relax as the second crullah swooped in for the kill. His delah wouldn't move. The main thrusters were offline.

"That's it," David said bitterly. "I'm tired of looking death in the face. Yavana, take me home!"

A trelemar flash blinded him a second time. It faded, revealing a delah stationed between David's ship and the approaching crullah. The new delah's laser expertly pierced the crullah, triggering a catastrophic explosion.

"Delah David to unknown delah, please identify yourself."

"Delah Rammar: I was told you needed a little help on Morsala."

"Rammar! Ha! You came in the nick of time," David lapsed into English. "How did you know I needed you?"

"Delah Rammar: Naphema knew. He told me to go get you."

"Delah David: I can't tell you how many times I thought I was dead."

David stared at Morsala. She was stunningly beautiful from here. Although his long time on her had been difficult, punctuated by moments of sheer terror, he had survived— and grown. Deep within him, adversity's hammer had forged a solid confidence. God had been with him all the way. David knew he would never be the same.

"Delah Rammar: We'd better leave before more crul-lahs arrive. I will stand guard until you've made your jump to Arana."

Joy poured over David as he gazed out at Morsala one last time. He had finished his task! "Delah, take us to Arana."

The humming noise increased. Good thing the trelemar equipment still functioned. Smiling, David pictured Gyra, Philoah, and Brusaka, rushing to the landing lawn to greet him. He hadn't seen a phantera in ages!

"Prepare for trelemar," the computer announced.

As the white light engulfed the delah, David cried out, "Ramara Yavana!"

# Preview of
# Blackwell's Wrath
## Book 3 of the Vadelah Chronicles

# 1. Back to Trenara

Clutching the ship's control yoke, David breathed a prayer of thanksgiving as the stars reappeared. At least the battered delah had been able to make the jump. His crippled ship hovered now above a great planet.

"Due to damage sustained to main thrusters, wings, and tail, descent to Arana's surface is not recommended," the computer announced.

David drank in the jewel-like seas and painted continents. "Great, so it's 'look but no touch,'" he muttered. "There's got to be a way to get down there." Pressing the mike button on his control yoke, he asked, "Delah David to Arana Patrol, how do I get to the surface? My ship is badly damaged."

"Arana Patrol: We will send a cargo delah to assist you."

As he waited, David ran his fingers through his dark oily curls. It'd been days since he'd had a proper bath. A great flash of light obliterated the stars on David's right before fading to reveal a giant ship. Coasting in like a mighty dirigible, the cargo delah opened its enormous belly doors to reveal a cavernous hold and a large set of clamps. The great ship lowered itself onto David's delah like a brooding hen onto an egg. With a loud *thunk-thunk* the clamps latched on.

"Delah Ranjar: We will inform you when it is safe to exit your ship."

"Delah David: I understand." David rubbed his beard. Ranjar. Where had he heard that name before?

Once the ship closed its massive doors, air flooded the bay. David heard a knock on his window and spied the white feathered head of a phantera.

"Toorah barune," David commanded. The delah's door slid open. David nearly squeezed the life out of the poor phantera as he embraced the six-foot bird.

Blinking his red eyes in surprise, Ranjar said, "Welcome, Vadelah David. May I presume you are happy to be back?"

David released him. "*Dala!* It's been so long since I've seen a phantera."

Ranjar released a cooing laugh. "When you're ready, I'll take you down to Arana."

Maneuvering around the cargo bay in zero gravity was tricky. David shook his head as he examined his mangled delah. The left wing was shattered, burn marks streaked the hull, and only a stub remained of the double tail. "I didn't know it was so bad!"

"Yavana protected you," Ranjar commented. "One little breach in the hull and it would have decompressed."

Grimacing at the thought, David asked, "Can it be repaired?"

"Dala, but it will have to go to Thalona. The coralana are the best at repairing delahs."

David scratched his itching scalp once more. "How long will it take?"

Ranjar drifted inside and consulted the computer. "I'm afraid the coralana are quite busy right now. Their repair schedules are so backed up that the waiting periods are longer than the actual repair time itself."

"So, how long will it take?" David prodded.

Snapping his pink bill in a display of annoyance, Ranjar perused the delah's status files. "You will be grounded for quite awhile—at least two days."

David laughed. "On Trenara, our mechanics would take months to fix something like this. Two days is nothing!"

Entering a corridor, they propelled themselves along using the railings on the walls. Ranjar was amusing to watch as he hovered without using his wings. He glanced back at David. "I need to tell my wife before we leave. I hope you remember her. Panagyra said your memories are funny."

David racked his brain. Where had he seen Ranjar before? The *dalaphar* ceremony! Ranjar was the groom. What was his bride's name?

"Layan, come see the vadelah!" Ranjar called.

Clutching a tiny phantera chick, a female phantera peered out from a nearby doorway. David had never seen a chick so young. The infant blinked her alert blue eyes and bobbed her fuzzy head. A thick layer of yellow down covered her delicate frame.

The mother smiled. "We are honored that the vadelah attended our wedding."

Stroking his chick tenderly, Ranjar added, "The phantera in the Marza Village had not done a dalaphar in Ramatera for a long time. It made ours special."

David put a hand over his mouth, stunned. The wedding had not been performed in Dalena, the phantera native language, but in the trade language of Ramatera. Ranjar and Layan had altered their ceremony for him!

Finding his voice at last, David replied, "That was long before I bore the title *vadelah*. I was a stranger, an alien in your world, yet you treated me as an honored guest. I am deeply humbled by your hospitality. Your dalaphar was one of the most beautiful things I have ever seen. I may not have a great memory, but I will never forget that experience as long as I live."

Pleased, the couple bobbed their heads in unison.

"I'm taking Vadelah David down to the surface,"

Ranjar told his wife. Turning, he guided David further down the corridor. "We were surprised when you turned up at Dalena to rest."

With burning cheeks, David remembered Ranjar had guarded him in orbit above the planet Dalena. He'd never forget that name again!

Ranjar babbled on. "Panagyra and Philoah will be thrilled to see you. We've all been very busy translating and spreading the Great Revelation."

David entered a smaller bay containing a standard delah. Gliding inside the ship, he stowed his bag. He eyed the u-shaped avian chair in the cockpit. "Um, do you have any extra...chairs?"

"No problem!" Ranjar tossed out in English. He typed a command into the computer and a lump rose out of the floor.

David watched, fascinated, as the green material molded itself into a chair suitable for a human.

"Belts are in the panel to your right," Ranjar instructed. The enormous bay doors opened and the delah flew out, paused, and faced the huge cargo ship. Ranjar smiled. "I like to bless my wife's ship whenever it leaves. She does the same for me." Placing his red scaly hand against the glass of the windshield, he whispered, "*Sarena* [Peace]."

The great ship disappeared in a blinding flash of white light. Ranjar began his descent. David was a little disappointed he couldn't see the great desert or the Pendaram's City from orbit. A dense cloud layer blanketed the area. Entering the clouds, they descended into a gray gloom. The delah broke through just above the well-lit city.

"You came at a good time," Ranjar commented. "It's not raining."

As the delah settled on the landing lawn, David spied Arachel, his duca. With up-raised head, the giant duck-like bird trumpeted a welcome. David grabbed his bag and hopped out. Arachel rumbled affectionately as he rubbed her smooth flat bill.

"She only alerted the whole city," came a voice behind the duca's great bulk. A phantera in a gray cloak stepped into view.

"Gyra!" David bolted into his friend's arms and held him fast. "Many times I thought I'd never see you again!"

"Hey, don't crush him," teased another voice, "He's the only brother I have." Philoah strode around the duca, followed by Brusaka.

After they exchanged hugs, laughter, and tears, Brusaka invited David to the guesthouse. "Come and refresh yourself," the black phantera cooed. "We can share horlah bread and drink falatirah together. Tonight you can sleep in the most comfortable bed on Arana."

Grinning, David patted the black phantera's cloaked shoulder. "Brusaka, many times I longed for that bed."

"Arana Patrol said your delah was badly damaged," Philoah spoke in an excited voice.

David's smile turned into a wince. "It was almost destroyed, but Rammar rescued me at the last minute. I owe him my life."

Brusaka bobbed his head solemnly. "Rammar is a good shot. He is very skilled in warfare."

After bidding Ranjar farewell, David headed across the lawn with his friends. They strolled through the city and entered a stone guesthouse. David enjoyed a relaxing swim in the atrium pool. Philoah joined him and David soon learned why it is never wise to pick a water fight with a phantera. Calling a truce, David washed his hair—his nose still stinging—and hauled himself out.

He grinned at his companions. "I can't tell you how good it feels to bathe in warm water!" He walked with dripping curls to his room. After changing into clean clothes, David strolled into the dining room and froze. "What is *this*?"

The three phantera stood behind the table, grinning.

"Do you like it?" Brusaka asked with eager orange eyes.

David approached the piece of furniture resting before the table. "I've never seen anything quite like it. This is a most unique chair." He sat in the green molded form. It was surprisingly more comfortable than he expected.

"We had it made so you could sit when you eat at the table," Philoah explained.

"Whose idea was this?" David asked, smiling broadly.

"Panagyra's," Brusaka and Philoah chorused.

Nodding toward Gyra, David said, "*Ramara*."

A yellow tear slid from Gyra's eye. "We hoped you would return to sit in it. We missed you."

David swallowed. "And I missed you."

"Tell us what happened from the time you left," Philoah prodded.

Brusaka placed some horlah bread and a bowl of falatirah on the table as he watched David expectantly.

Leaning back in his chair, David closed his eyes. "Just let me rest a moment." He felt their eyes burning into him with eager anticipation. It was useless to rest now. He sighed and sat up. "All right." As he pulled his journal out of his pack, he muttered, "I suppose I should tell you as much as I can before my feeble human brain forgets!"

Setting the worn journal on the table, David recounted his dangerous missionary journey to the three dark planets. He described the conversion of the first mel-balahrane on the planet Wicara and the controversy it created. Many mels had abandoned their demon gods to worship Yavana, the One True God. In two days, David's message had thrown Wicara's dark religious system into chaos.

Although his encounter with the mel-dijetara on the planet Cruskada had been even briefer, one of their species converted before David was forced to flee.

On the third planet, Morsala, David had lived for several months and witnessed the conversion of nearly a hundred mel-hanor. But life on Morsala had been very difficult for him.

"As soon as I arrived, I was made a slave," David recounted. "My mel-hanor master threatened to kill me daily."

Brusaka shuddered. "Oh, David! You must have been terrified living among those cruel mels!"

Toying with the pages in his journal, David continued. "Haltek was my first convert. He created quite a stir when he killed a huge skatolar, a dangerous beast. Since Haltek is only a cub, he got the mels' attention, setting the stage for me to preach."

"What prompted Haltek to follow Yavana?" Brusaka asked, eyes riveted on David.

David chuckled. "It's rather ironic, but a sheep played a role in that."

Gyra's feathered brows lowered into a deep scowl. "A *sheep*?"

"On Morsala I found sheep and horses." David shook his head. "Somehow, they were imported from Trenara."

The phantera all snapped their bills as the feathers rose on their heads, displaying alarm.

"And when I accidentally blundered back to Trenara, I found crullahs patrolling my own planet!" David added. "I never expected to see those nasty black ships in my own backyard." He pushed the journal toward them. "Here, read the details for yourselves. I'm going to take a nap."

Sauntering off to his old room, David lay down on the wonderful spongy bed Brusaka had prepared for him. When he awoke, the shrouded sun had set. He stretched, yawned, and wandered back into the dining room for a snack. His friends instantly barraged him with questions.

Wincing, David raised a hand to fend them off. "Hey! One at a time!"

Brusaka went first. "What concerns me most is the crullahs stationed near Trenara. I do not like it."

"Nor I," Gyra added.

Philoah scratched around the collar of his gray cloak. "David, you said the mel-hanor admitted being in contact with Trenara. That must mean there are other humans who know about them."

Brusaka's worried eyes blinked. "But are they humans or *mel*-humans?"

All three bills turned toward David.

"I don't know," David answered, rubbing his eyes. "I would guess they're mels. An unbeliever would be more likely to make an alliance with the mel-hanor."

Philoah lowered his voice. "Pendaram Ariphema must know of this. It could affect all naharam, not just humans, hanor, and phantera."

"Dala," Brusaka agreed. "But Pendaram Ariphema won't be back from Dalena for several days."

"We could call him back," Philoah suggested.

But Gyra cut him off. "*Myute!* His business there is important too. We will send him a message and wait until he returns. That will give David time to rest."

The next day, the gentle pattering of rain awakened David. He rolled out of his deliciously comfortable bed and stretched. Wandering out to the atrium, he gazed up at the canopy of dark lead-colored clouds covering the sky and sighed. He strolled into the dining room. "How long until the rain stops?" he asked his three friends.

Philoah tilted his head slightly. "When the rainy season ends."

David frowned. "And how long is that?"

"About five months, Earth time," Gyra answered in English.

"You mean it's going to rain continuously for *five*

*months*?" David cried.

"Myute," Brusaka soothed. "There will be some days when it does not rain. You may even see the sun on occasion."

"On *occasion*? What is there to do when it rains?" David asked, frantic.

"You can do everything you did before." Philoah cocked his head the other way. "I don't understand your distress."

Huffing, David retorted, "Humans don't like to be wet all day long. We don't have feathers like a phantera, and we don't live in the water like a haranda!"

"Your cloak should keep out the rain," Brusaka pointed out calmly. "Your shoes are waterproof too."

Gyra tapped the end of his pink bill. "Why don't you take Arachel and go flying? It would be good for both of you. You've hardly seen her since you returned."

Massaging his forehead, David confessed, "I've been under a lot of stress."

"Dala, David," Brusaka entreated gently. "That is why you need a little *enar*, 'a break' as you say in English."

As David remembered his duca, he smiled. "Okay, today I'll fly Arachel. She missed me and I missed her too." He broke off a piece of cooked vegetable to eat and paused. "Wait a minute," he whispered. "This doesn't make sense."

Looking up at his friends, David asked, "How did Arachel know I was coming? You said she trumpeted it across the whole city, but how did she know it was me? And how did Gilyen's duca know that the crullahs were coming the day I shared the Great Revelation?"

Brusaka cast a rebuking scowl at his comrades. "You mean they didn't tell you?"

"I thought Gyra told him!" Philoah protested.

Gyra aimed a purple scaly finger at Philoah. "Brother, you were negligent in your tutoring!"

"Wait a minute!" David cut in. "Just tell me and it will be all right."

Gyra and Philoah looked at each other.

"Okay, I'll tell him," Philoah said in English. He turned to David. "The ducas know."

"What do you mean 'the ducas know'?" David asked in exasperation. "*What* do the ducas know?"

Philoah's scalp feathers undulated. "They know when a ship is coming out of trelemar. They can tell if it's a crullah or a delah. Arachel recognized yours because of its unique shape—even though it was damaged."

David wore a skeptical expression. "How can they tell a ship's coming out of trelemar?"

"We do not know," Brusaka answered. "Yavana gave them one gift when He gave us our gifts. We did not understand it at the time because we had no spaceships, but Yavana said they were given a gift of hearing."

Pondering this, David wagged his head. "But that still doesn't make sense. Gilyen's duca bellowed that a crullah was coming *before* it arrived. If a crullah takes no time in trelemar, then Gilyen's duca heard it before it entered trelemar!"

"Dala, David," Gyra said, head bobbing vigorously. "Now you understand why it's such a mystery. That is how we know it's Yavana's gift!"

Breaking into a wry smile, David remarked, "A prophesying duca?"

Philoah laughed. "That's a strange way of looking at it."

David drummed his nails on the table as Brusaka watched, fascinated. "There's still something that bothers me," David said. "Why was there no warning when Gilyen's village was attacked?"

Philoah waved his bird hand. "We've already investigated that. Ducas can only hear a ship approaching in trelemar if that section of the sky is visible. The ships didn't come out of trelemar on this side of the planet, but on a side where there are few ducas.

"We found a barren listening-post with a dead duca. In our eagerness to share the Great Revelation, we allowed ourselves to be spread too thin. The mels happened to find our weakness and exploit it."

David frowned. "So, they killed the duca and flew in search of a village to attack."

"Myute, the duca became ill and died; otherwise we would have had a warning. Since then, Pendaram Ariphema has ordered at least three ducas to be on guard at each listening-post."

Blowing out his breath in frustration, David hung his head as he remembered the ghastly raid. What rotten luck. The one time the planet's guard was down they got massacred. If only the duca hadn't died!

Brusaka noticed his distress. "David, all events are in Yavana's hands. He alone has the power to bring good out of tragedy."

"I still feel like Gilyen's village died in vain," David exploded. "It all seems so pointless!"

"Myute, David." Brusaka's tone turned serious. "If you had not seen their slaughter, you would not have known the mel-hanor for what they were. You had to see them in all their mel-ness.

"The mel-hanor needed someone to show them Yavana's love, but that naharam would have to know the depths of their depravity. If you had not known the blackness of their hearts, you would have been unfit to show Yavana's grace to them."

Brusaka snapped his bill. "The death of those phantera was not in vain. Out of their suffering, Yavana has brought life to the mel-hanor. If those villagers could speak, they would testify that their sacrifice was an honorable one."

Bowing his head, David spoke in a subdued voice. "You're

right, Brusaka. My willingness to go—in spite of my knowledge of the massacre—had a profound effect on the mel-
hanor. Shektul, my former master, took part in that raid."

After breakfast, David donned his cloak and goggles.
He set out for Arachel while Gyra and Philoah followed.
The rain fell harder now. In the gray distance, three ducas
waited on the landing lawn. Arachel, Treasar, and Echo
rumbled their greetings. Lowering her crested head, Arachel
helped David onto her back.

"How do you see with all this rain?" David yelled to
Gyra.

Gyra fluttered onto his mount, Treasar. "We use sonar."

As Arachel ran across the landing lawn, David wondered if he'd made a mistake. The wind blasted the hood off
his head and the rain stung his face, forcing him to bend
down. Lightning flashed somewhere to his left. The duca
rose into the air. Holding on with his legs, David covered his
ears as the thunder roared out from the gloom. He
instructed Arachel to follow Treasar and Echo.

The rain slammed back harder. David hoped he
wouldn't run into any hail—at this speed it would be quite
painful. All he could do was stare at Arachel's sleek white
neck as the rain drenched his curls. At least his goggles
didn't fog up. When the air grew cooler, David plunged his
hands into Arachel's warm feathers.

The rain stopped, and he looked up to see nothing—no
horizon, sky, or ground. He couldn't even tell which way
was up! Arachel continued with steady confident
wingstrokes. The gray ceiling thinned, giving way to a
sudden brilliance.

David shut his eyes, and then squinted in the light. As
his eyes adjusted, his mouth dropped open in awe before he
closed it to the frigid wind. Like mighty fortresses, thunder-
heads towered around him, ignited by the sun with a daz-
zling white light. Treasar and Echo frolicked around the

lesser sky-castles and pierced through their vapor forms. David directed Arachel into a dark "cavern." He admired the blue and silver shadows. Turning his duca once more, he chased after his companions, darting in and out of the ever-changing skyscape.

Treasar came alongside Arachel. "Be sure to avoid the large cumulonimbus clouds," Gyra shouted. "They contain strong winds and hail."

David nodded. The dark clouds had a foreboding look about them anyway. Grasping Arachel's flying straps, he told her to roll. A whoop of joy burst from his throat as she turned onto her back and righted herself again. A thunderhead billowed up like an atomic blast in slow motion, developing into a powerful storm cell. It was followed by a second cell and then a third. The cold thin air began to wear on David. He told Arachel to take him back. Gyra and Philoah followed. Arachel swooped through the silver veil of water vapor, plunging them into the gray world below. The rain slapped his face raw. Within the watery haze, the vague shapes of buildings came into view as the landing lawn blurred by beneath them.

Flaring, the duca settled onto the soaked turf. David's wet curls drooped down and stuck to his goggles, making it hard to see. His hair was getting long. Who would cut it? As he slid off Arachel's back and into a deep puddle, David was glad his shoes were waterproof.

*I've spent the last three days flying Arachel, swimming in the sea, laying on the beach (on the one afternoon the sun came out), and relaxing in the guesthouse.*

*Using his super memory, Gyra cut my hair to the same length it was the day I first met him. Then he tried to trim my beard. I can't complain about his work because no one around here has any mirrors.*

*There were a lot of curls on the floor when Gyra finished.*

"David!" Brusaka called.

Capping his writing brush, David asked, "What's up?"

"Pendaram Ariphema has returned. He requests an audience with the vadelah immediately."

"On my way!" David crammed the journal into his pack, threw on his cloak, and ran with Brusaka through the incessant rain to the council chambers. Once inside the impressive building, he hurried down the great hall, shoes squeaking in protest over the polished stone floor. Brusaka's nails clattered beside him, keeping perfect pace. At the end of the hall, they both stopped. Pulling open one of the great double doors, David stared at Pendaram Ariphema standing in the middle of the cavernous chamber. Apparently this meeting was a private one. Only Gyra, Philoah, and Brusaka made up the rest of the audience.

Ariphema bobbed his head and faced him. "Come in, Vadelah David. Tell me about your mission!"

The feathers on the pendaram's head fluctuated as David recounted his adventures. Ariphema rejoiced upon hearing of the birth of the naharam movement on the three dark planets. Other times during David's report, Ariphema snapped his jaw or remained strangely silent. When David finished, the pendaram paced beneath the soaring dome. A circular skylight set in a triangle lit the great room.

"I am concerned about the large number of crullahs stationed near your planet," Ariphema began. "It cannot be good. Even more alarming are the horses and sheep on Morsala. Yavana forbade contact with Trenara for a reason, and the mel-naharam place everyone in peril by their actions."

David nodded. "I agree they must be stopped, but how?"

"One must become an alien among his own people, an exile in his own land," echoed a voice off the high ceiling.

Another phantera stood in the doorway, wearing a dark cloak. David recognized him. No other phantera had eyes so brilliant and piercing.

"Come, Rammar, your insights are always welcome, your prophecies firm," Ariphema said in greeting.

The phantera prophet strode up to the small group. "David must go back to Trenara. He has another task to complete. It will be his hand that sends the mel-naharam away from Trenara."

"Oh, David!" Gyra cried with concern. "I wish I could go with you."

Rammar's black bill turned to Gyra. "You shall. You alone of the phantera are prepared to face Trenara, but trials and hardship await you both."

"Will we return to Arana?" David asked, trembling.

Peering into David's face with his burning orange eyes, Rammar said, "You must trust Yavana for the unseen. Even if the path is to death, do not waver in doing what you know to be right. Remember what you learned on Morsala!"

Ariphema's eye-rings faded, indicating deep distress. "When should they leave?"

"Immediately," Rammar answered in a grave voice.

Gyra shivered. "Brusaka, grab David's travel pack and meet us at his delah. *Fly!*"

Brusaka dashed out of the chambers.

"I will tell Pendaram Ariphema what else is to be done," Rammar informed Gyra. "A great battle is coming. Go now and take your post."

Bowing his head respectfully, Gyra grabbed David by the hand and pulled him out the door. Philoah followed.

"Gyra, why are we running?" David asked, struggling to keep up with his friend.

"Because when Rammar says *immediately*, he means it!" Gyra cried. "Great peril comes to those who do not heed a prophet!"

They reached David's newly repaired delah and opened the door as Brusaka winged his way back.

"Yavana *hamoth* Panagyra and David!" Brusaka prayed as he landed.

"Ramara, Brusaka." Gyra grabbed the bag and hurled it into the delah.

David gave Philoah and Brusaka a quick hug and sprang into the ship before Gyra could protest. After shutting the door, he changed into his flight suit in record time.

"I'll fly. Hang on!" Gyra warned as David fumbled with his belt.

The sudden acceleration of the ship pinned David to his chair. He finally buckled himself in. "Well, at least I have company this time," David mused. "It was real lonely being the only naharam on a planet."

Gyra turned up the soft corners of his mouth into his subtle phantera smile. "We missed having a human to poke fun at us."

Gazing down at the planet's receding surface, David whispered, "Arana, I will miss you. May I see your beautiful land soon!"

"Perhaps we will see Todd," Gyra remarked.

"Perhaps."

As they reached the departure zone, the cabin grew quiet. Gyra had the weapons ready should they need them.

"Yavana guide us," David prayed in Ramatera.

"Amen," Gyra added in English.

David stared out the window as a brilliant white light swallowed the black void of space.

# Fast Facts

## Alien Characters

**Arachel:** David's female duca.
**Ariphema:** Pendaram (ruler) of the phantera colony on Arana.
**Belrah:** Female mel-balahrane and David's first convert on Wicara.
**Brusaka:** Black phantera host serving at a guesthouse in the Pendaram's City.
**Dah-378:** Blue-gray mel-dijetara worker, also known as Dah the Inefficient.
**Gilyen:** Phantera courier.
**Halora:** Pendaram of the haranda on Arana.
**Haltek:** Mel-hanor cub. David's friend and hunting partner.
**Hasket:** Shektul's hunting partner.
**Jearam:** Mel-balahrane high priestess and ruler of Wicara.
**Mojar:** White female phantera physician.
**Orajar:** Silver phantera, Master Breeder of Arana's ducas.
**Panagyra:** White phantera marooned on Earth. Nicknamed Gyra.
**Philoah:** White phantera, Panagyra's brother.
**Rammar:** Black phantera, prophet and warrior.
**Ranjar:** White phantera from Gyra's village. Married Layan and works on patrols.

**Shektul:** David's mel-hanor master.
**Sintwar:** Female mel-balahrane friend of Belrah.
**Treasar:** Panagyra's duca.

## CLASSES OF LIFE-FORMS

**Aradelah:** Spiritual beings. Angels (**mel-aradelah:** Demons)*
**Naharam:** Mortal sentient life-forms*
**Chelra:** Creatures on a level between animals and naharam, possessing crude language skills
**Dalam:** Animals without developed language skills
**Tearel:** Plant life

*The plural forms of aradelah and naharam do not use an *s*

## RAMATERA NUMBERS

| | |
|---|---|
| ni (nai) | zero |
| tren (trehn) | one |
| dar (dahr) | two |
| cere (**sehr**-uh) | three |
| dil (dihl) | four |
| pinnah (**pin**-nuh) | five |
| sha (shah) | six |
| deel (**dee**-uhl) | seven |
| augo (**ah**-go) | eight |
| nena (**nen**-ah) | nine |
| sint (sint) | ten |
| trenten (**tren**-ten) | eleven |
| pendar (**pen**-dahr) | twelve |
| trencere (**tren**-sehr-uh) | thirteen |
| trendil (**tren**-dihl) | fourteen |
| tren… | |

## ALIEN SPECIES

| Naharam | Home World* | Description |
|---|---|---|
| Coralana | Thalona | Large butterfly-like creatures with blue wings. Very high tech. |
| Haranda | Arana | Seal-like aquatic mammals. Males have a curved horn protruding from base of skull. Low tech. |
| Mel-balahrane | Wicara | Dinosaur-like creatures with smooth blue skin. Bipeds with long tail and a fan-shaped bony head-crest. Devout polytheists, they have an affinity for precious metals and jewels. Moderate tech. |
| Mel-dijetara | Cruskada | Large crawling insect-like creatures with long snouts, four arms, six legs, and tail ending in four tentacles. Come in three colors: bluish gray, brown, and khaki. Very high tech. |
| Mel-hanor | Morsala | Brown wolf-lion mammals. Very fierce and undisciplined. Low tech. |
| Phantera | Dalena | Large dove-like avians with arms and wings. Come in white, black, or silver feathers. High tech. |

*Native language named after home world

# Ramatera–English Dictionary

**ab** (ahb). Or

**adrana** (uh-**drah**-nuh). Sea.

**Agaria** (uh-**gair**-ee-uh). The large white moon of Arana. Literally, "big light."

**agera** (uh-**gair**-uh). Large.

**aireah** (**air**-ee-uh). An artificial overhead light.

**Alamar** (**ah**-lah-mar). Arana's sun.

**alawa** (**ah**-lah-wah). A spongy turf-forming plant that grows in pink or lavender. Native to Arana.

**aradelah** (air-uh-**del**-uh). Angels. Also see mel-aradelah.

**Arana** (uh-**rah**-nah). Home world of the haranda. Also home to a large colony of phantera.

**awal** (uh-**wal**). Hot.

**ayeen** (ah-**yeen**). Pain. May also be spoken to express discomfort. Often shortened to "ayee." Literally, "Oww!"

**ba** (bah). A suffix which forms the plural of the noun it follows.

**balahrane** (bah-lah-**rayn**). See mel-balahrane.

**balatren** (bah-lah-**tren**). Discipline.

**balith** (bah-**leeth**). Master breeder of ducas.

**balute** (bah-**loot**). Why?

**barune** (bah-**roon**). To open.

**boolee** (**boo**-lee). A large mollusk two to three feet long, native to Arana. A favorite food for ducas.

**boosah** (**boo**-zuh). An expression of disgust, akin to "gross" or "yuk."

**bot** (bot). To stop.

**caleah** (kah-**lee**-uh). To eat or drink.

**caruk** (kah-**ruk**). A versatile laser tool and weapon.

**castulshep** (**kast**-ul-shep). A strong word expressing deep revulsion. Literally "abomination."

**cerepanya** (sair-uh-**pahn**-yah). Heaven.

**charane** (cha-**rayn**). To come.

**chelra** (**chel**-ruh). A group of lifeforms possessing crude language skills. One level of intelligence below naharam, and one level above dalam.

**cipal** (**sip**-al). A unit of time just under an hour in length. Part of the cipatrel system. One cipal equals fifty ciplets.

**cipatrel** (**sip**-uh-trel). A galactic-standard time measurement system.

**ciplet** (**sip**-let). A unit of time just over one minute in length. Part of the cipatrel system. One ciplet equals fifty cipras.

**cipra** (**sip**-rah). A unit of time about one and a third seconds in length. Part of the cipatrel system.

**cirilla** (sir-**ril**-ah). Silver.

**Cirilla Pala** (sir-**ril**-ah **paul**-ah). The Milky Way Galaxy. Literally, "silver plate."

**cirilamar** (sir-**ril**-ah-mar). An extremely strong alloy composed mainly of marza, silver, and aluminum.

**clishtip** (**klish**-tip). A vulgar swear word.

**coralana** (kor-uh-**lah**-nah). An industrious butterfly-like naharam whose home world is Thalona. Their technology is unrivaled in the galaxy. Great architects and scientists, they discovered trelemar travel and designed the delahs.

**corune** (kor-**roon**). A large cauliflower-shaped tree with hard blue wood. Native to Arana.

**crealin** (**kree**-uh-lin). A vital phantera organ that can rupture and cause death during a time of intense mourning. Used to perform falarn and rhutaram.

**crektul** (**kreck**-tul). To die, or be dead.

**croto** (**krow**-toh). A large oily tree, native to Morsala, that has the ability to mask scents.

**crulhiya** (krul-**hy**-yah). Hell. Literally, "black flames."

**crullah** (**krul**-luh). A spaceship built by the mel-dijetara, used by the mel-naharam for space travel. Literally, "dark ship."

**Cruskada** (crus-**kah**-duh) Home world of the mel-dijetara.

**dahmoo** (dah-**moo**). Mother.

**dala** (**dah**-luh). Yes.

**dalam** (duh-**lahm**). Any animal that has no developed language skills.

**dalaphar** (**dah**-luh-far). Bonding covenant, e.g. marriage. Literally, "yes covenant."

**Dalena** (dah-**lee**-nuh). Home world of the phantera.

**dee** (dee). To bring, send or give.

**del** (del). A message.

**delah** (**dee**-luh). A spaceship built by the coralana, used by the phantera and other naharam for interplanetary travel.

**delaram** (**del**-uh-rahm). Leaders who traverse large areas of a planet to ensure the well being of their subjects. The next level of authority under the pendaram. Literally, "traveling rulers."

**dijetara** (dih-jeh-**tar**-uh). See mel-dijetara.

**Dilari** (dih-**lahr**-ee). The small red moon of Arana. Literally, "little light."

**dilu** (**dee**-loo). Small.

**doiyal** (**doy**-ahl). Female. Doiyal was the first phantera female, their "Eve."

**doloom** (doh-**loom**). A cave. Also an enormous system of caverns under the great Arana desert.

**dowel** (**dow**-wel). A stick with a lighted orb on top.

**drea** (**dree**-uh). Water.

**driya** (**dry**-yah). A fermented drink made on Morsala. Literally "burning water."

**duca** (**doo**-kah). A very large flying bird, resembling a giant duck with a bony crest. The phantera's chelra.

**elah** (**el**-ah). A cry for assistance. Help!

**enar** (**ee**-nar). To rest.

**fala** (**fah**-lah). A sweet purple fruit grown on Arana.

**falarn** (fuh-**larn**). The phantera ability to share the current thoughts of another naharam.

**falatirah** (fah-lah-**teer**-uh). A drink made from the fala fruit.

**hamjea** (hahm-**jee**-uh). The protective third eyelid of a phantera.

**hamoth** (**hahm**-oth). To protect.

**hanor** (hah-**nor**). See mel-hanor.

**harana** (ha-**rah**-nah). To give praise.

**haranda** (ha-**ron**-dah). An aquatic seal-like naharam whose home world is Arana.

**hayan** (**hay**-an). All lifeforms, sentient and non-sentient.

**hoowah** (hoo-**wah**). A phantera expression of joy, similar to a cowboy's hoot.

**horlah** (**hor**-lah). A chalky tan vegetable found on Arana.

**hiya** (**hi**-yah). Fire.

**Hiya Amada** ( **hi**-yah ah-**mah**-dah). Volcano. Literally, "fire mountain."

**jarune** (juh-**roon**). Cold.

**jea** (**jee**-uh). To see.

**kunah** (**koo**-nah). The ruler of the mel-hanor on Morsala.

**lampar** (**lam**-pahr). A large, deer-like dalam found on Arana.

**lar** (lahr). The same as; equal to.

**lastor** (**las**-tor). A slave.

**loomar** (**loo**-mar). An edible fish found in the great caverns (dolooms) of Arana.

**maha** (**mah**-hah). Who?

**Majeram Amada** (mah-**jeer**-um ah-**mah**-dah). A mountain range bordering the great desert of Arana. Literally, "look-out mountains."

**manar** (mah-**nar**). What?

**marana** (mah-**rah**-nah). Where?

**marza** (**mar**-zah). A rare element used to make cirillamar (a very strong metal).

**matrel** (mah-**trel**). When?

**mel** (mel). Those who rebel against Yavana. Unbelievers.

**mel-aradelah** (mel-air-uh-**del**-uh). Demons.

**mel-balahrane** (mel-bah-lah-**rayn**). A reptile-like mel-naharam whose home world is Wicara. The prefix "mel" shows their rebellion against Yavana.

**mel-dijetara** (mel-dih-jeh-**tar**-uh). An industrious insect-like mel-naharam, whose home world is Cruskada. The prefix "mel" shows their rebellion against Yavana.

**mel-hanor** (mel-hah-**nor**). A fierce mammalian mel-naharam, whose home world is Morsala. The prefix "mel" shows their rebellion against Yavana.

**mel-naharam** (mel-nah-ha-**rom**). Mortal intelligent life-forms who do not serve Yavana.

**melcat** (**mel**-kat). A giant arachnid dalam native to Arana's deserts.

**meno** (**meh**-no). A lie.

**Morsala** (mor-**sah**-lah). Home world of the mel-hanor.

**myubala** (mee-**yoo**-bal-ah). Wild passion. Literally, "no discipline."

**myudel** (mee-**yoo**-del). To have no purpose. Literally, "no message."

**myute** (mee-**yoot**). No.

**nachel** (**nah**-chel). Children of naharam.

**nadrea** (nah-**dree**-uh). A large marine mammal on Arana. The haranda's chelra.

**naharam** (nah-ha-**rom**). Mortal intelligent lifeforms, for example, humans and other species. Also used specifically for those who serve Yavana.

**najaran** (nah-**jar**-ron). Truth.

**nal** (nahl). And

**Naphema** (nah-**fee**-mah). The "True Spirit" of Yavana.

**pagaruna** (pa-guh-**roo**-nah). A large warm-blooded aquatic dalam found on Arana.

**pala** (**pah**-lah). A serving plate.

**panatrel** (**pan**-uh-trel). A funeral.

**paru** (pa-**roo**). Yours. Belonging to you.

**patu** (**pah**-too). Mine. Belonging to me.

**pendaram** (**pen**-dar-rom). The ruling leaders of the phantera. These twelve are each responsible for the phantera populations on their planets. Also used by other naharam as a title for their highest leaders.

**phantera** (fan-**tair**-uh). An avian naharam whose home world is Dalena.

**pharuna** (fah-**roo**-nah). A solemn covenant or promise.

**phema** (**fee**-muh). Spirit.

**pinnah** (**pin**-nuh). Five.

**plumos** (**ploo**-mohs) An edible bulb found on Arana.

**pulmar** (**pul**-mar). To sleep.

**ramara** (ruh-**mar**-uh). To give thanks. Literally, "Thank you."

**Ramara nal harana sa Yavana** (ruh-**mar**-uh nahl ha-**rah**-nah sah yah-**vah**-nah). A formal blessing for a meal. Literally, "Thanks and praise to God."

**Ramara sa Yavana** (ruh-**mar**-uh sah yah-**vah**-nah). An informal blessing for a meal. Literally, "Thanks be to God." In the company of close friends the word "sa" may be dropped.

**Ramatera** (ram-uh-**tair**-uh). The language of the flexible tongues. Spoken by all naharam and mel-naharam (except humans) who have the ability to form words.

**rhutaram** (roo-**tar**-um). The phantera ability to learn a foreign language instantaneously through contact with a naharam's head.

**rusoph** (**roo**-sof). To learn.

**sa** (sah). To.

**salan** (sah-**lon**). To go.

**Sanor** (**san**-or). The name for Earth's sun.

**sarena** (sah-**ree**-nuh). Peace. Often used as a blessing.

**shalar** (sha-**lar**). To forgive.

**shar** (shar). To mix, stir, or agitate. Used to describe a storm.

**shardrea** (shar-**dree**-uh). A rainstorm.

**shartara** (shar-**tar**-uh). A sandstorm.

**skatolar** (**skat**-oh-lar). A huge bear-like dalam found on Morsala.

**steen** (steen). To close.

**ta** (tah). Is

**talaram** (**tah**-lah-rom). The main leader of a naharam village. This is the next level of authority under the delaram.

**tara** (**tar**-uh). Sand or dirt.

**tearel** (teer-**el**). Plant life.

**teayoo** (tee-**yoo**). Down.

**Thalona** (tha-**lohn**-ah). Home world of the coralana.

**toorah** (**too**-ruh). Door.

**tor** (tor). From.

**trean** (**tree**-an). A knife or blade.

**tren** (tren). One.

**trelemar** (**trel**-uh-mar). A form of deep space travel discovered by the coralana. It allows one to jump from one point in space to another with no lapse in time.

**Trenara** (tren-**ar**-uh). Earth, the home world of humans. Literally, "first planet."

**vadelah** (vuh-**dee**-luh). Literally, "Vashua's messenger."

**Vashua** (vah-**shoo**-uh). Known as "the Mystery," "the Provision," and "the Restoring One."

**wesarel** (**wes**-uh-rel). Canopy trees native to Arana's jungles, whose leaves contain compounds which inhibit life-scanning equipment. The leaf fibers are used in phantera cloaks.

**wesar** (**weh**-sar). Wind or breeze.

**Wicara** (wih-**kar**-uh). The home world of the mel-balahrane.

**yal** (yahl). Male. Yal was the first phantera male, their "Adam."

**Yaram** (yah-**rom**). Father God.

**yarama** (yah-**rom**-ah). A naharam father.

**yatala** (yah-**tal**-ah). Family.

**yataphar** (**ya**-tah-far). The adoption ceremony. Literally, "family covenant."

**Yavana** (yah-**vah**-nah). The Creator of all naharam. Combination of *Yaram*—Father, *Vashua*—the Mystery, and *Naphema*—the True Spirit.

*Julie Rollins* resides in Washington State with her husband and their three daughters. In addition to writing, her interests include canoeing, painting, and raising ducks. An active member of her church, she sings on the worship team, composes worship songs, and leads a home group. After teaching in a Christian high school for eight years, she now homeschools her children. She has a B.A. in Art and holds a commercial pilot's rating.

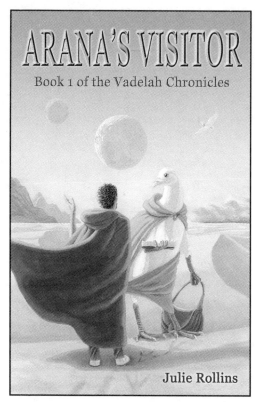

David Decker is stunned. Driven by his Christian compassion, he has just rescued a marooned space alien, but the alien's mere existence threatens to shatter David's worldview. How can he reconcile the two? When David learns the truth, it will astound him. But David has other troubles. Shadowy government forces are desperately trying to capture the alien. In his quest to follow his convictions, David must battle enemies—seen and unseen—and travel to incredible places he's never imagined.

# Coming soon…

# Book 3 of the Vadelah Chronicles

David and Gyra must return to face a nightmare: Earth. They tremble at the pronouncement, but Rammar the Prophet has spoken: only David can sever Earth's secret link with the dangerous mel-naharam, and Gyra must help him. Who are the humans involved on Earth? How will David stop the contact? Will he come out alive? David doesn't know. But Rammar has warned that David will suffer…greatly.

# Want More?

Be sure to visit the author's colorful and informative website at **www.JulieRollins.com** for

- **Vadelah Chronicles** alien "photo gallery" with computer screensavers
- Bonus chapters (not in printed books)
- Short stories by the author
- Book descriptions and release dates
- Feedback and questions to the author
- Links to order books

Or you can order books in the **Vadelah Chronicles** series by contacting the publisher directly at

Essence Publishing
20 Hanna Court
Belleville, Ontario, Canada K8P 5J2
Toll-free: (800) 238-6376 ext. 7575
Fax: (613) 962-3055
Email: publishing@essencegroup.com
www.essencebookstore.com